RISE OF TH

THE

JIM MURDOCH

A ROC BOOK

ROC

Published by the Penguin Group
Penguin Books Ltd, 27 Wrights Lane, London W8 5TZ, England
Penguin Books USA Inc., 375 Hudson Street, New York, New York 10014, USA
Penguin Books Australia Ltd, Ringwood, Victoria, Australia
Penguin Books Canada Ltd, 10 Alcorn Avenue, Toronto, Ontario, Canada M4V 3B2
Penguin Books (NZ) Ltd, 182–190 Wairau Road, Auckland 10, New Zealand

Penguin Books Ltd, Registered Offices: Harmondsworth, Middlesex, England

First published 1995
1 3 5 7 9 10 8 6 4 2

Roc is a trademark of Penguin Books Ltd
Set in 10/12 pt Monophoto Melior

Printed in England by Clays Ltd, St Ives plc

18865

VANDYKE UPPER

ACKNOWLEDGEMENTS

The author would like to thank the following people for their help in making this book happen:

Sean Griffiths and Mirage's Instinct Design team for creating the Rise of the Robots computer game. Sean Naden and Kwan Lee for their inspirational artwork. Andy Wood and Peter Jones at Mirage for all their support, including the financial variety. Special thanks to Julia Coombs at Mirage for her faith and for trailing round book publishers with me. Dave Cotton at Mirage for allowing his name to be abbreviated. He is a cyborg. Pete Dabbs at Mirage for his name. Becky Jackson for being prepared to struggle through the unexpurgated draft and make helpful comments. Jeff Tawney at Time Warner Interactive for thinking that the book was a good idea. Ravi Mirchandani and Andrew Welham at Penguin Books for their enthusiasm for the project. Arne Peters at Sunflowers GmbH for patiently waiting for his translations. Gina Jackson for her moral support and being genuinely interested in my daily word-counts. Last but by no means least, my son Robert for no doubt losing some *quality time* with his father, and Eileen for being heavily pregnant and still letting me bash on to write to the deadline.

'THE CHROM... ...OID, WE CALL HER THE *SUPERVISOR*, IS LIKE NO OTHER DROID IN EXISTENCE,' RAKUSSEN REPLIED.

'The robot is a complete departure from commonly held machine-design philosophy. Although she has all of the standard components of any robot; a CPU, neural systems, server motors etcetera, they have all been engineered from base molecular level.'

'And she's a *she*, Dr Rakussen,' Clowes smiled. 'She sounds like progress.'

'An understatement, Ms Clowes ... She's the mother of a whole new generation of droids, of a new era of engineering in fact ... This is no good, I'll see if we can go along and see her ... you have to see the Supervisor to really appreciate what I'm saying.'

ABOUT THE AUTHOR

Jim Murdoch was born in Stockport, England, in 1956. He began writing in 1961 but it was some thirty-three years later before a publisher gambled on putting him into print. *Rise of the Robots* is his first published book and is only a slight divergence from his more regular work of creative writing and translation within the computer games industry. A graduate of the University of Cologne students' refectory, he has an interest in all matters linguistic along with a love of ancient motor cycles and brass musical instruments. He has two children, a Royal Enfield, two trumpets and a valve trombone.

INTRODUCTION

The Einsam Archipelago was a scattering of planets, twenty in all, locked into orbit round a minor sun, some five light-years distant from the home planet ... Mother Earth. The EA was a heaven-sent discovery for the migrant humans from Solar System I. Here was a close grouping of habitable planets which mimicked their own science and presented an opportunity to begin over again, a new anthro-ecological history for the human species.

When ecological catastrophe finally proved to be unavoidable, man at last united across the home planet and began the Migration Project. The huge Chrysalis Class vessels were constructed and became the last locations on Earth which could support any mass population. The ships were modular and were steadily enlarged, section by section, for two hundred years. Over this period Mother Earth's thinning atmosphere and weakening gravity slowly allowed these craft to part from the planet's surface and begin their journey through half a century to the new worlds of the Einsam Archipelago prospected by the Pathfinders.

The Einsam planets were colonized by a new generation of man, a dynamic breed of mixed-race humans who saw nothing to fear in these new worlds. Their science and philosophy, cultured in a lifetime of space travel, equipped them perfectly for the task of building a super-civilization across this new solar system.

By the thirtieth century, the new humans' command of

science had established a thriving advanced-technology society across the planet chain. Powerful interdependent city-states grew up, focusing sprawling populations in islands of vitality amongst the deserts of the plundered mineral-rich crusts of the planets. Metropolis 4, on the prime planet of TI Creda, was the oldest and most successful of the Archipelago's city-states.

CHAPTER ONE

Metropolis 4's security services occupied the tallest building in the heart of 'Central 1'. The massive flagstaff structure drove into the dull haze that hung over the city; its rotating aerofoil command floors cruised silently round the central column, brushing in and out of the mist. Command Floor 3 hummed with routine monitoring activity. It was early evening, Friday Newjune 1st 3012.

The Floor Commandant, Piaget, was making his way along the walkway between the comms monitoring banks, heading back to his desk up on the mezzanine in the glazed bow section of the department. He'd had a hell of a week: his teams had logged an unprecedented increase in illegal transmissions, and the senior staff assembly which he'd just left had all but carpeted him for not coming up with conclusive source and solution action. He had mobile units out all over the city and into the Wastelands, but had gained no significant intelligence. These latest insurrectionist transmissions were operating under a new generation comms code, making their content impenetrable to his decrypt team. As he walked past Kraemer, Section Leader of mobile units, he caught the end of a voice link with Lander 6 out in the Wastelands.

He bellowed to the surprised SL, his message also unmistakably for the rest of the section. 'Tell those guys not to bother coming home until they've got something to justify their pay credits!'

3

'They reckon they might have something for us, sir,' Kraemer replied promptly, 'but they're having problems uploading the data. Coton is going to retry when they've cleared the Newmines Ridge and they've got better topography.'

'What's Coton doing out there? He was supposed to be with Decryption all this week!'

'I believe he was there until this morning, sir, then he decided he wanted to get nearer to the new transmission source we'd found. He's with Walker, you don't need to worry, sir.' Kraemer smiled at the reassurance he'd just given the Commandant.

'I need to worry, and I consider your recommendations to be a section one impertinence, Kraemer. Do your job and keep your assertions to yourself or I'll have you back on the screens . . .'

Piaget strode off, his thoughts now back on the assembly.

The open treads of the metal stairs up to the management mezz trembled as the heavy man powered towards his workstation. Piaget swung himself round the final 180-degree turn and crested the flight. Over at his station he could already see his e-mail icon flashing up on the screen.

'More crap to sort out . . .' He was vocalizing his thoughts: *stress counselling session one, spot the signs . . .*

Sitting at his station, Piaget took a long, deep breath and swung round in his chair to take a look over the city. He needed to chill a little before he started the next chapter of hassle.

Friday evening was breaking out over Metropolis 4. Piaget glanced at his watch and noted it was already 7.30. He could see the Wonder Theme Park over near his home in West Central 3: strobes and holoprojectors beamed up the evening's theme but he couldn't make out what was on tonight – after all, he was at almost the same altitude as the focus plane for the projectors and from this shallow angle they lit the haze like pools of coloured mercury. He thought of his son pestering his mother to take him along . . .

Command Floor 2 came cruising round the central mast and obscured his view, Logistics Planning and bad air-con. They also said that CF2 vibrated like hell, though he'd never noticed it, and if any of the wings were going to fly off the Big Mixer, then CF2 was candidate number one. Piaget screwed back round to his desk and winked at the e-mail icon, the cube shattered with a sampled popping noise and he read the news.

The menu displayed all the usual stuff, exec assembly minutes, staff productivity codings and field team activity reports. He muttered 'FTA' to the machine and scanned the list for Lander 6's bulletin. He followed the log of reports down to the point where Coton had made his positive ID on a suspected insurrectionist transmission. The location was the Lorus Depression, about 250 ks out from the National Minerals site over the Newmines Ridge. That put the source about 300 ks from M4 itself. It seemed a long way out for the regular anti-social elements to be operating; the Azzis were not normally so mobile, he pondered; it could be a group from M2, some further 100 ks to the north. Piaget winked at the last voice link box and listened to the transmission. Coton's voice came through on what was obviously a messy comms link – the Lorus Depression was notorious for bouncing signals all over the place.

'Fix made on ... transmission 632 ... High power signal ... radio ... VHF, and ...'

A loud crack interrupted the communication.

'... am ... decrypting and loading to sat-link ...'

The transmission broke completely in a blast of static – Piaget leaned back from the terminal, grimacing at the noise. Then the message continued, almost completely jammed ...

'Up-load ... not ... possible ... Heavy mineral ... atmospheric contamination breaking ... sat-link ... Losing all comms ... Will retry nearer home ... expect transmission –' The message cut off, dead.

Piaget noted the time entry: 19:15. It was now 19:45, and there was no further news. He rose from his station and walked to the mezzanine rail, from where he could see Kraemer leaning back in his chair and looking down his nose at the master comms terminal. Piaget bleeped the Section Leader on his portable and watched him jerk back to answer his call.

'Anything from Coton, Kraemer?'

'Nothing at all, sir. Met. reports heavy weather in the Lorus area, pretty well all air links are down.'

'OK, Kraemer. I'll be leaving in half an hour, let me know as soon as you get something. If it's after 20:15, reach me in my mobile.'

'Very good, sir.'

Piaget returned to his station and flicked off his display. Turning back to the view of the city, he watched the auto-wash trigger across the massive expanse of glass, thin rivers of sandy water scribbling over the curvature. Beyond the rim of M4, the western horizon was a blank bright orange.

By 8.15 Piaget was somewhat happier. He had re-booted his terminal and completed his action returns for the exec assembly, and he had found another message on his e-mail informing him that he had succeeded in being selected for stage two executive selection, a staff ranking that would finally get him out of this nitty-gritty routine *and* get him an apartment in Sunnyside, upwind of the city centre.

The city below was now well illuminated: tracks of lights splayed out from under the tower, here in the centre of M4 the tree-lined boulevards moderated the hard edges of the route system and the city looked quite inviting, like somewhere in the movies a thousand years ago. 'Distance lends enchantment to the view,' Piaget muttered to himself, quite proud of his spontaneous lyricism and this evidence of his culturedness. As he descended to the walkway above the monitoring floor, he searched for Kraemer at his terminal, but saw only an empty chair and his screen in secure mode.

'Anybody know where Kraemer is?' the Commandant barked at the two duty staffers at the far end of the row of comms terminals. Their blank expressions were answer enough and Piaget did not even wait for a reply. Making a mental note to check the SL's productivity code first thing Monday, he set off apace in the direction of the mess room. Bursting through the air screen into the mess reception, Piaget wheeled around and scanned the log-in table.

'Can I help you, sir?' The 'duty monkey' had come up behind the Commandant and caught him unawares.

'Kraemer,' muttered the flustered officer. 'Have you seen Kraemer in here in the last half-hour?'

'No sir, he's not logged in and I certainly haven't seen him . . .'

'Right, Duty Staffer, put a bar on anyone else from Comms Monitoring coming in here, and if you see

7

Kraemer, tell him I want to see him immediately. I'll be in Met. Central, Floor 5 ... And relay that order to Comms.'

'Very good, sir!' The duty monkey turned smartly and headed for the internal information panel. Piaget was actually impressed, a duty monkey acting like a serviceman.

'What's your name, Duty Staffer?'

Not pausing in his attention to the panel, the monkey replied, 'Landucci, sir!'

'Very good, Landucci, carry on!'

The Commandant turned out of the mess room and marched briskly along to the elevator bay. Pushing past a crowd of end-of-shift operatives, he thrust his priority card into the slot, gaining some satisfaction from the barely audible groan that his action aroused. This group would probably lose at least half an hour of their Friday evening now that Piaget had commandeered one of the six already-overworked main tower elevators. The prioritized elevator, somewhere down around the fiftieth floor, had now stopped, no doubt disgorging another squash of disgruntled occupants. Heralded by a racing floor indicator and a piping alarm, the elevator presented itself for Piaget's disposal. The Commandant stepped in, turning to smile at the dismayed faces as the doors hissed shut.

The elevator dragged on Piaget's stomach as the priority mode acceleration took the big man by surprise, and he rocked back and caught hold of the rail round the polished cylindrical capsule. He remembered that he hadn't eaten for six hours. The thought did not mitigate his brooding annoyance at the absent Kraemer. 'SL Kraemer, you're back on the screens, no question about it!'

The soothing female voice announced, 'Command Floor Five,' the doors parted and Piaget stepped out into the elevator bay. As he approached the registration desk across the reception hall, an incongruous whiff of food caught his nostrils, further stirring his stomach. Compass-like, his nose panned for the source. Immediately on entering Meteorology Central his opinions concerning the sloppy management of the department had been reaffirmed.

'See to it that your mess area air screen's looked at!' was Piaget's opening statement to the bewildered staffer at the security panel.

'Sorry, sir?'

'Your air quality stinks, Duty Staffer, the air screen on the mess area is inoperative. I am recommending that you pass on this information to your maintenance section.'

The staffer craned her neck to look at the entrance to the mess area just round the corner, then ducked back to the Commandant. 'Of course, sir, I'll enter that straight away.' She bowed her head to address the terminal below the counter.

Piaget interrupted this action, flattening his palm on the ID pad. 'Piaget, Floor Commandant Comms CF3, I need to see the supervising officer in Met. Observation ... Leave the maintenance for later and check me in now.'

'Very good, sir.' The terminal emitted a peep. 'You may enter. Please use gate eight. Do you know the way, sir?'

'Thank you!' Piaget was already halfway towards the security gates.

Crossing the flux mat into the moving wing section of the department, Piaget found himself on a side mezz above the top level of Command Floor 5. To his right was the glazed bow section, starkly monochromic in orange light from the sunset. Following the arc of the roof ribs back from the bow, the vast hall darkened and he could see the balcony rail silhouetted against the top edge of the enormous Met. screen which hung, all five levels high, in the trailing edge section of the command floor. Piaget made his way down on to the level and reached the balcony rail. He paused, leaning on the steelwork, and took in the giant picture in front of him, a real-time satellite view of Metropolis 4 and about half the continent. Right over the Lorus Depression was a huge brownish vortex. As he watched, text overlays appeared over the various weather systems, giving local pressure, wind speeds and temperature. Lorus recorded a 0.2 pressure, 240 kph winds and 30 degrees ground temp. Atrocious flying conditions, atrocious any kind of conditions . . . He'd go down to the screen monkeys and get them to do a zoom for him.

'Commandant Piaget!' Kraemer's voice, a little breathless, broke into Piaget's thoughts. 'I'm glad you're here, sir. I've been trying to reach you in your mobile.'

'What the hell are you doing here, man! Why did you leave your station?' Piaget wasn't going to let his anger just vanish, although he already suspected that Kraemer, a cocky but competent officer, would have some rational explanation for his presence on the Met. Floor.

'Well, sir, I'd received a transmission from Lander 6, very broken. Coton reported rapid weather deterioration and stated he was losing his navcoms. He gave me a position over Lorus, then I lost him completely.'

'And you chose not to relay this information to me . . .' Piaget leant with his back to the rail, arms outstretched along the curved top section.

'I was unable to reach you on voice, sir, so I e-mailed a notification.'

'I didn't receive it, Kraemer . . .'

'I don't understand that, sir.'

'So why did you leave your station?'

'I went down to Air-Traffic. I couldn't get them to send me a screen, they were having all sorts of trouble with the entire north and western sector navcoms. All the ground beacons were out – still are, I think – and sat-nav was dropping out because of the mineral storms. I wanted to get some hard information for you, sir, before I contacted you again.'

'This is Met. Central, Kraemer. Air Traffic is on CF1 . . .'

The interrogation was broken by a paging announcement asking Kraemer to go to Met-Mapping.

'Sorry about this confusion, sir, I think Met-Mapping has something for us.'

Piaget grunted an acknowledgement, nodded for the SL to lead the way and followed him, zigzagging down the flights of stairs to level 1.

At the bottom of the stairs Kraemer led the way to a trench of monitor banks directly back from the centre of the massive Met. screen, which now stretched above them like some huge graffiti-covered wall. Artificial colour rendering had switched in to compensate for the onset of night; the weather cocktail swirled seductively. Piaget halted as Kraemer dropped down the short flight of steps and approached an operative at one of the larger screens in the middle of the row. He touched the man on the shoulder and the latter turned around and nodded. Piaget saw the operative key in a command on the code pad as Kraemer made his way back along the row of screen monkeys.

'The Section Leader has the last two hours' met. for us, sir, and he's got some infra-red tracking which he thinks could show Lander 6.'

Piaget stepped past his subordinate and negotiated the steps down into the monitoring trench in a couple of strides. Behind him, Kraemer felt the floor spring.

The Met-Mapping Section Leader was already running the weather history as Kraemer caught up with his Commandant.

'Take it from 19:15, SL. That's our last transmission log from Lander 6.' Piaget hulked over the operative's back, completely obscuring Kraemer's view of the screen. Kraemer edged round the pair to where he had sight of the display. Piaget's lump-hammer face shone smooth in the reflected light, a flash from the dark pits below his brow betraying a glance in Kraemer's direction.

The Met-Mapper started his commentary, pointing a strikingly long manicured forefinger at the screen. A typical 'gene-genie' trait, Kraemer could spot the sons of the rich bastards a mile off.

'This is Lorus at 19:15 and you can already see there's a massive pressure drop going on by the rapid cloud build. If I take it to 19:25 and zoom out, you'll see that we've already completely lost the physical topography . . .' The screen showed a great swath of orange cloud covering the circular Lorus Depression. The Met-Mapper continued, 'Then, just ten minutes later, we see these anti-cyclones swinging around as they move to rush in to fill the low pressure, creating turbulence, which if you look at the bottom of the screen is given as winds measured by our ground stations at between 180 and 250 kph – hurricanes . . .'

Piaget interrupted. 'You've got some infra-red as well. Show me that!'

'Correct, sir. Our infra-red is primarily for ground temp, but a strong heat-source such as a Lander exhaust should give us a discernible trace – that is, as long as it's not running with shields on . . .'

'Run it, man! I've seen these things before. What was the fix, Kraemer?'

Kraemer rattled out the co-ordinates.

'Give me a zoom on IR, as close as you can at that location at 20:00!'

'One moment, sir . . .' The Met-Mapper winked at the screen and punched another code into his pad. The screen brightened into a mass of red. 'One moment, sir, I'll adjust the palette.' The red shrank to clotted pools contoured by rippling oranges and yellows. 'And here's the topography . . .' A green-toned mat unrolled under the paisley of the IR mapping; to the south, the New-mines Ridge was a dark olive fold.

'Give me a cross-hair on the co-ordinates.' Piaget couldn't see a thing.

A white circle, a centimetre across, appeared in the centre of the bottom half of the screen.

'More zoom, er . . .'

'Anderson, sir!' The Met-Mapper turned and virtually beamed at Piaget. The Commandant wanted his name . . . Kraemer thought for a moment he was going to kiss the superior officer, after all he was close enough . . .

'I can't get any more natural zoom, sir. I can go enhanced, but it's less accurate.'

'Do it, Anderson!'

The white circle bloomed to the edges of the monitor; in the centre was a tiny blue-and-white cluster of polygons.

'Bingo! That's L6!' Piaget leant even closer, brushing Anderson's shoulder with his breast ID.

'I agree, sir,' the Met-Mapper chimed in.

'Now run the scan from there at one-minute samples . . .'

Just two screens flashed up, and the polygons vanished. The screen locked at 20:03.

Kraemer felt a jolt of *déjà-vu*. 'I'll try Air-Traffic again, sir,' he said, picking up the desk comm-set.

Piaget swept the crumbs from his trousers to join the scatter of debris building round the base of his chair. Quite unconsciously, but to the amazement of the duty Flight Officer in Air-Traffic, he'd solidly gorged his way through two men's carbohydrate rations – the only thing AT could offer at that time on a Friday evening.

'You enjoyed that, Commandant?' Johnson, the duty FO, enquired. 'Sorry I couldn't spare anyone to go down to the mess.'

'Just something to fill me up a little, Johnson. As I said, first an exec assembly and then this. No time to get a damned thing.'

The two men sat in the executive office on the mezz above the Air-Traffic floor; through the full-height glazed partition, the controllers below were setting up re-directs round the storm-locked north and west of the city.

'It's a bad night, never mind your own guys. I've not seen anything like this since we had the meteorite hit. I've lost another Lander on the coast somewhere and there's a stratoflight that can't come in. No sat-nav and too much crap in the air for airtorque motors . . . It's heavy dust, my samplers give it all as heavy metal ore . . . It'll be those bastards at National Minerals blasting another strip. They haven't a clue what they're doing, no idea about the weather . . . I'm going to ground all of their stuff when this lot's over ... Look, you can't even see the Electrocorp tower from here.'

The eastern industrial quarter of M4 was unusually dark. Electrocorp's robotics tower was *the* landmark in the east; Lander pilots used it as their first visual fix when coming in from the Wastelands.

'... Oh yeah, sorry, nearly forgot ... Your man Kraemer voiced through, asked me to tell you that your wife had called, she knows something's on. Kraemer said that he'd explained you were up to your ears ... Is that Kraemer your "Mobiles" man?'

'Yes, a good officer, good on initiative. Gets off his ass and does things,' Piaget replied. 'Now tell me about my Lander. Is that the traffic log?'

Johnson had been leaning back in his chair waving a print-out as he gestured at the invisible Electrocorp tower. 'Yep, it sure is. Pull your chair over and I'll take you through it.' Johnson spread the plotted sheet out on his desk; clicking away his workstation console, it retracted into the desk top.

'Now this is the way I see it ...'

Johnson was typical of the jocks who inhabited the flight sections of Metropolis 4's organizations. Outwardly casual, scruffy even, and with a manner to match, the Flight Officer (1st Class) was almost an exaggeration of that breed which was a petty annoyance to the corporate mentality running through the whole fabric of the city's organized society. The real problem with these people was that they were good. Piaget had never met one who didn't know his stuff – hell, he'd even met women FOs who had impressed him.

What disturbed Piaget about Johnson was that he felt he genuinely liked this man. He'd first met him at some exec assembly where Johnson had given a briefing on aerial surveillance of civil disturbances; it was a couple of years ago and he, Piaget, had just been given two sectors in M4's south-east, filthy underclass residentials. Johnson had come up to him after the meeting and had assured him that he could give him crews who could get down below the building line, technically illegal and dangerous space. Together, over the next months they developed a clean-up strategy which cleared more Azzi dens than in any other sector. Johnson's pilots would take the Landers between air and ground traffic control, giving Piaget's on-board anti-insurrection teams an opportunity to monitor and smash entire floors of dregs and anarchists in the 'wohn-blocks', the tenement-housing schemes. Virtually undetectable, these patrols were blind-eyed by both the air and the ground traffic authority. He got some trouble at first from Ground Security, but when they saw how the tactic drove the Azzis out of the blocks into lower, less secure hideouts, their kill-rate put on pounds and everyone was happy. He still worried about Johnson though: he never seemed interested in the kill-rates, he just loved his Landers performing on the edge of their spec. Piaget had called in Internal Services to look at Johnson's flaky side, but called them off when they started to over-investigate his work practices, threatening the Azzi clearance project.

Johnson had now worked through the routine of Lander 6's out-flight; the print showed a conventional search sweep over a section of the Lorus Depression, mostly new territory for Piaget's Comms Monitoring teams.

'It's a long way out for your guys, Piaget, but no problem for the Lander though.'

'My decrypt specialist, Coton, had got a good fix and

went out there with Walker to nail it down. Walker knows Lorus as well as anybody: he trained with National Minerals. He loves it out there – he's not really a city jock. Joined us just after I transferred from the South-East job.' Piaget smiled at Johnson.

'That was some naughty project, Piaget. D'you know, I was getting some heavy Internal Services attention over that one?'

'Really?' Piaget's eyes flickered from Johnson's gaze. 'We were doing too good a job.'

'I guess so – but not nice, those "Internal" slimeballs give me the creeps.'

'They have their job, Johnson. You had nothing to fear, did you?'

'Nothing they could find!' The Flight Officer snorted a laugh and shook his head. 'I worry about you, Piaget . . .'

Johnson brought his attention back to the print-out.

'Now here's where things start to get funny.' There were blank spaces in the plot of Lander 6's course. 'This is where we start to get some comms drop-out, probably heavy minerals blowing across the beacon paths. You see how the course goes intermittent and then we get this weird deviation, then nothing, that's heavy weather. Look at the time on the matrix: 19:19, four minutes after his last voice-link. Now here I reckon that his navcoms have gone completely.' Johnson swept his pointer in a curve from the Lander's position. 'He's hit some really fast air and has put on speed to avoid a stall. The Lander goes with the wind trend and comes around in a shallow curve north, instead of maintaining his straight-line easterly course. He may even have lost his airspeed indicator and not realized he was going so fast, because to land up where your Met. guy loses him, forty-four minutes later, he's way off where he should have been and he's got there more like a Stratocruiser, must be at least 750 kph ground speed . . .'

'So what's your conclusion, Johnson?'

'Bad weather, dust jammed motors, Piaget. He'll be down where Met. plotted him. Your alert will have terrestrial search and rescue out there by mid-morning, depending on the weather. I can't see it, but if these storms blow out by daybreak we can have a Lander out there too. I couldn't recommend a landing though, not until I knew what the surface dust was like. We lost one, a year ago, on a similar recovery job. The pilot brought her down on what looked like a solid mesa – the whole thing caved in – took an Electrocorp droid team a week to dig the machine out . . . the crew just suffocated.'

Piaget looked at the plot again. 'Why was Walker going east after he lost his navcoms?'

'Your pilot knew the Wastelands, Piaget. He was flying purely on visual and he knew that if he could get a better angle and find some clear air, he could pick up a Metropolis mirage and get a good idea of where he was.'

'I've seen the mirages on a media flick,' Piaget commented. 'How reliable are they?'

'There's several places where you can get them, Piaget. If conditions are right and if you know your way around, they're good enough to show the way home. Your pilot, Walker, was going for a long shot, but it was probably the best he had.'

CHAPTER TWO

The 'Airtorque' motor was an elegant feat of engineering, a descendant of the old jet engines that had first given man the freedom of the sky centuries before. In its simplest form, the ATM was a series of turbines and compression chambers which sucked in air at one end and blasted it out at the other, by which time it was moving very fast and had reached a very high temperature. The amount of thrust developed was governed by venting the compression chambers and allowing cooler air to slow the whole process. ATMs were very efficient, requiring no fuel other than air itself.

The 'dense-air' planets of the Einsam Archipelago were particularly suited to ATM-powered travel, the atmosphere offering high aerodynamic buoyancy and an optimum gas balance. In clean air the ATM was unsurpassed for medium speed/distance mobility.

'Oh shit. That's no mirage, it's a genuine dust-wall!'

Walker, the pilot, pulled the Lander into a steep climb, throwing Coton away from the comms terminal hard, back into his seat. Coton leant forward against the acceleration, bringing his head level with the pilot's shoulder. He caught Walker's eye as the pilot glanced back to check on his intelligence officer's status.

Walker's tone was fevered as he continued, responding to Coton's unspoken demand for more information.

'You know I said that we'd chase a Metropolis mirage

and get a top. fix pretty easily ... Well, we've screwed up!'

'Correction, Walker!'

'OK, I've screwed up!'

The stall-warning alarm blipped and flickered as the pilot held the Lander at the limit of its climb-rate. Intermittent thuds through the airframe settled into a rhythmical drumming, announcing the craft's contact with the pressure wave generated by the looming dust-wall.

'We'll be into powder any second if we don't crest this baby!'

Walker was now thinking out loud; his commentary needed no lucid response, he just needed a reply to assure him he wasn't alone.

'Right!'

Coton barked the reply as if this would somehow discharge the apprehension flashing between the two men.

'We're not gonna make it!'

Walker was croaking through clenched teeth. He kicked a foot-load of right rudder through the control pedal; the Lander hung for a second, then lurched greasily into a full stall, nosing towards the scratched desert plain below.

Coton had been on 'Decrypt' for three months; he was good at it, it was like reading music. He could listen to a transmission, watch a wave-form and have a picture of the sender running his hands across a keypad or cross-patching a scramble box. They could compress or interpolate all they liked, there was always a fundamental rhythm to be felt. The new colour stuff was good though, it was an adaptation of a system used by the Internals, specially designed to merge with the Security

Service's own code. The Internal guys even bounced it around for the Azzis, beaming messages on to the required sector. A lovely system, elegant cheek.

Coton had managed to crack the random palette selector almost by chance. He'd been doing a little research and had found an ancient prime-number generator used for testing early computer types; it was basic, but quality maths. Take a twenty-nine-digit prime number, find another, splice them with simple arithmetical code – the key function – and use it as a palette address from the millions available. He never touched his vectorscope to frame-match like the Internals, completely up the wrong alley . . . Hours of processing . . .

Once he'd cracked the colour code though, things began to get dull, he was turning into a desk jock. All the other decrypt guys would just feed him stuff, he'd turn it around then sit back and wait for the field report. When the reports came in, he'd find that the field teams had completely missed the source; something was missing, the dumbos on the Landers weren't following through. They were lazy sons-of-bitches: give them a few vectors and off they went, they never cross-checked, never looked for patterns or red herrings. He'd memo'd Piaget up on his mezz, told him he needed to check his field teams' ops methods, but the big guy was only interested in getting his promotion out of there. Piaget was going to feel some heavy exec assembly download before that happened though.

When Walker came over to his workstation that Friday morning, Intelligence Officer Jon Coton was in the process of reviewing his weekend plans. He was off-hours for the first weekend in the month – always the best one to get, everyone in the central district had a full credit float and there was plenty of life in the 'real-clubs'.

'Hey, Coton, you've another eight hours before real-time!' Walker dropped down into the decrypt pit and perched himself on the ergo seat next to Coton's preferred standard tilt-and-swivel.

'You'll be dropping prod. codes in a minute; you know the old man monitors the lean rate on those exec chairs . . .'

'Get out, Walker, I'm out of prod. code range by Wednesday every week. I'm the only guy on the whole floor that actually goes positive every month!'

'Don't forget Kraemer, league leader, ears, eyes and nose of CF3!' Walker interjected.

'Kraemer's all admin, I'm talking about intelligence work. Y'know, using both sides of your brain at the same time . . .' Coton raised an eyebrow at the flight officer.

Walker ignored the reply cue and leant across Coton's workstation; he stroked an entry code into the blank palm pad. 'Here's some intelligence for you, Cot. We've got a new sub-net . . . Take a look at this.'

A new icon appeared on the row on the bottom of Coton's screen, a small skull and crossbones.

'Very original, Walker. Whose is that?'

'Dunno . . . Go on, open it!' Walker was winking crazily.

'You've been doing too many nights, Walker; that's a terrible twitch you've got there.'

'Open the damned box, Coton!'

Coton winked at the icon and a menu appeared. At the bottom of the standard list were two additions: *Contacts* and *Nightlife*. Coton smirked at Walker and opened the Nightlife box. There was one entry.

22

'*Real Club Azzocial*? What the hell's that?'

'Look where it is, Cot, look at the link number!' Walker was jigging up and down on the backless ergo seat like a circus sea mammal.

'That's Industry Two, Dodge City . . . You wanna go, don't you?' Coton had turned back to Walker.

Walker hushed and flipped up the comms monitor audio, then he got up and leant over the main screen, hissing under the data wash.

'Two guys from Flight went there last week . . . Too good . . . No cybies, no holomorph crap, real booze! It's a real real-club. They've got everything . . .'

Coton cleaned the screen with another wink and hissed back at Walker. 'You're mad . . . Two guys from Comms Monitoring going to a place like that. Hell, we'd finish the night in a garbage tube. They can sniff Big Mixer dudes a mile off!'

'Think about it, man . . . There's everything, absolutely the works . . .'

Coton killed the audio – he had spotted Section Leader Kraemer coming down the walkway. Walker straightened from the screen and turned to follow Coton's eye.

Kraemer skipped into the pit. 'I see a perfect team, gentlemen!'

'I was just saying the same to Coton, SL.' Walker patted the intelligence officer on the back.

'Oh, you've received the latest source rangings then, sir?'

'No, Kraemer, Walker's just being his usual presumptuous self.' Coton had adopted his superior officer's tone, wary of Kraemer's sometimes over-familiar style. 'What've you got?'

'A new transmission, from upcountry. Smack in the

middle of your old territory, Walker, the Lorus Depression.'

Walker sat himself back down on the ergo seat and cocked his head at Kraemer. 'You sure? That's a hell of a way out for our Azzi buddies ... Which sector?'

'I have a scan which suggests central. They're putting out VHF, loud and proud.'

'You know Lorus, Kraemer, one beautiful big mixing pot – your ranging could be miles out.'

'Well, Mr Walker, I have a lovely signal with regular ghosting – and I'm sure that IO Coton will back me up – it shows all the signs of coming right out of the middle of the Depression.'

Coton lit the comms monitor and scanned for the Lorus Depression. He read the multi-display and confirmed Kraemer's hypothesis.

'Looks very clean. These guys are out in the open somewhere, the co-ordinates stack up, it could be an easy hit for anyone who gets out there.' He paused. 'I'd like to know what the hell they're putting out though, something long-range ... I don't really understand why they'd be transmitting so strongly, obviously beyond the Lorus rim.'

'Source and solution action, Coton,' Walker cut in. 'Time to stretch your legs, I guess! Finish the week on a high note. Get Piaget off our backs, give the ungrateful bastard some promotion points ...'

'Walker's due out, sir. And this is the best TR we've had this morning.' Kraemer thoughtfully ran his finger around the monitor moulding as he spoke. 'Probably the best we'll get all day, sir ...'

Coton's curiosity had been aroused and it was a long time since he'd been out on field team activities. Krae-

mer, he also knew, was under a lot of pressure from the
Floor Commandant, the whole floor was. He, Coton,
was up to date with all the desk decrypt stuff, and a
blast out over the Wastelands would certainly be a
welcome end to the week. Moreover, Walker was
damned good, not one of those crazy ravine jocks that
had scared the shit out of him on the residential clearing
ops.

'OK, for the honour of CF3, I'm in ... Clear it with
Piaget, Kraemer, while I get down to Flight.'

'Very good, sir, I'll get you on the Field Ops Board.'

Kraemer knew that Piaget never really checked the
Ops crew lists. He would find his moment in the course
of the morning to tell the Floor Commandant that his
lead decrypt specialist was out on field ops. If he was
going to have any objection, Coton would probably be
already homing in on the TR ... It'd work out OK.
Coton was No. 1.

Down in Flight the Lander bays were all empty apart
from Slot 6. Walker and Coton had come nearly the
entire circumference of the 'Big Mixer' tower to find the
last available craft.

'Hell, how was I to know we were going to get L6?
I've been flying L1 all this cycle ... Anyway, the walk'll
do you good, Coton; your ass has been hardening up,
sitting at that station these past months.'

'You could at least have got the right elevator,
Walker!'

'I just wanted to get away from that roster staffer –
*Sorry FO Walker, I have no listing for your Intelligence
Officer on my ops list.* – shit-wit admin jock ... What
the hell's Kraemer been doing all this time? Goddam
SLs, they're all society plants, *gene-genies* ... What's

his father do? Super Senior Exec, Sec-Services, Chairman of Electrocorp . . .'

Coton interrupted Walker's spleen-venting.

'Kraemer's OK. He's a career guy, I don't think his folks could even afford a look at a gene map, his old man's some kind of tech manager in a theme park.'

'He's off the ball this morning, Cot. I don't need that crap from the roster dudes. They'll have us doing all sorts of report shit when we get back . . . And we need to be out on the town tonight, brother . . . Fresh and early . . .!'

'Forget the real real-club idea. I told you it was a bad plan, just listen to your *Intelligence* Officer! And don't worry about Kraemer, I'll voice him from the Lander.'

L6 sat in its park slot, still hooked to the service gantry, while two maintenance droids clicked and whirred along the walkway round the waist of the ship. A maintenance staffer stood at a monitoring console watching their progress. Walker swung away from Coton and spoke to the staffer.

'Should I be nervous, Ralph?' Walker's eye hadn't left the droids.

'Hell no, Mr Walker. These are Electrocorp's finest, we've been running them for the past two weeks on L6, just basic stuff, they're cute little workers.'

'How basic is *basic stuff*, Ralph?'

'Just routine, sir, cleaning, inventory, connecting umbilicals. Look at Droid 1 with that electrostat on the front screen: he's programmed to polish it until he can see his own retinas in the reflection.'

'You *are* joking . . .'

'Well, kind of . . . But they do have some sort of opti-sensor system which lets 'em know when the job's right. We've had no complaints.'

'What do you think, Coton?'

The Intelligence Officer had joined them at the console.

'They're good. I've seen these models at Electrocorp, they've got a combat droid based on this system type.'

'I think we're ready for your pre-flight, Mr Walker, Droid 2's dropping the umbilicals, my values on the console are all good.' The maintenance staffer scrolled the check screen as he spoke.

Walker scaled the gantry ladder as the two droids retreated round the far side of the ship to their docking point. The pilot started at the rear of the ship, checking the ATMs' intake filters. Coton moved under the belly of the craft and climbed through the crew hatch.

While Walker made the external visual checks, *the most important 50 metres you'll ever walk*, as it said in the flight manual, up and down both sides of the craft, Coton booted the comms systems: everything checked out 100 per cent. Some minutes later, the hatch seals hissed, announcing Walker's entry; his face appeared over the comms console, set in a ridiculous smile. He swept a flattened hand over his face in an exaggerated movement, wiping the smile and replacing it with inane blankness. Uttering a mechanical growling, he rose to his full height in a passable droid imitation and stuttered his way to the front of the cockpit and settled in the pilot's seat, laughing. 'Droids away! Coton.' He gave a wave to the maintenance staffer through the side-window and the gantry lifted, clearing the view ahead to the slowly opening exit port in the side of the tower.

The Lander rocked gently as the skid anchors engaged, and the docking platform carried the craft towards the exit port. Walker switched in the turbine spin and pre-heat, the heavy current hum woke the airframe and Coton felt his stomach flutter in sympathy.

'One, and two!' Walker announced the turbines as they ran up to speed. The oxygen injectors snapped open, Coton watched the rev counters catapult as the gas hit the turbine blades with a twanging whine. The docking platform was now locking outside the cliff face of the security services tower, while the roar of the turbines slammed hammering, oscillating echoes against the blast wall.

The docking panel indicators flashed green. Walker's intercom cut through the din.

'Oxy off ... Compression ... Combustion ... Lift thrust forty K ... Release ...!'

The Lander dipped momentarily as it left the plat-form, then pitched back as Walker wound on the power, and the craft surged away from the Big Mixer.

'A hundred and fifty K on one and two in less than half a second! This baby's got new ceramics ... Sweet little ATMs ...!' Walker's voice whooped over the intercom.

Coton replied: 'I've been checking the log, complete new main turbines one and two, fifty hours back, you crazy bastard!'

'You do that every trip, don't you!'

'What?' Coton bellowed.

'Check the maintenance log back to the last motor refit, you suspicious mother!'

'Well, I can't ask the hostess, can I?'

Walker banked the Lander into a steep climbing turn and exchanged a course code with Air Traffic. Coton could see the 'Big Mixer' below moving across the cabin window-frames like an animation flick. The smog haze was just building over Industry 1, the prevailing wind marshalling it in a wedge-shaped wave, driving the filth west towards the Central District.

Coton turned his attention back to the comms console and put in a link to Kraemer. The SL's face flashed up on the personal monitor.

'Good morning again, sir! I was watching you clear on AT.'

'No thanks to you, Kraemer! What happened to the entry on the field ops list?'

'Sorry, sir, there was some delay. FC Piaget was logged on to the list when I got back to my station; he'd just run a full print for an exec assembly and I didn't want him to have to change it.'

'Well, Flight Officer Walker's after your ass, Kraemer, he was getting some grief from the flight roster staffer — no record of Yours Truly. It was only Walker using some of his *very expensive* persuasion technique that got us up here. He now owes flight ops one; *ergo*, you owe Walker one-cubed ... Sort it out ... Or I can accurately predict some kind of ass-and-sling scenario ensuing. *Compris?*'

'Crystal, Mr Coton ... Don't worry, tell FO Walker it's in hand and please pass on my sincere apologies.' Kraemer paused and waved a data cart. 'I'm uploading the Lorus transmission data on the sat-link, sir. You'll have it any time now.'

'Thank you, Kraemer, I'll let you know if it's dirty. Speak to you at 12:00, out.'

As the Lander levelled at its cruise height, the comms console twittered the download. Coton switched in the nav-comparator and watched the Lorus Depression build across the screen.

'Was that Kraemer on the personal?' Walker called back from the cockpit. He'd backed off the throttles

29

and the crew deck was quiet against the dull rumble of the ATMs.

'He extends his sincere apologies, Flight Officer! Administrational difficulties . . .'

'He'll be extending more than that when I see him!' But Walker's face betrayed no malice as Coton flicked on the personal and caught him on vision.

'You're full of shit, Walker! I'm putting the TR data through on to your nav-panel. I'll come up and hold your hand!'

Coton climbed from the comms pit and joined Walker on the flight deck, snapping into the number 2 seat. The Lander was now over the northern edge of M4; they were crossing the weather walls, a series of ramp structures that protected the city limits from the shifting dunes in the summer and the snows in winter. Over the last century TI Creda's weather had worsened measurably, polarizing into a hot dry summer season and a bitterly freezing winter. Super-storm-force winds regularly lashed the low-lying northern city fringe and carried the seasonal debris, smothering the residential wohnblocks. The weather walls and the traps between them were routinely cleared throughout the year. Coton watched the dozers stitching red scores of fresh-turned sand against the bleached herringbone lines of the defences.

'How's the Met. for today? I want to run it over the nav-panel.'

'Looks fine, a couple of anticyclones to watch, quite normal for this time of year.' Walker cross-patched the Met. data, so that it patterned over Coton's TR plot.

'Straight on, driver; is that Newmines coming up?'

'Ghosting, Cot. That's a mirage, we'll get the ridge busting through the haze in about ten minutes.'

Coton settled down to observe this phenomenon, fixing his eyes on the shimmering brown strip. The comms monitor ticked on the open VHF frequency.

Walker announced their arrival at the Newmines Ridge with a sharp pull on the control column, automatically blasting the throttles. Coton just caught a glimpse of the hard brown of the escarpment splashing through the haze as the soft curve of the Lander's climbing nose interrupted his view.

'Heavy wind rotor on the ridge.' Walker spoke, holding his gaze on the altimeter. 'Did you feel that tremor just then? That stuff'll smack you in like an insect if you don't get some height.'

'Thanks for the warning!' Coton replied, his stomach just returning to its customary location.

'Five thousand . . . Passengers may smoke . . .' Walker smiled at Coton. 'There you are, the beautiful Lorus Depression . . . Did I tell you that there was smoke at that club . . .'

'Can the real real-club idea, Walker! I am not going to risk my ass . . . career . . . my freakin' life . . . for a night out with you in Industry Two! End of story . . . End of transmission . . . I'm going to admire your beautiful Depression . . .'

Cradled by the ragged arms of the Newmines Ridge which now arced away into the distance on either side of the Lander, the depression swept out to the vague horizon. It was featureless, save for the ancient scarring of mineral extraction, softened by centuries of heavy dust sweep. Walker played the Lander across the waste, enjoying the crisp new ATMs as Coton watched its shadow scudding across the geology through the floor observation prism. Its progress was effortless, distorting and snapping back into shape like some strange beetle.

31

He had gazed fifty minutes away when sharp data snap from the comms monitor broke into his fascination.

'Ho, ho! It's Azzi radio time, Cot. Man all consoles!'

'You bet!' grunted Coton, raising himself from the deep number 2 seat. 'I can see the logger going crazy already.'

The comms console was already issuing a search scan permutation as Coton slipped the headset over his ears. He immediately detected some other signal behind the VHF he was expecting.

'You got that course perm, Walker?! Three-thirty degrees, seventy-eight point . . . er, two clicks!'

'On the dial already, IO. You're not quite as quick as the nav feed!'

Coton looked at the multi scan and clamped his hands over the headset to concentrate on the noise under the prime signal. He could see a tiny peak on the light compression wave.

'Goddam! We've got some shielded light compression! What's on ground-scan, Walker?'

'Zippo, Cot, only National Minerals forty clicks south-west, and that's always been there, way off your TR source.'

'How far off from the search sweep are we? I'm going to change the sensor heads.' As he spoke, Coton unclicked from the comms pit seat and reached up to the overhead locker.

'Five minutes.'

'Give me . . .' Coton broke his intended request for more time as his eye fell on the empty clips that should have held the light compression sensor heads.

'How much, Cot?' Walker turned back to look at Coton. 'What's up?'

'There's no freakin' LC heads in the locker!'

'You checked the tech log?'

'Of course I checked the freakin' tech log – it was a hundred per cent!' Coton began to rattle open the other lockers, and the rest of the kit checked out.

'See if you can voice up Kraemer. We're going into the search sweep anyhow.'

As the Lander climbed to the scan altitude, Coton sat back at the comms console and logged in a report code, as there was no voice link available. Not unusual for Lorus, but the beginning of a suspicion nagged at Coton as he hammered an urgent request for clarification on the key pads.

Kraemer's reply flashed back on the screen, declaring no knowledge of the missing LC sensor heads but promising prompt investigation. Coton cursed the bland syntax of the message and concentrated back on the Azzi VHF. Walker was going into 'guidebook of the Lorus Depression' mode from the cockpit: the ship was on auto and he was bored.

'Your *Mysterious Mesa* was three hours back, you boring old bastard ... Or are we going round in circles!' Coton had been feeding Walker intermittent insults in order to keep him company, or was it to keep him awake? Whatever, the light compression vestige was still present and the VHF was coming in now and again, but it seemed to have no real form. They were certainly now closer to the source, but the stuff wasn't telling Coton anything – nor was Kraemer, as all his returns on the absent LC heads were negative. Coton would be joining Walker in a Kraemer ass-kicking session when they got back home.

'Weather's dirtying up some, Coton. I'll give it two more sweeps, then we'd better wrap it.'

As Walker took the Lander back on to manual, Coton felt the ship yaw, the action seeming to trigger a node on the ground scan.

'Take us round to one-two-zero, Walker, I think we've got something!' Coton peered back at the dunes rippling in the exhaust wash, as unpromising as all the other million . . .

The Lander was burning a crystal trail through the rising dust-eddies over Lorus. Flying at the scan altitude, the wash was clear to see from a good twenty kilometres by any observer in the dunes.

'We have the Lander at two-eight-zero, seventeen clicks. Do we hit him, sir?'

The weapons master's officer was standing at the opening of the canopy over the test station, holding the front half of a dust helmet over his face. Without dropping his gaze on the horizon, he replied to his NCO. 'No, they have no visual contact. We'll send them a final message from their comms officer. If we get no response, we will see. Our work is nearly finished and we don't need any extra complication.' The officer paused and turned back to the weapons master, rubbing his eyes. 'The weather may well be the best screen we have – this damned sand is building to a storm condition.' The officer walked back into the dark of the tenting, past a stack of droid cases, and climbed down into the half-buried command shell.

Walker now had the Lander off the scan pattern and was following Coton's course; they had dropped to 500 feet to reduce unfriendly visual detection and the craft buffeted on the waves of hot air sweeping up from the dunes.

'This is getting a bit wild, Coton – these boomers are flipping us all over the freakin' place!'

'Just a few clicks more, Walker ... Come on, you Azzi bastards, give us another TR!'

A Met. warning from Kraemer underlined the screen, demanding a mission abort.

Walker called back to Coton. 'You got that, Coton ...? Kraemer's doin' his job ... Actually got an accurate Met. report!'

'Keep going, Walker ... Any minute now ...'

Coton voiced a message to the sat-link buffer; it would get back to Kraemer and hold him off, once they'd pulled a bit more altitude. He'd just clicked the auto-encrypt when the Lander winged sharply to the right, a blast of white light from the port view prism behind him bleaching out the crew deck.

'Holy shit, Walker ... Pulse fire!'

Walker was in no position to answer. Coton could see his upper body wrenching the control column to pull the Lander out of the rapid side-slip. Another flash terminated directly ahead of them.

'Get your ass up here, Coton ... I can't see a thing!'

Coton gripped the edge of the comms console and flung himself up and across the crew deck. The vent system choked him with a hard noseful of burning something or other. Walker had the Lander on full power and climbing, as he made it to the number 2 seat.

'Just hold her steady, Cot, I'll be all right in a minute or two ... Freakin' light compression means pulse fire capability, that was military shit down there ... What the hell are they playing at!'

'Just steady? We're yawing like hell and I can't seem to correct!'

'Leave the rudder, Cot ... Back off on the stick and get her level. What's our altitude?'

'Two point five!'

'OK, ease off, relax, the motors are fine ... Now just hold the horizon ...'

'There is no freakin' horizon, it's all gone orange!' Coton peered ahead but couldn't make out a single detail.

'Better than me, Cot. It's all gone bloody red! Read the artificial ... The artificial horizon ... In the middle of the panel, you dork!'

Coton hadn't flown a Lander for over two years and he needed some practice. He also now noticed that there were no auto systems available ... and no nav-comms. He hadn't a clue where they were, or which direction they were going in. He held the Lander level while Walker fumbled with the first-aid pack and bathed his eyes.

When Walker finally managed to get some vision back, they were rocketing down what looked to Coton like some kind of spinning tube of smoke, and the collision strobes on the wing stubs pulsed their progress through the vortex, making his head ache.

Walker reached out from his seat, his head still tilted back, and flicked off the lights from the nav-panel. 'Thank God, I thought it was me ... You'll have us tripping out if you keep those things on ... Give me control.'

Coton relaxed on the column and watched the pilot trim the throttles to straighten the craft.

'We need to get out of this dirt fast, Cot – the ATMs won't take too much of this powder. We should be able to pull above this stuff and get some clean air and some freakin' topography.'

Coton climbed out of the number 2 seat and crouched by Walker's shoulder.

'I'll get back and see if I can get something out of the comms console. You OK now, Walker?'

'Getting there, Cot . . . No problem, we've still enough time to get out of this and get a top. fix, or pick up a mirage.'

Piaget was surprised when he heard that L6 had been located by an Electrocorp field test outfit. Nobody seemed to have known they were operating in Lorus, not that far out anyway. When he did a check on the movement records, though, there was a full security-coded log. Coton was a big loss: the field medics had him stable, but he was smashed to bits. There was no trace of Walker, rather like Kraemer. But the Section Leader's absence was more understandable. He would wish he was dead after he'd surfaced to answer for this disaster.

CHAPTER THREE

Ursula Clowes' chosen discipline of cybotics was – and she was the first to admit it – a strange one for a woman. The field was populated almost exclusively by males, all fascinated by the rather narcissistic theme of creating subservient anthropoid machines to service their whims. A personal interpretation, maybe, but she had put together a sufficiently sturdy argument based on this postulation to gain her the senior assistant's post on the Thin Doctor's latest research project. The TD hadn't yet gone into any detail about this new cybotics opportunity, but he seemed to be in no doubt as to her abilities to make a significant contribution. What the hell, if the Thin Doctor, the planet's leading sci-medical authority, valued her, who was she to argue?

She had declined the offer of an apartment from the Sci-Medical Foundation. An acceptance would have gone against all her principles of independence, not to mention her better judgement. She'd only once lived in a tied accommodation block, and that was during her early college days, ten years ago, back in Metropolis 2. The constant knowledge of being somehow always connected with an institution, even in her most private moments, was a feeling she found too claustrophobic.

This private apartment wasn't particularly grim, however. It shouldn't have been, either – the bursary from the Foundation was significant and was renting her a fortieth-storey view over East Central M4: a neat address, according to all the people she'd met so far. The four rooms: living area with balcony, bathroom, bedroom and study, were bright and fitted with pleasing, natural-finished furniture, attractive and comfortable. There was good security on the building and a twenty-four-hour cater-net link, where food could be vacc'd up in a capsule from any hooked-up outlet in the district. M4 seemed a good place to be. It was living up to its reputation.

It was a quick October outside, the month when TI Creda's condensed seasons competed with each other to gain the initiative for the day's next few hours. Inevitably, summer always lost through the single autumn month and now, in that early evening, a firmly cold blast of air from the balcony had swelled the curtains into the living room. There was no air-screen across the opening to the balcony, but Clowes liked it like that, the curtains were old-world and cosy. Clad only in her drape from the shower, she moved across the room to grab the billowing material, remoting the sliding glass closed from the palm-clicker. She looked at the time display on the compact device: it was seven-thirty, her date would be here in an hour . . . Still plenty of time. She went back into the bathroom.

The shrilling of the apartment doorbell made Clowes jump. She was expecting a softer announcement from Reception that her date had arrived – if this was her date . . . She flicked the large ent-screen on to door monitor and was surprised to see the frame fill with the unmistakable shape of the Thin Doctor, his back towards the security eye.

The Doctor turned and addressed the door. 'Sorry to catch you unawares, Ms Clowes. I always enjoy a little game with block security systems. I like finding the holes in the fence!' The Thin Doctor blew a little snigger down his nostrils. Clowes subconsciously registered that the Thin Doctor seemed to be initiating a face-to-face conversation, impossible through the security eye.

'Oh, no problem, doctor, I was just playing with the holobuilder. Please come in.' Clowes squeezed the clicker.

The Thin Doctor entered the living room from the vestibule, first making a quick sweep at eye level before dropping his scan to Clowes, now sitting upright on the sofa.

'I love your apartment: the doorbell ... and curtains ... terribly retro, very cosy.' The Thin Doctor moved down the steps into the sitting area, gesturing expansively with his right arm. 'Oh, you've killed the holobuilder; show me what you were doing ... I love these things.'

Clowes felt slightly uncomfortable, even more than usual with her new boss ... Well, what was usual? She had only met him three times ... She threw off the thought and replied to the Thin Doctor, who was now sitting across the play deck on the other sofa, his eyes full of anticipation.

'It's only a landscape, doctor, I started on it last week when I moved in. It reminds me of home.' Clowes waved the silicon shaper blade over the table and a beach-scape grew out of the play deck: perfect waves crashed on to a white crescent of sand and a tiny surfer tubed repeatedly in a looping cycle through the curling breakers.

'The man in my life ... I've only animated five seconds up to now, but he's cute, isn't he?' Clowes studied the Thin Doctor's face as he now knelt on the floor, his head level with the hologram. He was squinting down the shoreline, smiling at the progress of the surfer.

'He's very fine, I love your plane vector management; it's quite flawless — I hadn't realized you were so artistic. Does your résumé contain any other gaping omissions?' The Thin Doctor rose from the kneeling position as he spoke and he backed, slightly awkwardly, on to the sofa opposite.

'It's really only a hobby with me. I know that, once I get out more, I won't touch it for months.'

'Now I feel quite guilty,' the Thin Doctor replied. 'I shouldn't be taking you away from this work of art.' He paused. 'But I do have an evening planned for us ... I'll try and make it as stimulating as your wonderful landscape here. Are you ready to go? ... May I?' The Thin Doctor picked up the shaper blade and, flicking open the programming pad, he entered a few rapid clicks and shut down the hologram.

Beyond, the street was dark; tracers of diagonal rain shot across the pool of light under the block reception canopy and spat as they terminated on the hot lift-guards of the Thin Doctor's mobile. The door of the vehicle popped open and Clowes stepped inside, the Thin Doctor joining her from the traffic side. As the flux lift engaged, a close blanket of steam drew itself over the bonnet of the machine and then melted away as the mobile left the kerb. The Thin Doctor guided the vehicle to the end of the street, then pressed in the autoroute as they joined the leftwards traffic stream, towards Central 1.

'So what do you think of Metropolis 4? Our New Chicago.' The Thin Doctor rotated his seat to face Clowes.

'I haven't had time to see very much. Would you be

offended if I said it was much like any other city? A little grander perhaps,' Clowes replied.

'I could hardly be offended by such an honest reply, Ms Clowes.' The Thin Doctor tilted his head back and squinted up at the light-splashed dome of the mobile's roof. He spoke again, addressing the craze of colours. 'I owe no particular allegiance to this city-state, but it impresses me daily with its life and possibilities. I enjoy this place immensely, it gives me great freedom and choice. I think that once you begin to discover these opportunities for yourself, Ms Clowes, you'll begin to enjoy it too. Metropolis 4 is a great enabler, and we scientists are those it enables most . . .' The Thin Doctor returned his look to Clowes. 'There, a sorry, selfish confession from an old romantic. I'd best continue letting you gain your own impressions. Our own perceptions are, after all, the best messengers to our soul.'

'I'll agree with you on that final statement, doctor, but I don't perceive you as an old romantic, if you don't mind me saying . . .' Clowes laughed lightly. 'And I don't mean to invite the question, *Well how do you perceive me?* I'll only answer politely if you ask . . .'

'Fine, Ms Clowes. As I suspected, I believe we're going to work very well together.'

The mobile drifted right, out of the traffic stream, and came to a gentle halt at the kerbside. They were in the heart of the Central District, on the edge of a vast, tree-planted space. Across the square, over the top of the gently washing traffic flow, the 'Big Mixer' tower shot out of the dark soft far edge of the parkland like some forced vegetable, its lower blank fat stalk bleached by powerful floodlights.

'Impressive, isn't it, even on a miserable October

42

evening like this, Ms Clowes.' The Thin Doctor joined Clowes on the sidewalk as she took in the massive structure.

'The Security Services tower . . . *The Big Mixer*. It's a rather friendly sort of name for such a serious organization's HQ, don't you think, doctor?' She turned to the Thin Doctor.

He smiled and replied. 'It's the people's name, much nicer than the *Steel Finger* or suchlike. A little irony softens both the building's *and* the organization's existence perhaps? Come on, we'll get a better view from our table . . . And a drier one!' The Thin Doctor took Clowes' arm and guided her into the foyer of the building behind them. The rain was renewing its intensity.

Tiny lights like luminous pebbles guided them to the table at the edge of the restaurant. Clowes could see the white napkin on the arm of the Maître d' ready to flag them in on their final approach by the wall of glass.

'Good evening, doctor. A pleasure to have you dine with us again. Good evening, madam.' The man was immaculate, his accent strangely neutral.

They were settled at the table in Metropolis 4's most exclusive restaurant, the *Ouest La Plage* at the top of the Minerals Exchange building. Mist, smoking round the tower, dulled the view.

'You can't control the weather, doctor, you don't need to apologize.' Clowes stopped the Thin Doctor in midflow as he has bemoaning the seasonal elements. 'The Maître d', he was odd, like some kind of a . . .'

'A cyborg, Ms Clowes . . .?'

'Yes, he was unreal, quite bizarre . . . something about him just wasn't right.'

'His name is Pechard, he has a prosthetic face and

trachea. He was involved in an accident two years ago, when he was subjected to a blast of liquid gas full in the face. We rebuilt the front of his head and upper respiratory tract at the Foundation; he has full micro-hydraulic expressional articulation, but is virtually blind. At the time we could not repair or substitute his optic nerve.'

'I read your paper, doctor. I remember now, you synthesized the entire facial nerve cortex ... with great success, obviously.'

'Yes.' The Thin Doctor was thoughtful. 'We're very proud of Pechard. We now have an almost flawless system for constructing such subtle structures. We can now give our robots similar systems. The only thing that still needs refinement is the grey lump that makes it all work.' The Thin Doctor smiled across the table at Clowes. 'A little demonstration. Come with me to the bar. There's something I'd like to show you, something you won't find anywhere else except M4.'

The bar was a sunken, circular affair at the hub of the restaurant, populated by three male staff in crisp shirts and bow ties. As the Thin Doctor and Clowes neared the counter, one of the young men smiled and moved around to the quarter to where they were headed.

'Watch the barman, Ms Clowes,' the Thin Doctor whispered conspiratorially as he took her elbow and sharply changed direction.

The barman's expression flattened as they turned, and his colleague caught sight of the customers advancing on his section of the bar. The second barman, this one mustachioed, laughed and uttered a cheery, 'Hello, doctor, good to see you again!'

'And once more, Ms Clowes.' The Thin Doctor

changed course to circumnavigate the bar. 'That was the funny one!'

'They're all droids, doctor, they've all got your faces!'

'In one, Ms Clowes. They're rather fun, aren't they? I suppose we should have a drink and a chat, now we're here. Rude of me not to have offered before.'

They returned to the droid with the moustache who was now smiling again and polishing a tall glass with a cloth.

'Your usual, doctor, and something for your charming companion, good evening, madam. A terrible evening out there tonight, *still*, not unusual for our October.'

Clowes listened, fascinated by the odd rise and fall of the cyborg's speech. The machine had a phenomenal repertoire of small talk and conversed steadily, dropping quirky idioms into the flow of banality to humorous effect. The Thin Doctor was right: this droid was the funny one. When they laughed, the cyborg would pause, apparently registering the response of his interlocutors, then burst into a peculiar giggle which only had the effect of making her and the Thin Doctor laugh even more. It was a contagious loop, which was broken by the arrival of the menu borne by Pechard, who also seemed to exercise a calming effect on the droid.

The restaurant's menu was remarkable for the fact that every item on it was natural produce; Clowes could only speculate privately as to the cost of a meal here. She made her selection, taking guidance from the Thin Doctor's interpretation of the ancient language, and they returned to their table, ushered by the slightly over-attentive Pechard.

Throughout the meal the Thin Doctor philosophized and joked on a prodigious range of subjects, and Clowes felt herself falling under the man's notorious spell of charm. She admitted to herself that she had never before met a man of such obvious knowledge tempered with an instinctive wit. It was an intoxicating cocktail, and she wondered how old he was ... fifty, sixty? Too old for her in any case, but she couldn't help but keep imagining him when he was thirty years younger.

When they exited the elevator in the brightly lit sub-floor, the mobile was waiting for them, both its wing-like doors open. The Thin Doctor offered Clowes his arm as she slipped into the vehicle. Once he had joined her and the mobile was moving up towards the street level, the Thin Doctor surprised her with a question.

'Would you like to see a little more of M4's night life, Ms Clowes?'

Clowes had fully anticipated that they would be heading back to her apartment; after all, it was after midnight. She hesitated a little, toying with the thought, before answering.

'Why not ... This *is* my first proper night out in the city. Thank you, do show me the sights!' Clowes realized she was feeling a little drunk, or caffeine-blasted, the rich wine and the coffee peaking in her system.

'Very good, I'll take us over the Skyway so you can see some of Central. I know a fascinating place, just off the ring. We won't bother with the real-clubs, you'll have plenty of other evenings to visit them.' The mobile diagonalled into the traffic. The Thin Doctor moved the stick on manual and, after filtering off the city square, gunned the mobile up the sharp ramp on to the Skyway centre ring route.

'You can do that in this mobile, doctor?' Clowes had fixed on the Thin Doctor's control of the machine.

'Oh, you mean the manual control in the traffic stream! Do you feel all right, Ms Clowes? I'm sorry – I

46

should have thought.' The Thin Doctor registered Clowes' controlled speech and pressed in an aroma code on the climate system, his hand on the sliders like a piano chord. A smell of fresh peppermint filled the mobile. 'This machine is slightly non-standard and I've found that I can beat the Ground Traffic Control. I'm quite safe, I assure you – if a little thoughtless, considering our recent stimulant intake. Do you feel any better now?'

'Yes, thanks, I was feeling a little queasy for a minute.' Clowes breathed deeply; the peppermint had had a rapid effect and she could feel her stomach relaxing as she spoke.

The rain had now completely stopped; the skyway ahead spread out in a sweeping banked curve. Clowes could see the water-vapour rolling off the surface and stacking in the dark hollows among the raked support frames. On the right and almost overhead, due to the steep angle of the Skyway, the Central District cruised past. The commercial buildings presented a crazy topography of curves and angles like an experiment with a bowl of fruit and a geometry theorem. Clowes checked her head ... From the inside ... The last few minutes ripped past in reprise. She felt a splash of panic as she pictured the wine bottle from the meal and she drank in the heavy peppermint air of the mobile.

'I'll change the air again, Ms Clowes; we're just about to come off here.' The Thin Doctor's voice brought her back round. 'I think maybe we'd better get you back home.'

Clowes sat forward in her seat as the mobile levelled and slowed down the exit ramp of the skyway. 'I'm sorry, doctor, I'm not used to secondary alcohol, I suppose.

Is this the exit for our planned destination? This is much better, being back on the level again.'

The Thin Doctor stopped the mobile at the foot of the ramp. He spoke again. 'The place I had in mind is just along from here, outside the ring. We can still go back . . . On the ground, on auto-route . . .'

Clowes smiled at the Thin Doctor and replied, 'I'll be OK now. I could do with some iced water . . . I'm a little dehydrated, that's all.'

The Thin Doctor gently pursued a few more enquiries about Clowes' condition as he cruised the mobile along the flat boulevard which led off from the skyway. Open space on either side of the route eased the sensation of movement.

'Honestly, you can rest assured, I'm all right, doctor. Is it much further?'

'Just along the block coming up. I hope this hasn't been a bad choice on my part, Ms Clowes.'

They were entering an industrial sector and, as the mobile reached the first building after the open land, Clowes noted the large twin humps of freightway tubes rising out of the ground and butting up to the blank end of some kind of warehouse.

'Where are we, doctor?' Clowes let a little anxiousness show in her question.

'Industry Two, Ms Clowes. I planned a little contrast for our evening. As I said, I hope I've judged correctly. I wanted to show you another side of M4; there's a very interesting club just down here.'

The Thin Doctor stopped the mobile outside a metal-fenced enclosure on the corner of a side street. A narrow red light beam ran over the vehicle from a monitor box up on the fence top and an opening appeared in the steel panelling.

'No proper parking facilities around here, Ms Clowes, I find this Foundation store serves rather well, though.' The Thin Doctor chuckled as the mobile slid into the yard.

As the Thin Doctor guided Clowes across the dim, security-lit compound, he explained the ground rules for being in the *Real-Club Azzocial*.

'It's not really a real-club at all, the key thing about the *RCA* is that everything in it is actually real. Well, they do have some holomorph and cybie-type cabaret, of course, but everything they put on in that mode is pure parody.'

'Sounds fascinating, doctor. Is it much of a walk?' The October air was refreshing her body and spirits, but left a sulphurous aftertaste on the back of her throat.

'No, no, we just pop through the gate over there and it's across the street. Now I have to say that some of the clientele are not quite what you may be used to – it is a little *azzocial*, in fact. The club isn't officially licensed, but it's tolerated – well, for the present – by the Sec-services. It's an exciting place, but quite safe, I guarantee.'

Clowes smiled at the Thin Doctor striding along like a military droid and found she believed in the guarantee one hundred per cent. She felt no surprise.

'And one other thing: you are my niece for the rest of the evening. I shall call you Ursula and you must call me TD.'

'Uschi, TD, please call me Uschi. Only my mother calls me Ursula.'

The Thin Doctor went through some kind of formality unseen to Clowes in the shadowy entrance to the club, then they were inside. They descended a precipitous stairway and emerged on to a curving concrete raised area, about ten feet above a busy dance floor. The basement was large, apparently circular, and smoke hung in the air. There were a few flashing lights but no holoprojectors, and the farthest wall was only partially visible past a row of dim red lamps on the tables on the platform opposite. A hard-edged music struck Clowes' eardrums with its pure acoustic clarity.

The Thin Doctor was beaming at Clowes as he observed her looking for the source of the sound.

'Classical music, Uschi – jazz! There's a band over there, about twenty degrees from our twelve o'clock.' The Thin Doctor pointed and Clowes could just make out the flashing of bright metal against dark human shapes, slightly raised on a low stage.

'This is amazing, do . . . TD, it's so . . . so alive!'

'Come on, let's get you that ice water.'

The bar was thronged several bodies deep and Clowes hung back as the Thin Doctor worked his way through the mass. He was the tallest man in the crowd, by a good head the tallest, his silver hair and sleek dark suit contrasting sharply with the somehow cruder shapes of the other patrons. Clowes looked down at her own smart evening wear then back at the group at the bar. The majority of them were clearly underclass – UCs. She felt a little nervous as she noticed more than one or two of them looking at her; she was a trespasser. Clowes moved away to the rail over the dance floor. As she observed the dancers, she could spot more like herself: professionals taking in a little wild life. She felt more comfortable as she enjoyed their uninhibited dancing – obviously they felt no threat.

She felt a touch on her arm.

'Evening, Genie.' A low voice, not the Thin Doctor's, belonged to the toucher. 'You're with him, then!'

Clowes turned to find a solid, youngish UC man uncomfortably close; cigarette smoke wound from his hand and stung her eyes. She glanced around for the Thin Doctor.

'He's still at the bar . . . This your first time here?'

Clowes found herself tensing irrationally as she mentally balanced to control the encounter.

'Yes, it is . . . My uncle wanted to show me a really good club.'

'Your uncle? Not a lot of family likeness, Genie . . . You wanna buy anything? Smoke?' The man raised his cigarette.

'Er, no thanks, I don't do tobacco . . . or anything else.'

'Not a lot of fun, are you? Mind you, you must be fun for something . . . you're with him, aren't you . . .? You wanna watch who you hang with down here . . .' The man moved away and back to the bar, passing the Thin Doctor as he returned with the drinks.

'Did you buy anything, Uschi? Sorry, I should have warned you about the dealers, some of them are Sec-services plants. They use this place as a net for their insurrectionists.'

'It's all right, I'm just annoyed with myself for being fazed by him, he took me by surprise. Can we sit down anywhere? Somewhere quieter maybe?'

The Thin Doctor led the way to a series of alcoves almost hidden by the spread of people at the bar. The crowd seemed to screen the noise of the music and Clowes found she could speak without having to raise her voice.

'Is this a regular haunt of yours, TD? My UC friend . . . I don't know, he seemed to know you.'

'Really? Well, I do come down here from time to time, it makes a refreshing change from Central. It's a fine place for just observing people. You'd be surprised who you see . . . And who sees you, I suppose. I sometimes speak to perfect strangers, perhaps he was one of those.'

Clowes peered out into the grey smoky hall; she thought she might glimpse the man from the bar. In the same visual sweep she noticed that the roof of the club was perfectly domed – the whole space represented a complete hemisphere, in fact.

'What did this place use to be? It's not a purpose-built ent-centre, is it, TD?'

'It's a disused pressure reservoir from the freightway. You saw the tubes on the boulevard. It was abandoned during the last redevelopment. Underneath the dance floor is the other half of the sphere, and the floor laminate makes a very effective diaphragm for the sound system.'

'Then what's below the floor, just space?' Clowes had an image of the floor caving in and the bouncing dancers tumbling into a black void.

'More or less, Uschi. There are some services for the club and ports to the freightway, well sealed; a few hundred psi of propellent gas would certainly upset the dancing, if it were not so!'

'Makes me feel a little nervous, perched on the edge of it, all the same. How do you know all this? Have you been down there?'

'I just ask questions, much like you do, Uschi. I took a look once, there's an access hatch behind here.' The Thin Doctor gestured vaguely behind them. 'I too have a naturally enquiring mind – essential for our profession – essential to exist in this society, I believe. Now tell me some more about yourself, I know a little from your résumé and your file. Tell me about your family.'

In the dim red glow from the table lamp, the Thin Doctor watched Clowes' expression change from one of enquiry to a deeper seriousness, as he had expected.

Ursula Clowes was one of two children in a professional-class family in the city-state of Metropolis 2, TI Creda's second city after the dominant Metropolis 4. Her parents were both medical doctors, individual specialists in psychology and neurology. Ursula Clowes' mother, the psychologist, was quite eminent in her field and had founded a clinic which brought in sufficient income to allow her and her husband comfortable semi-retirement. They now spent most of their time in their island home just off the coastal city of M2.

Ursula was the younger of the two children, both naturally conceived and born within three years of each other. Ursula Clowes was now nearly thirty years old; her brother Georg was dead. She had been eighteen years old when Georg died, his death the spur to her taking up the study of medicine. Up until this event she had decided to herself that she wanted a career away from her parents' discipline; she had wanted to be a physicist. TI Creda's technology was on the brink of developing a faster-than-light-speed space propulsion system and it was this leading-edge field of science which had captured her imagination. She could have made it, too: Clowes was the right material, her logic was clear, and computation was the strongest academic subject in her education assessment at the time.

By contrast to his studious younger sister, Ursula

Clowes' elder brother was wild. He had joined the military academy as soon as he could, at the age of eighteen, in bitter conflict with his parents' aspirations for him. They had finally conceded that it was a better plan to have Georg's adventurous nature channelled by the system; the alternative would have been to run the risk of an unknown outcome for their wayward child at the hands of an authoritarian society which frowned on the type of independence Georg displayed so strongly. Georg had been an academy cadet for only a month when the accident occurred. It seemed that he was involved in some extra-curricular activity, high on some kind of stimulant, high on the roof of one of the training academy's barrack buildings. He slipped and fell while attempting a leap to an adjacent block, and he suffered a severe head injury in the fall. There was much official to-do surrounding the incident and Georg, then weeks into a deep coma as a result of the event, was expelled from the military. The academy took no responsibility for the accident and the parents were forced to hospitalize their son at their own expense.

The Clowes parents were lucky in that they were both well connected as medical professionals, and Georg had the best attention through their contacts and their comparative wealth. A whole year of repeated surgery was spent on Georg's damaged brain, and much was achieved in restoring many of the basic functions which had been lost.

Fourteen months after the accident, Georg came out of his coma. He came out of his coma, but he emerged with a variety of disjointed consciousness; the most accurate diagnosis that his parents and the specialists could make was that their son was now suffering from a form of autism. He was back in the world: he could see the world, feel, touch and act in it – but he could not logically relate to it. The family was devastated, they seemed to have got so far, and now this.

Their father, the neurologist, was worst affected. He had taken part in some of the surgery, and he entered into a depression that still haunted him, even now, years on from the event. His wife found herself torn between supporting her husband and her brain-damaged son. It was at this time that Ursula Clowes took on the lead role in caring for her brother, two years of painstaking care that saw a steady improvement, then the shock of his sudden death.

The Thin Doctor had been silent while Clowes told her story; he was measuring her signals from the profound events and balancing them against the weight of the proposal he was about to put to her. His judgement on the evening's entertainment had seemed to be sound, but he now started to question his choice of Clowes for the project he had in mind.

More drinks had arrived at the table, a bottle of ice water and the Thin Doctor's chosen spirit. The Thin Doctor refreshed Clowes' near-empty glass.

He spoke as she brought the drink to her lips. 'So, after all the time you'd spent restoring your brother's consciousness and then witnessing his sudden decline and death, it was then that you decided to go into medicine?'

'Yes,' Clowes replied. 'I felt cheated, and I believed that there was more that I could have done.'

'You did everything in your power, it would seem. Teaching Georg to relate to the world again, you achieved an amazing amount, and besides, his death was outside your control. So then you took up medicine, and just as you had graduated – in neurobiology, no less – you then elected to switch to cybotics. Why the change?'

Clowes let out a sigh and rolled the narrow glass of water between her palms; this gesture and her clear, attractive face, lit by the table lamp, made her seem iconic, her tone of honest revelation compounding the image.

'I realized that I was doing things for the wrong reasons. I had wanted somehow to go on doing something for my brother, and at the same time I was following my parents' wishes. My choice wasn't rooted in what I was logically interested in – it was too emotional, not the right basis for me to rest my future on.'

'Not a scientific choice, Uschi – and at base you are definitely a scientist.'

'True, TD, I originally applied to join the Light-Speed Project, but I was rejected in selection, I don't think they wanted me with my recent background. So then I got into cybotics, which I saw as being the next best thing: pure research and a dynamic discipline really going places, and I've no regrets, I love this field, it's brought me to M4, the centre of excellence . . . And now, here I am with you, the most famous scientist on the planet and I'm going to work on one of your projects, a dream come true . . .'

'My project, Uschi.' The Thin Doctor hesitated. 'I think we should discuss that in the morning. Can you come to my study tomorrow, shall we say at eleven o'clock? I've kept you from your bed far too long already . . . And thank you for telling me about your brother, it was important that I heard your story.'

It was just on three when Clowes flopped down on

56

the sofa in her apartment. Her head was still spinning from the evening – the meal, the funny cyborg, the embarrassing sickness in the mobile and then, to cap it all, her telling her life story to the Thin Doctor in that weird club.

'Oh, my stars . . .' She breathed the words out loud as she tried to remember what she had said.

She poured herself a glass of water from the flask on the table and popped a z-powder to calm her head. As she stretched out on the cushions, she felt something dig into her back. Slipping her arm behind her, she pulled out the holobuilder shaper control from where the Thin Doctor had left it. Clowes reached out, fanning the shaper over the play deck, and watched the beach-scape rise out of the plate. The little surfer still tubed through the breakers; then she noticed he wasn't alone, he had a double – a silver figure had joined her original character, following a parallel path through the waves.

'Wow, a new man in my life . . .' Clowes could feel the silliness coming on from the powder. She was asleep in seconds.

CHAPTER FOUR

Metropolis 4's accepted working day spread over twenty highly productive hours. Most of the working population were occupied in four-hour job-share slots, rarely running concurrently, so that for a large part of the day people were on the move to the location of their next share slot. This arrangement worked well for M4, and it operated with small variations in the other city-states of TI Creda. The system kept the public service and transport systems fully utilized and in profit, but, more significantly, it kept the population busy.

The process of the population being in employment was more important to the city's managing fathers than any product of the employment itself. The people in the job-share system, eighty per cent of the working population, were underclass and were engaged in service industries or administrational occupations. The work was generally self-serving, since real wealth generation took place in the wide-ranging automated industries and their powerful trading and research institutions.

In order to maintain the punishing schedule of the job-share system, workers routinely relied on stimulant drugs either to keep them going or to allow them to rest. The more-or-less-constant state of either upping or downing therefore kept the bulk of society sufficiently dulled not to question too hard the wide social inequalities that undeniably existed. There was no state benefit safety net for those unwilling or unable to work; all services, education and healthcare had to be financed by the individual. For those unable to find other means, job-share was the only way to survive.

UCs, underclass society members who made up most of the job-sharing group, had their own sub-set, broadly referred to as *Azzis* by the ruling politico/technological elite. The Azzis themselves were no straightforward group; the classification conveniently embraced those who were involved in crime and insurrection, or who simply didn't work for a living in any visible way. There were people from all strata of society who had landed up in this section at the base of society. Many had their own individual agendas and the grouping was an ever-present irritation to the smooth running of the city-state machine. They were therefore the main focus of attention for the Security Services in all of the planet's city-states, the biggest fear being that the widespread Azzi groups might begin to act in concert with one another across TI Creda. This was the planet-wide driver behind the Security Services' overwhelming preoccupation with communications monitoring.

Piaget had finally made it, his days in Comms Monitoring at last seemed numbered and new pastures beckoned. Now he just had to get through the damned traffic congestion that the twenty-hour system was supposed to even out.

For two days now, the feeling of anticipation had overwhelmed Piaget, triggered by the summons from the Executive Selection Board. He was about to conclude Stage Three, the final step to full Staff Officer status. Now the millstone of direct departmental responsibility could be removed, executive autonomy was within his grasp. He would take his own initiatives, lead his own special projects. But this anticipation was a dreadful and useless emotion.

Piaget had fired his stress counsellor, who had been muttering about *acceptance* and Piaget's need to reconcile the *child* with the *parent* side of his character.

'Crap, absolute neonized crap.' Piaget was vocalizing his thoughts as he waited for his presently stationary mobile to filter into Skyway Central 1's subscription lane. This was the first day of real winter cold, and the traffic was heavy; two weeks ago in this situation, he'd have let his vehicle auto-route it into the parking frames while he used Central's powered sidewalks. Now he could see frosty eddies of precipitation spiralling over the queue in front, it was zero plus wind-chill outside. A meaningless traffic control indicator nagged at his peripheral vision on the skyway's guard rail. Piaget turned away and idly scanned the infotainment channels, then flicked the console back to trafficom, but there was little movement in Central.

Ursula Clowes had woken early with a stiff upper body from her night on the sofa. She was still muzzy from the effect of the z-powder she had taken just four hours earlier. She had no memory of the evening before, but she knew that this would return, once the drug had worked through her system.

As she showered she felt the tension drop away and slowly the events of the previous evening began to rearrange themselves in her mind. Z-powders were curious drugs: they could obliterate and rebuild memory in serial time; the parent pharmaceutical was used medically in psychiatric treatment. Under expert usage, events in the subject's life could be pinpointed and then be suppressed or removed altogether. Clowes used the domestic product rarely and then only in its weakest form, to help her sleep.

As the recollection of her morning's appointment with the Thin Doctor fell into place, she enjoyed a definite buzz of anticipation. The two weeks since her arrival in M4 had left her with a slight sense of disappointment, as she seemed to have been almost totally ignored by the great scientist. This was it, though; today all would be revealed. She would be able to start work at last.

Clowes dialled a breakfast order into the cater-net then wandered over to the window. As she clicked back the curtains she was surprised to see a fine powder of snow dusting the balcony.

Clowes pushed her face against the glazing which was slightly cooler than the room. 'Intense ... Snow in October.' The little patch of condensation from her breath spread then rapidly evaporated with each word. In her native ocean-side Metropolis 2 it was rare to see snow before January.

Piaget smiled at the security staffer at Command Floor 6's reception. She seemed to have recognized him from his previous visits to the exec floor.

'You're already logged in, Commandant. Could you please just confirm with a palm-scan?'

'Certainly, Duty Staffer.' Piaget pressed his right hand on the soft opalescent pad. 'Which gate today?'

'Gate one. Your meeting's on level five, sir, suite three. I'll let them know you're on your way.'

'Thank you very much, Ms Flute.' Piaget had taken the trouble to read this woman's ID; it was surprising what influence even a duty staffer could have on CF 6. They were very well screened to get such a plum job –

she could even be sleeping with some Staff Officer, so a little prudent familiarity now could pay dividends later. You simply never knew.

Command Floor 6 was the uppermost of the Big Mixer's rotating aerofoil extensions, and level 5 was its top level. As the glass-panelled elevator carried Piaget on the short haul up through the hallowed floor, the spacious cube steadily filled with natural light from the sheer glazed roof of the executive level. Piaget felt for the blocker tab in his trouser pocket which his wife had dropped in there this morning. He swore to her that he never used calming drugs, but now he found himself popping the blocker into his mouth. Damn that anticipation . . .

Clowes watched the ball of white appear in the bottom of the deep slot which cut Central 1's wall of commercial buildings, a click or so distant. As the A-train neared the station, the fluffiness of the shape steadily hardened and took on a more geometric form, growing larger up the snow-dusted track.

Clowes remained at the head of the platform, enjoying the spectacle of the last few seconds of the A-train's approach. She stood, rapt, as it sent long cones of powdery snow pluming from its chisel front over the lip of the track. The whole dramatic event was markedly silent. The damping effect of the snow and the dullness of the ranks of commuters soaked up any sound-effect that this arrival should have had. Only the residual whiff of naphtha and sulphur, pollutants released from the melting ice-crystals, left a tag on the event. It was a new spectacle for Ursula Clowes, but nothing out of the ordinary for her tired fellow-travellers who witnessed this prosaic event, day in day out, every commuting winter. Clowes moved with the crowd through the nearest open passenger-car door and managed to find a seat across by the far window. The doors closed and the flux lift surged the train smoothly back towards Central.

She had a different feeling today: she felt a part of the city machine, and she smiled to herself at the prospect of the new chapter opening in her career. On the seat opposite, an oldish UC woman glanced at Clowes as she scratched a long fingernail in a plastic tab cartridge. Eventually she hooked out a small red pill and nonchalantly brushed the button of chemical into her mouth. By the time Clowes had reached her stop, the woman had completely out-smiled her by ten to one.

In Central, the power sidewalks ran black against the dusty snow and Clowes played a game of identifying the building entrances just by noting the degree to which the snow had been mashed by people stepping off the power track. When she arrived at the Sci-Medical Foundation, she could see that she was early: only three or four identifiable sets of tracks led up to the building's curved narrow frontage. The Foundation building was deceptive. From the street, the onlooker could see only the vertical composite and glass cylinder which formed the main supporting structure. Behind this rather lean tube, floors fanned out radially from the rear of the structure in leaves of pie-section plateaux.

Clowes logged in at the security desk and made her way down to the mess area in the number one basement. She was going to treat herself to a real coffee; she had plenty of time, it was not yet nine o'clock.

*

Piaget settled himself calmly in the chair in front of the executive selection panel. The four Selectors opposite him sat in the shadow thrown by the partial polarization of the glass ceiling. Piaget glanced up at the clear section over his head and saw nothing but grey sky. If the selection panel were going for some kind of dramatic effect with this choice of illumination, he didn't feel fazed by it. He smiled inwardly, then tensed for a moment as he worried that the blocker tab he'd taken might relax him even more. If he could hold it as he was now, this session would be a cruise.

The chairman spoke. 'Mr Piaget, this is your final attendance before the executive selection panel. My fellow panel members and I have reviewed your progress so far and have, I will tell you now, made certain decisions about your suitability for full Executive Staff Officer appointment.'

Piaget felt the effect of the blocker disappear. They were going to reject him. He leant back in his seat, unable to arrest his hand which had already risen to stroke his chin nervously.

'We have all of us been impressed by your progress within the service to date. Your wide experience and obvious loyalty and commitment to our common aims have led us to the conclusion that you are indeed the right material for a staff appointment. Yet certain events this year – the loss of two experienced officers in the service of your department, no less – have caused us to have reservations about your readiness for the executive autonomy that comes with Staff Officer status. Do you understand, Mr Piaget?'

'I understand, Mr Chairman.' To launch into a defence now, Piaget knew, would be the kiss of death to his career.

The chairman continued. 'However, Mr Piaget, we do

not wish to deter you from pursuing your ambitions in the Service with the vigour which you have clearly shown so far. We are very keen that you continue to demonstrate to us that you will make Staff Officer grade and therefore, to assist both you and ourselves in the selection process, we are relieving you of your present command in Communications Monitoring.'

It was getting worse. Piaget saw his dream of the Sunnyside apartment melt away. The chairman noted Piaget's clear dismay; the ex-Floor Commandant's now fidgety body-language belied his neutral expression.

The chairman spoke again, his tone of voice noticeably lighter. 'Take heart, Mr Piaget, we *are* offering you a promotion. We wish to raise you an increment and give you responsibility for a specific project. This is not a full Staff appointment, you will not have complete autonomy; but you should consider it a stepping-stone to the Staff Officer position which you will doubtless achieve eventually.'

Piaget had regained his confident posture, and he smartly acknowledged the chairman as the session continued its progress.

'And that, gentlemen, is all I have to say ... Mr Piaget, I wish you good luck ... I now call this session closed ... Would you please remain, Mr Piaget, Staff Officer Pepper will brief you on your new appointment.' He gestured to the panel member on his right. 'Thank you, gentlemen.'

The chairman and the two other anonymous panel members rose and filed out of the room through a door which Piaget had only just become aware of in the gloom. Pepper stepped round the curved table and greeted Piaget with a handshake.

*

The Thin Doctor's office was decidedly stark. He sat at a square, traditional timber table, framed in the hemisphere of glass that formed the end of one of the stubby wings of the Foundation building. The table was clearly a genuine and very ancient antique, and it contrasted sharply with the workstation sprouting out of the floor at his side. This was also quite individual: all the purplish green interface surfaces folded out from a central stalk, crowned by a paper-thin stereo screen which curved from the top of the tree like an oversized leaf. Clowes thought to herself that it looked slightly ridiculous. The only other item in the room was a curious sculpture sitting in the centre of the table. This was a clear plastic vessel, filled with liquid in which floated an overgrown, shallow, truncated eggcup affair, some ten or so centimetres across. It seemed to be made of a strange, oxidizable material of indeterminate colour, or maybe just grey.

'Good morning, Uschi. I trust you managed to get sufficient sleep after last night. I saw that you were here in good time. How do you feel today?'

'Fine, doctor, I took a little assistance from a z-powder. Thank you for last night, I enjoyed myself very much.'

'Not at all, your company was charming – but I *was* worried about you on the Skyway.'

'High living, I'm just not used to it.' Clowes smiled apologetically.

The polite exchanges continued for some minutes, then the Thin Doctor reached out and pushed the sculpture across the table towards Clowes.

'What do you make of that, Uschi?'

The eggcup thing rotated gently in the fluid and Clowes could now see that the inner surface of the cup was made up of thousands of tiny soft flaps of what looked like algae. In between the swirling texture she could see hundreds of tiny metallic pinheads, possibly some kind of securing studs for the peculiar lining. The thick stem was similarly lined and hollow.

'I thought it was a sculpture when I first noticed it, but, looking more closely, I would say it's some kind of device, partly organic? It looks like it could have another piece to it – something that goes on top or sits inside maybe?'

'Very good. It's a bio-laminate, a spin-off from our tissue-growth programme.'

'It's some kind of organ?' Clowes interrupted.

'Not quite ... It is virtually organic and is very sensitive to the atmosphere, hence the fluid. It's a synthetic cranial floor ... A carrier for a human brain.'

Clowes drew back from her examination of the object and looked squarely at the Thin Doctor. She wanted to see his reaction to her next question.

'And this, er, *cranial floor* is key to your new cybotics project?'

'Pivotal, Uschi. If you pardon the slight pun. I believe I can now locate a human brain in a cyborg chassis and have full cerebral functionality – motor functions and complete sentience.'

Clowes saw the utter confidence in the Thin Doctor's face. She didn't doubt that he was right, but the consequences of being able to achieve such a feat were inestimable.

The Thin Doctor granted her some time to take on board the concept, then he continued. 'We have already had long-term success with animal adaptations of this model. I can show you our cats and apes. You'll be impressed.'

Clowes was still finding it difficult to grasp what she was hearing; the full import of this quantum scientific leap was overloading her thought processes.

'I'm sorry, doctor, I'm having a problem taking this on board. You've just told me that you have it in your power to virtually customize the human race . . . I know we have genetics and we're already doing some stupid things to ourselves on that level, but if we go down this path, then the consequences could pervert the whole development of our species.'

The Thin Doctor studied the open concern on Clowes' face then fixed his eyes, clearly full of a kind of devotion, back on the specimen vessel. He spoke gently, seemingly addressing only the cube of fluid. 'Of course you're entitled to your interpretation, Uschi.' He flashed a look at Clowes. 'You have very valid fears for your race. This technology exists, and I'm offering you the opportunity to have some control over its destiny . . . Don't you see that if *we* don't exploit this field, then sooner or later someone else will, and you'll have no control. That can't be what you wish.'

'I wasn't prepared for this, doctor. This is something else . . .' Clowes paused for a second. 'You know I really hadn't any idea of the nature of your project . . . Cybotics, yes, but nothing quite . . . Well, I couldn't even have conceived of this . . .' She withdrew her hands from the table top and looked hard at the Thin Doctor. She sensed a real discomfort at this project the Thin Doctor was introducing . . . something amoral and seemingly already irrevocably under way.

The Thin Doctor made no response to her stare, and Clowes found herself continuing.

'Maybe I need to reconsider your offer. How can I be of any real use to you? There must be others, people on your project already, who are more experienced and qualified than I am . . . Why did you select me, doctor?'

The Thin Doctor hesitated noticeably at this question, then he rose from his chair and paced the short distance back to the window, staring out into the back lot. He ran his hand slowly from his forehead through his ample silver hair and turned, addressing Clowes in a softer, fatherly tone. The confidence he'd exuded in the last few minutes was lessened considerably.

'Uschi . . . I chose you for the assistant's post *because* of your experience. You're highly qualified in all the relevant technical fields, you have proven rapid learning abilities, and you have something more. I hope you will understand me when I tell you this. You have your past . . . Your experience with your brother, Georg.'

'Georg? How do you link Georg to all this, doctor?' Clowes felt a gut defensive reaction to the Thin Doctor's reference to her brother.

'Last night in the RCA, when I asked you tell me about your family, and you did . . . You told me all about Georg . . . His death and the time you spent with him leading up to that event . . . the two years you spent helping him to understand the world again after his coma and his terrible brain injury. I have to confess that I knew about these things already.'

'I had a suspicion, doctor. Especially after I'd told you. Please continue.' Clowes clipped the phrase, controlling a sense of anger at the Thin Doctor's manipulation of her.

'I'd heard from an associate in M2 that you had had some tragedy in your life; this associate was a colleague of one of your referees, Uschi. My initial discovery about your past *was* pure coincidence, I assure you.

Then I made further straightforward enquiries, and I learned about Georg.'

'You still haven't told me how this fits in with your selecting me as an assistant. Why should my personal life suit me for your purposes? Pardon me, doctor, but I need an explanation. I respect you very highly as a scientist, but I feel I'm the victim of some calculated manipulation ... I'm not happy about this, I have to tell you, doctor.'

'Hmm ...' The Thin Doctor lowered himself back into his chair and offered his upturned palms in a gesture of guilt. '*Manipulation* ... Yes, I can understand your anger. But, you see, I needed to check for myself.'

'Check what?' Clowes interrupted him.

'Sorry, Uschi, I've not handled this very well ... Please let me explain my project more fully. Then you'll understand why you are so important to its success.'

Clowes calmed herself and settled back to listen to the Thin Doctor's explanation. She had nothing to lose now, even if she'd already blown it with the Thin Doctor – but then again, she surely hadn't. The great scientist seemed to be going all out to get her on board, albeit badly. The idea of her being critical to the man's plan was both flattering and fascinating, but the thought of Georg being involved had spun a thread of personal horror into the possible plot. She was beginning to think that the Thin Doctor was capable of anything: he could have her brother's DNA or his brain-maps, or God knows what at his disposal. She suddenly remembered the gossip of the Foundation's lab people from the time when she had first arrived: the *mad professor*, not quite human. She could see it in him now.

The Thin Doctor began to tell her about his cyborg

models like those at the *Ouest La Plage*. He explained that they were pure electro-mechanicals, severely limited by their base intelligence architecture and unadaptable to functioning beyond the circular bar which was in fact their whole notional world. If one of them moved beyond the bar, if that were possible, he would be unable to interact with the new environment and would be completely useless.

There were only two routes for a cyborg to go down to be fully functional in the wider world: the path of total artificial intelligence using a synthesized and incredibly complex brain-emulating processor, the existing route chosen and still being pursued by Electrocorp's R&D people; or the Thin Doctor's own choice of locating a human brain in a machine and creating an effectively bio-mechanical cyborg. The Thin Doctor's choice was, he knew, fraught with profound ethical dilemmas.

The Thin Doctor paused in his lecture and flicked on his workstation, moving the screen around to where Clowes would have a clear view. As the picture filled the screen, she saw that it was a personnel file from the Security Services. She read the name under the ID hologram of the subject: *Jon David Coton*. A status box flashed under the file code line, indicating that the file was suspended.

'Who is he, doctor?' Clowes stared at the intelligent face of a man around thirty.

'He's an Intelligence Officer, a decryption specialist with the Security Services.'

'And the significance of your having his file, doctor? Is he a member of your team?' A preposterous thought snapped into her mind. 'He's not a volunteer, is he?'

'Not exactly.'

'Please explain, doctor.'

'Coton was involved in a Lander crash, earlier this year. He's alive, supported in a military ICU. He has a perfect brain scan, but his smashed body is beyond our surgeons' present skills. There's a tissue build programme already initiated, but at present we estimate at least a ten-year growth period before we can begin any transplantation.'

'And you want to use him in your cyborg project ... He's conscious? Does he know about your proposals?'

'He's in a coma. We can't be one hundred per cent sure of his sentience, but his scans are perfectly normal – no damage.'

'And you want to use his brain and then have me work with him when you move his brain to a cyborg chassis ... if I understand this scheme correctly?'

'Correct, Uschi. You're ideally qualified to support him, both technically and psychologically, post-transplant.'

'Do you know what you're proposing? You want to use this man like a laboratory animal. It's against every ethical code, although I know that abuses have been common in some Sci-Med fields.' Clowes looked for a reaction from the Thin Doctor, just a hint of acknowledgement. The Doctor remained impassive, waiting for her to finish her statement. 'How can you interfere with him? He's stable and he'll have a life again – eventually.'

The Thin Doctor flipped through a few screens and brought up a medical file. He pointed to Coton's haematology report.

'Coton is displaying high levels of several blood-borne toxins, a build-up resulting from his body's poor condition. We can't be sure that we can control the situation indefinitely; we can only guarantee to protect his brain from this danger if we isolate it very soon. You know yourself that even tiny levels of toxicity can cause profound damage to the cortex's delicate structures.'

'You're telling me that there's some urgency in this whole thing, doctor, and, if I don't want to be involved, you're going to go ahead anyway.'

'I'll have to, if only to save this man's life, Uschi.'

'I have to have some time to think about this. Give me twenty-four hours. You do appreciate what you're asking me to get involved with . . .'

'We have that long. But there's one condition which you have to agree to.'

'What's that, doctor?'

'This is a highly secret project. Only myself, my technician and certain people in the Security Services know about this. You cannot leave the Foundation until you have made your decision. If you contract to join the project, all well and good . . . If you don't, then you'll have to submit to a removal of the memory of this discussion . . . You already use z-powders; I trust that you'll co-operate if that's your choice.'

'You've done well, Piaget.' Pepper, the Staff Officer, shook the ex-Commandant's hand. 'You've landed a serious project. What do you know about robots?'

'As much as most of my Floor Commandant grade. They're dumb but obedient, useful if properly programmed.'

'OK, Piaget, so what about robots!' Pepper interrupted with a laugh. 'Nah, sorry . . . So you're not especially clued in, but you soon will be. We want you to manage a project which is going to revolutionize the way we all think about our droid friends. In fact, our droid friends

73

themselves are going to be revolutionized through this project.'

'Could you be a little clearer, Pepper.' Piaget was already beginning to grow annoyed by this smart young Staff Officer.

'You hit upon the fundamental problem with droids in your first statement, Piaget. *They're dumb but OK if properly programmed*; but, even then, you know their limitations. You know what a combat droid's like once you take it out of its known environment: they lose their parameters and then they're useless. Imagine what you could do with a droid if it had real human intelligence.'

'It would be a near-perfect combat and security machine, Pepper. It could render most of our people redundant overnight.'

Pepper's eyes lit up. 'Exactly ... Now, I don't know if you're aware of this, but Electrocorp have a droid which has something approaching a human level of cogniscent intelligence. They're calling it the *Chromium Programme*. Apparently this droid is already running half their manufacturing plant and their people are confident that it'll be out of trials in less than a year.'

Piaget had heard about this robot, but just casual rumours, and he hadn't paid much attention to them.

Pepper continued with his briefing. 'Now, you know what Electrocorp are like. They're the biggest commercial gangsters in the Archipelago; as soon as their droid's signed off, they're going to have them in production and exported to every state and corporation between here and Andromeda. We need a competitor product to diffuse their droid's impact and to slow the market, or they'll run away with it altogether.' Pepper booted the workstation with a remote from his pocket. 'Here's the baby that's going to spook their project.'

Pepper was now guiding Piaget over to the large hologram deck on the low platform where the selection panel had sat earlier. A full-size silver metal humanoid rapidly built out of the plate, which crackled loudly with the current rush.

Piaget winced as the cyborg slowly rotated, accompanied by more snapping from the electromagnetic field. 'Is that thing safe, Pepper? It's making a helluva noise!'

The Staff Officer smiled at Piaget. 'It's because it's all one colour, there's a slight overload on the guns. But what d'you think? Impressive or what!'

Piaget was impressed, but this was only a hologram – anybody could create a hologram.

'It looks good, but does this thing exist for real, though?'

Pepper turned back to the workstation and clicked up a laser pointer from the monitor screen. A pure, narrow, white beam of light now shot from the remote and Pepper swung it round the room, bringing it to rest on the cyborg hologram. 'Now this is the really interesting part, Piaget, watch this . . .'

Pepper held the remote at eye level with two hands and described a line through the hologram's head. He then moved the resulting stripe some centimetres to the right. The cyborg's head parted, revealing what looked to Piaget like a human brain.

Piaget turned to the enraptured Pepper and spoke. 'Is that what I think it is?'

Pepper replied, smiling again. 'Do androids dream of sheep?'

'So you're telling me that what we have here is a robot – with a human brain . . . Is this for real?'

'It soon will be ... The Sci-Medical Foundation has all the components, a chassis – and a brain. We've entered into a partnership with them to sponsor the project ... Your project, Piaget ...'

Piaget looked again at the hologram then back to Pepper. The Comms Monitoring department suddenly seemed very attractive again.

'This is surely very sensitive: the state – the Security Service entering into a commercial arrangement with a research institute. Who's behind all this?'

'Electrocorp has steadily become a serious security concern, Piaget. It threatens the economic stability of Metropolis 4, its growth is frightening. The company has doubled its global influence in the past year; its turnover now accounts for nearly half of M4's gross domestic product. Its trade across the Archipelago is seemingly unstoppable, and they now have an effective monopoly in the whole automation and droid sector. We cannot allow the imbalance to grow. M4's General Council of Fathers has given the green light to the Thin Doctor and his Foundation team. They have to progress this project as fast as possible. It's our aim to render this latest Electrocorp droid technology obsolete before it can hit the market ... And we need to have the right person in place on the project to look after the city's interests ... Someone with unquestioned loyalty to the state ... You're a lucky man, Mr Piaget; this appointment will set you up for the rest of your career.'

Tecchies ... Piaget had a few pet hates. He knew it, though: young ambitious officers, filthy stoned UCs, the traffic system – but probably at the top of the list were technical people, and the Thin Doctor, the planet's most eminent scientist, had to be the number one character in this sub-set. Weird, arrogant, smart, all of Piaget's hate adjectives sat perfectly with this man, and now he was going to have to work with him.

Piaget addressed Pepper again. 'So it's the Thin Doctor's baby. I should have guessed.'

'Yes, we have the planet's most eminent scientist working for us. Have you ever met him?' Pepper was obviously a TD fan.

'No, never.' Piaget suppressed the negativity he was about to express on the subject of the Thin Doctor's tecchie empire. He let Pepper continue.

'Well, you'll be meeting him soon enough. I'll give you all the schedules and your full brief from the General Council. I have it all on paper, can't risk a leak on an e-system. Any questions just now, Piaget?'

'No, Pepper. I think I've seen enough.'

'Right then, we'll call the briefing closed. Come with me to my station, and I'll give you the notes.'

The Thin Doctor had given Clowes a document pad containing the project summary and had personally ushered Clowes to the Sci-Medical Foundation's quarantine section, where she would have to remain until she had made her decision about joining the Cyborg Project. The whole scenario was quite bizarre, and now she found herself in an isolation suite, feeling like some condemned criminal being given a last taste of living before being coma'd. The set of rooms was incredibly well appointed and Clowes wandered around in a kind of daze checking out all of the facilities as she wrestled with the Thin Doctor's proposal. She kept telling herself that she had twenty-four hours and she decided to take some rest before finally making up her mind. She had after all only managed a few hours' sleep the night before.

The isolation suite boasted a fully equipped bathroom complete with a jacuzzi, and Clowes found the prospect of a relaxing soak too tempting to pass by. She programmed the suite's domestic console and heard the distant hiss of the tub's plumbing as she confirmed her option. Some few minutes later the console announced that the pool was ready and Clowes strolled through into the sleek, steamy bathroom and slipped into the water. She lay back against the padded rim of the tub and let her legs rise on the pulsing currents. She reached behind her and felt for the document pad the Thin Doctor had given her; she located the composite tablet and slid it past her shoulder into the tub. She spun the floating document pad in the lumpy water and watched the face of Jon Coton blur and re-form with the rotation. She spoke out loud to herself.

'If you weren't such a handsome bastard, Coton, this might be a little easier ... We're going to rip your head to pieces and stick your brain in a damned robot, and you can't do a freak about it.'

She sighed and considered the irrationality of her thoughts. She was now looking at Coton in quite ridiculous terms, whether he was good-looking or not – crazy ... But at the same time she was, quite rightly, unable to shrug off the fact that the Cyborg Project was going to use this man, his human life, like a simple component in an arguably whimsical scientific exercise ... Her decision-making process was going to have to go way beyond the application of logic and reason ... In so many choices, especially about life itself, logic had to take a back seat – certainly when it came to dealing with fellow human beings ... Logical reasoning always carried the stamp of scepticism; it was anti-vital, and surely vitality – life itself – was the key issue here, the continuance of a life and her ability to influence it.

'Wow ...' Clowes spoke out loud again. 'Abandon all logic, we're going down.' She grasped the floating document pad and flicked off the power, then brought her foot up and sent the tablet surfing across the pool, at the same time letting herself submerge beneath the foam. She suddenly felt a z-powder flashback and saw the silver surfer in her hologram – the Thin Doctor had put him in there ... He'd only held the controller for a few seconds but in that time had managed to build a whole new figure. How could he have done that? He was giving her a clue to the project, but he couldn't have known that she'd see it before their meeting. She surfaced from the confusion of the jacuzzi bubbles and looked at the document pad jerkily trapped in an eddy across the pool.

'That's it, then.' Clowes tilted her head back and peered up at the cluster of ceiling lights through the aroma-laden steam. 'We have a decision ...' She couldn't leave Jon Coton alone to the devices of the *Mad Professor*.

CHAPTER FIVE

There were a number of matters to tidy up in Comms Monitoring, and Piaget had a week to clear out his things and prime the task list for his successor. It was all routine stuff, perhaps one or two little unfinished projects that were better shut down and deleted now, before some smart new guy turned them up. The main priority had to be to make sure all of the Lander 6 enquiry files were ordered up properly: he'd have to double-check the subtle re-configuring of the log and the roster tables. He was still in a position where he could probably do a deal with Kraemer. OK, Kraemer had done time for his insubordination, but he, Piaget, had lost a certain direct promotion. He could better judge Kraemer's standpoint on all this when he picked him up from the detention centre, any time now.

Det. C2 was located on the northern fringe of Metropolis 4. It stood back from the Outer Ring, a flat concrete dome on a single angled strut, giving it the appearance of a giant distressed mushroom sprouting out of the miserable wasteland. There was no auto-route guidance on this part of the Outer Ring, and Piaget had to concentrate as he took the mobile on manual down the steep exit ramp. At the bottom there was only one turn available; on his left, the Ring underpass was blocked by some abandoned route works, while the right led in a dead straight line to the foot of the prison's massive supporting strut.

The security control was bleak and efficient, matching the surroundings of the dismal entry hall. The staffers processed his authorization with the minimum of verbal communication, grudgingly acknowledging his central office status. The final staffer accompanied him to a well-worn armoured door which tore open, dryly grating on its track. Piaget entered and found himself in a bare elevator cage; when he turned around, the staffer had disappeared. The cage jerked into motion in an unexpected sideways direction, beginning the diagonal climb up the strut.

Although it was Kraemer who had caused all this trouble in the first place, even Piaget couldn't help but feel a twinge of sympathy for the Section Leader for having spent the last three months in this place. Det. C2 was a high security prison for politicals and psychos. As the iron lift cage ground steadily up the incline inside the bare concrete hollow of the strut, Piaget pondered that this entry to the main dome was surely grim enough to have even a psycho ruing his misdemeanours. The cement floor of the cage was stained and tacky under his feet and, as the elevator climbed higher, weak draughts of air chased round the half-barred cubicles, lifting a sweet stench to his nostrils. Piaget peered up through the cage roof to see how much further there was to go.

'They must have sent you up the *Stairway to Heaven*, sir.' Kraemer smiled at his commanding officer. 'The staff have a certain sense of humour in this place. Once you're in the cage, there's no communication unless you've got a portable.' Former Section Leader Kraemer was sitting with his commandant in an interview room off the prison's main reception, listening to the officer's account of the climb up to the dome.

'I'll be reporting this back to the warden when we get

out of here. This is a hell-hole. How did you end up in this place?'

'Overcrowding, sir. The big Azzi sweep in August filled all of the inner city det. centres and they didn't want me, a Sec-services guy, to be in with them. They were doing me a favour.'

'Some favour, Kraemer. If you'd let me know, I could have fixed something. I could have had you coma'd.'

'They wouldn't coma someone for a three-month stretch, sir. It can take that long at the end to bring someone out. I'm not sure I would have appreciated the treatment either, sir.' The thought flitted through Kraemer's mind that the Floor Commandant had himself been coma'd. The big man's solicitude was strongly out of character for the FC Piaget who had ripped him to bits at the enquiry. There had to be an angle to this new personality.

The door to the interview room burst open; a staffer entered and thrust a write-pad on the table. The man offered Piaget a grubby stylus for him to sign the document. Piaget declined the well-worn stick disdainfully and used his own titanium instrument to slew his signature across the glowing mat.

'And palm it, please, sir.' The staffer pushed a button on the side of the pad. 'Right, then left.'

Piaget complied, staring hard at the staffer all the while. The staffer was unmoved.

'Thank you, sir. It's security, sir. We don't take chances in here.' The staffer offered his explanation.

'I can see that, Duty Staffer,' Piaget replied. 'Is that everything now?'

'The prisoner will need to have his tag-band removed. The bottom gate personnel will do that. I can switch it to amber now from the pad.'

Kraemer offered his left wrist to the staffer, who connected the pad's trailing lead. The red diode on the wristband turned orange.

'Please display the band clearly as you pass through with your commandant, Kraemer.'

Kraemer nodded and the staffer left the room.

The mobile's route-logger display flashed green from blue and announced guidance system lock-on.

'Thank God!' Piaget uttered the phrase with feeling as the auto-route switched in to relieve him of the concentration of driving. 'This Outer Ring needs some sorting out. Fancy not having guidance all the way round.'

Kraemer shared Piaget's relief – the Commandant was not a natural driver.

'Well, Kraemer, you've really screwed things up for yourself, haven't you?'

'That's true, sir.'

'You know they never found Walker, and Coton's as good as dead in an intensive care unit.'

'Yes, sir, my rehab. officer told me about them. It was all a dreadful chain of events. I'm going to miss both of them very much, they were two of the best ... I can only repeat what I said at the enquiry. They really wanted to go ... I only made it possible for them.'

'And now we're paying the price.' Piaget checked ahead at the filter route coming up for Central and continued, 'I don't trust this junction ... I've missed the Staff position and you're back on the screens. You're damned lucky I swung that for you, standard procedure would have had you on job-share.' Piaget tweaked the mobile's stick to make sure of the filter.

'You can be sure I appreciate your doing that for me, sir. I hope we can rebuild the relationship that we had before all this. You know I'm still highly committed to the department.'

'I know that, Kraemer, that's why I fought to have you reinstated, but you won't be reporting to me in future, I have a new project to manage – outside Comms Monitoring.'

'A promotion, sir?'

'Hmm . . . Yes, a sideways move into a quite different field, a semi-Staff role. I'm unable to discuss the nature of the post.'

'Congratulations, sir. I'm glad the Lander 6 affair didn't wreck things with the Selection Panel. If there's anything I can do to assist you . . . I'm at your disposal.' Kraemer dropped the bait for Piaget to bite. The Floor Commandant was really not himself: coming personally to the det. centre, his obvious nervousness. This new job had to be something pretty heavy for him to be carrying on like this, and it was clear that he, Kraemer, had something that Piaget wanted. There was no other explanation. Piaget seemed to be giving his offer some thought anyway.

'You can help me, Kraemer. I've got a week left in Comms before I start my new role and, as you can imagine, there's a lot of stuff to be tied up. Routine bits and pieces mainly, but there's one specific task I'd like you to do for me.'

'Of course, sir.' This was it; Kraemer's simple gambit was coming in.

'Lander 6, the comms log. I want you to dupe it for me. All entries from all sources. I'm going to be under scrutiny in my new position and there'll be an Internals' archive squad coming in. I did make some adjustments myself – protocol stuff, that's all – to smooth out the enquiry audit. This will benefit both of us, Kraemer.'

'You don't need to explain any further, sir. I know the type of people who might want to do a retro-check.' Piaget was paranoid about the Internals and he had been damn-well convinced at the enquiry that Piaget had juggled some of the timings to put himself completely in the clear. The crafty old bastard.

'I know I can rely on you, Kraemer. I'll grant you an executive access code tomorrow.' Piaget knew Kraemer well enough. The former Section Leader would certainly be aware that doing a favour for Piaget now could only help him pick up his career from its present low point.

'Thoroughness with discretion, Kraemer, will always pay off in the future.'

'I understand perfectly, sir.'

'Pepper, I need to speak to you about the project document.' Piaget was hunched over his workstation on the Comms Monitoring mezz, thumbing the edge of the large wedge of paper in front of him. He held the portable clamped hard to his head as he half hissed the words into the mouthpiece.

'Easy, Piaget,' Pepper's voice intoned calmly down the link. 'Meet me for lunch ... in the front of the Mirage real-club. Bring the doc with you ... Twelve thirty.' The link clicked dead.

Piaget rose and walked over into the bright curve of the floor's bow glazing. Outside, the view was lost in yellow mist. On turning around, he was met by the figure of former Section Leader Kraemer, newly attired in the green uniform of a screen monkey.

'Good morning, sir. I'm reporting for special duty ...'

Kraemer chopped the sentence as Piaget seemed to ignore him, heading straight back to his station. 'Sir?'

Piaget stuffed a large document folder into a drawer and sat down, swinging his chair to face Kraemer.

'Sorry, Kraemer, I didn't log you there for a minute . . . The green staffer's uniform . . . Take a seat.'

'Yesterday, sir, we discussed the Lander 6 log, if you recall. You have some special duties for me for which I need access clearance.'

'Of course. The Internals' archive squad are due in any day, and we need to do our own checks before they freeze the files. You know how important this is.'

'I remember our talk, sir.'

'Very good. Now I'm going to allocate you an executive access code. Of course you realize that this is slightly irregular, especially with your reduced staffer status. Use your discretion, Kraemer – I know I don't need to labour the point.'

Piaget turned to the workstation and winked up a security icon, then clicked in the code. As the palm pad flashed, Piaget immediately covered the plate.

'That's it, Kraemer, you're authorized . . . Carry on.'

'The dupes, sir, do you still want them?' Piaget was obviously rushing.

'Of course, Kraemer, copy me daily, use a data cart.' Kraemer had reminded him of his request from the day before; it had completely slipped his mind.

As Kraemer disappeared, Piaget slumped back in his chair. The Cyborg Project was already giving him stress . . . '*Coton*, they're going to use *Coton*,' he breathed. He was vocalizing his thoughts.

Piaget saw Pepper at once as he stepped off the power sidewalk in front of the Mirage real-club. He was sitting in the window, already eating, and he nodded as he met Piaget's eye through the glass. When Piaget made it to the table, the Staff Officer was ordering another course down the voice link. He raised his eyes from the menu. 'You want to order, Piaget?'

'*Coton*, you want to use . . .'

Pepper cut Piaget's hissing dead, gesturing at the open voice link. He snapped at the switch. 'Are you crazy, Piaget? Sit down and shut up!'

Piaget, effectively silenced, lowered his large frame on to a stylish but flimsy chair, clasping the Cyborg Project document to his chest.

'You are a highly trained and experienced Services officer. Don't you ever do anything like that again . . .' Pepper's voice carried an authority that Piaget could never have imagined from his first meeting with the man.

'Sorry, Pepper, I wasn't thinking.'

'You are now at a grade where you are paid to think, Piaget . . . All the time . . . This is not some dumb Azzi sweep we're involved in. Enough said . . . Now order something to eat and tell me about your concerns.'

Piaget took the voice set and ordered a sandwich with real coffee. When the order arrived, the two officers were well on with their meeting.

'I can understand your ethical concerns, Piaget. All parties to this project are well aware of the issues at stake.'

'But why do you have to use Coton? He's been through enough.'

'Coton is the perfect choice. He has the ideal background for the job . . . A trained Sec-services officer, an impeccable record, highly intelligent. Need I continue?'

'He strikes me as over-qualified, Pepper, if you don't

mind my saying so. The project could easily use another subject: some long-term detainee with nothing to lose.'

'And a completely unknown quantity. No, Piaget.'

'He could be profiled. Christ, the Thin Doctor could sort his personality, if he's going to be fishing about with the guy's brain anyway. You would of course have checked out the subject's background.'

'How much of the document have you read, Piaget? Did you read the tech supplement?'

'Yes.'

'Then you'll understand the limitations of profiling.'

'Well . . .'

'Look, Piaget, I can well understand your personal reservations about the choice of Coton. Someone you've had on your Section for the past year. Look at it this way . . . You're getting him back.'

'Like some kind of robot zombie.'

'So you lack confidence in the project. You know you've a visit scheduled for the Sci-Medical Foundation. Reserve judgement until you've seen the prototypes. You can't flunk out of this thing now purely on the basis of your own subjective appraisal.'

'OK, Pepper, I accept your logic.' Piaget realized he was in danger of going too far with Pepper, who was clearly much more of a hard man than he had thought.

'Put it this way, Piaget. Your career won't stand it if you back out now . . . At the moment, this meeting's off the record.'

Piaget's suspicions were confirmed.

Pepper poured Piaget another cup of coffee, then he leant back in his chair and considered the older man opposite. Fifty-two years old, at the top of his departmental tree, still desperate to get his Staff appointment . . . at any price, a couple of days ago. Now he looked rather pathetic, out of his depth with this new project. If it hadn't been for his amazing loyalty record, Pepper would have trashed him from the selection process right at the start. The chairman had faith, though: the same school as Piaget, the same age. The generations, how they stuck together ... He had no choice but to carry on with the overweight Floor Commandant.

'So what was the other thing, Piaget? Political stuff?'

'I need a few things clarified about where we stand on this in relation to the Electrocorp lobby and the Chromium Programme.'

'Understandable. You know the influence that Electrocorp has with the Council.'

'Sure, I've always thought they owned the City Fathers.'

'That's not far off the mark. It's fair to say that there's a growing imbalance in step with their commercial success. It's not surprising, given the way our society functions.' Pepper scanned the radius of tables in the window. 'Let's walk, fresh air's better than this stuff.' The real-club was filling with lunchtime patrons.

'No, I'll get both of them, Piaget.' Pepper waved Piaget to put his card away as they passed through a toll gate into Central's Park One, below the Big Mixer. 'I hate that stuff, paying to use this damned space. You know the Internals make daily checks on the credits log. We think we're so free, but our cards tag us just like any UC.'

Piaget snorted his sympathetic acknowledgement. 'So you think that they'd log two Sec-services cardholders entering the park together.'

'I know they would, Piaget, they're like freaking bloodhounds ... So, what about our wonderful General Council of Fathers, the *Traditionals* and the *Tecchies* ... It's a mess right now ... and that's barely confidential. If you read the Infonet you can see straight through the lines.'

'Tell me about it. I think we both know where we stand.' Piaget sought Pepper's eye.

Pepper continued: 'At one time, all they used to worry about was greasing each other's palms for the next sector redevelopment; it was a nice, balanced market in corruption. Nobody ever lost out in the long term. Now, as you know, it's not property that backs the power, it's technology ... it's been going on for the past century, a steady sea-change in power politics. What's really upped the ante, though, has been the combination of the cash going into the Light-Speed Programme and Electrocorp's expansion of their sector, pushing droids into every application, in every colony in the Archipelago.'

'D'you know, we've got droids in Lander maintenance now?' Piaget interrupted. 'Coton's Lander was a test bed for two EC droids ... and even after what happened, they're still in service.'

'I think you'll find that our purchasing department is heavily sponsored by Electrocorp, Piaget. They cash discreet back-hander credits through to the buyers, which virus the system when the Internals do a check. So they don't do checks any more. Simple ...'

'And we know, but we can't do anything about it?'

'We're getting there ... another new system in development, but it takes time ... Anyway, we're both in the same camp, Piaget; you and I know what's right for this city-state, which is why we're having to play the Tecchies at their own game.'

'Using the Thin Doctor and his cyborg.'

'An arch-Tecchie, if you like.'

'That's what I thought.'

'Yes, Piaget, but the Thin Doctor is different. He has no loyalty to money or power, he's maybe the *only* guy in the whole of M4 who can't be bought.'

'You think so, Pepper?'

'I know so ... When the Thin Doctor was approached about this project, he submitted himself to psychometrics – any kind of personality and intelligence testing we could come up with. The Doctor came through one hundred per cent in *every* test. He is a *complete* – and I'm not exaggerating, believe me – a *complete genius*, and he has no motives that drive him other than science itself. I know that's tough for an old cynic like you to take on board, Piaget – hell, I'm not the planet's most gullible fool either – but there it is ... Proven beyond doubt. The man is so clean he might as well be an alien or a robot himself.'

'I'll have to go with you on that kind of tribute, Pepper.'

'Wait until you meet him. I guarantee you'll be converted. He's our kind of guy, a good job too.'

'So how's this all going to work? The document is not specific on the bigger picture, competing with the Chromium Programme.'

'The reason for that is that you don't really have to know ... We're in the process of setting up a state-financed company – completely illegal – but you understand the necessity. The company will support the project, and that's all you need to be aware of. Your own role is concerned purely with monitoring the development of the hardware and providing a security function to guard our interests. As soon as we have a functioning marketable droid, you'll be out of the project.'

'Tell me about the project team and how you see me handling them.'

'You'll be surprised at the small scale of the project. The Thin Doctor, his assistant and a freak of a technician.'

'Come again?'

'Three people, Piaget, all operating from the Sci-Medical Foundation.'

'And the freaky technician?' Piaget was getting involved in a tecchie circus and he transmitted the thought to Pepper with a look of distaste.

'Oh, a gene-genie disaster area, but a brilliant engineer. Don't worry, you'll meet him soon enough.'

'And what do they know about our involvement?'

'Only the Thin Doctor is aware of the whole picture. The other two will just do their job. They can't be allowed to know about our part in this. You'll be a representative of the sponsoring company, looking after their interests.'

'And Coton, what happens when he comes round and sees his former commanding officer? You reckon he's going to be completely sentient ... he'll have memory functions as well ... He'll blow the whole thing.'

'We can fix that. The Thin Doctor doesn't see it as a problem. And anyway he's not going to come round like he's just woken up. It's going to be a slow process getting him readjusted to his new body. He's going to be well freaked out to start with.'

'Sounds risky, Pepper.'

'Don't worry. The Doctor's got his assistant all geared up to deal with the readjustment programme. What's more, you forget that Coton's a Services man; he'll understand he has mission orders.'

Piaget thought about Coton as he had been: he was a great officer, but nobody's fool. This crazy scheme, if it was going to come off, would have him looking out for number one, straight off. Hell, if *he* were in that position, he knew where his first loyalties would lie. It was difficult to imagine the kind of profile that the Service had of Coton, to believe that he was going to go through with this thing like some meek little test animal. They couldn't be telling him everything about this whole mad project, but he'd go along with it until it was time to get out. Planned or otherwise. One last thought occurred to him as well . . .

'Now, if I'm going to be *Mr Droid-Company Man* on this project, then I can't be in uniform. Is that right?'

'I hear a penny dropping, Piaget! You're going to be, shall we say, kind of anonymous . . . We have everything planned for you, your ID will not be a problem. You can use your own name, this thing will be very low-profile, and any Internal Services interest that may possibly be shown, we can deal with at this end. We do have our own people in the Gestapo.' Pepper laughed at his use of the word. 'You can tell anyone who asks, that you've been given an admin job in scientific liaison – a demotion for your mess-up with the Lander 6 incident. You need to swallow a little pride when you're undercover . . . Treat it as a back-handed punishment from Staff, you'll get the right mind-set for your cover as well.'

It certainly was turning out to be like a punishment. The Executive were excelling themselves in their deviousness; they certainly knew how to get to him. Pay him more money, give him a crazy job and make him feel like shit. Piaget suddenly thought of Kraemer. What the hell will he have been telling people? He'd told Kraemer he had a special project – a promotion. He had to get to get to him before he blew the whole thing.

'Takes a little thinking about, huh, Piaget?'

'Yeah. I should have realized from the document. There was no specific mention of the undercover aspect.'

'It won't be a problem for you, you'll enjoy it. The Executive wouldn't have given you this job if they didn't think you could handle it. They have complete confidence in you, you know that. And we'll support you right through. If you have any problems at all, contact me. I'll be in regular touch anyway.'

They had reached the far end of the park and made their way via the subway back to the Big Mixer. Pepper prioritized the elevator to Piaget's Comms Monitoring floor.

'Make sure you get all your things sorted for the end of the week, Piaget. We can't have you coming back here after that.'

Piaget left the elevator bay and skidded slightly as he hurried across the flux mat into CF3's aerofoil section.

Kraemer spotted Piaget coming back from his long lunch, steaming along the walkway in characteristic fashion. He was surprised when the big man called out to him to meet him on the management mezz ... not exactly practising the paranoid discretion that he'd been ramming home to him ever since he'd collected him from the det. centre. When Kraemer made it up to Piaget's station, the big man was refreshing himself with a glass of water from the dispenser.

'I've not had an opportunity to get anything yet, sir,' Kraemer began.

'No. OK, Kraemer ... How's things? Are people talking to you?'

'Well, sir, it's a little different, just having my own single monitor bank.'

'But good to be back with your colleagues, though. Lots to update you with, I bet.'

'Fairly quiet actually, sir. It's funny to see the August Azzi sweep on the files. I saw half of the catch come in when I was in the first det. centre.' Piaget was back in his solicitous mode, Kraemer thought. Something was definitely wrong with him. 'Excuse me, sir, but is everything all right with you?'

'Er, actually not, Kraemer. I've had some bad news. My promotion's not going to happen.'

'Oh no, sir.'

'You didn't tell anyone I was going to be promoted, did you?'

'No sir.'

'Good, Kraemer. You can understand that that would have been an embarrassment for me, especially in the light of my now effective demotion to an admin job.'

'What, sir? That's rather harsh. You won't be on the Command Floor then?'

'I won't even be in the tower, Kraemer. I don't want to talk about it. And I'd appreciate it if you kept quiet too . . . If anyone asks, you don't know anything . . . Got that?'

'Completely, sir.'

'Now I'm going to be out of here at the end of the week and I need the other things from you for then. The archive squad will be here any time, as you know . . . Don't let me down, Kraemer.'

'I won't, sir. I'm really sorry, Mr Piaget.'

'Thanks, Kraemer. Dismiss . . .'

Piaget breathed a sigh, but halted in speaking out loud. He got up to get another drink of water.

CHAPTER SIX

As the elevator descended, the Thin Doctor explained to Clowes that the cranial floor testing programme had been located in the sub-basement of the Sci-Medical Foundation building for reasons of security. He had personally carried out all the work to date, supported by his technician Dabbs, an ex-Electrocorp droid designer. Dabbs had built all of the test chassis using a combination of proprietary Electrocorp components together with custom parts he'd developed in his Foundation tech-lab; the Thin Doctor had conducted the marrying of the biological components to the machines. When the elevator door opened on the main corridor of the subterranean lab complex, it was the curious figure of Dabbs, sporting a broken left arm in a strange alloy sling, who greeted them both.

'G . . . good morning doctor, and Ms C . . . Clowes I presume.' Dabbs gulped oddly as he spoke. He was a freak of a man: short and very thin, with a long neck that flared to almost create a chin. His hollow cheeks compensated in some way for his chinlessness by defining an otherwise absent jaw-line from above. Black sunken eyes projecting a wild intelligence flashed brightly below a thick fringe of jet-black hair. Clowes controlled her shock at his appearance and offered a hand which was readily shaken by Dabbs' free hand's spidery grip.

The Thin Doctor smiled at Clowes and formally introduced Dabbs. 'This man is a genius, Ms Clowes. Your knowledge of cybotics is set to enter into quantum growth, working with Mr Dabbs.'

'Please call me Dabbs, Ms Clowes, just Dabbs. I prefer informality.'

'Very well, Dabbs, then call me Clowes, or Uschi if you like.'

'U ... Uschi ...' Dabbs struggled with his gulping on the 'U' sound. 'No, I prefer Clowes ... my speech y'know ...'

'No problem.' Clowes interrupted the struggling technician. 'What happened to your arm?'

Now the Thin Doctor interrupted. 'He had an accident working on one of our subjects. Come, let me show you the facility.'

The Thin Doctor swept away down the corridor, followed by Clowes and with Dabbs trailing a little behind her. Without turning, the Thin Doctor addressed Dabbs and suggested he might like to attend to Subject 4, at which Dabbs did a prompt about-turn and disappeared into a side-corridor. 'See you later, Clowes,' he called over his shoulder in his gulpy voice.

'Dabbs is easily distracted, Ms Clowes. He doesn't get to meet many people down here, let alone attractive young women like yourself; he rarely leaves this basement complex.'

'The poor man. Can't you help him, doctor? You could surely do something about his appearance – and his speech.'

'He's very happy as he is: he has a healthy mistrust of surgeons – and, besides, he has an amazing social life on the Infonet ... I may as well tell you now, since you're bound to find out ... Have you ever used the virtual sex sub-net, Ms Clowes?'

'Er, only in voyeur mode, I have to confess.' Clowes felt stupidly embarrassed.

'Like everyone else, of course.' The Thin Doctor added with a smile, 'No, I can see you wouldn't need to use it. But Dabbs, Dabbs is *Lolita*, the most popular hooker on the system.' His smile broadened and he laughed. 'Hilarious, isn't it? But he takes it very seriously; he has regular clients and makes quite a tidy income ... So now you know, please don't tell anyone or let him know that you know ... Now let me show you our operating theatre. This is where we perform our transplants.'

Following the revelation about Dabbs, the operating theatre was something of an anticlimax. The layout and equipment were quite standard, except for the presence of some strange jig-frames in addition to the table, presumably for the subjects. There was also a bank of monitoring equipment that was not for any biological dependant. Next door to the operating theatre was a small tissue-growth facility, where the Thin Doctor showed Clowes the compact cranial floor assembly line. They then moved on to Dabbs' tech-lab, littered with robot parts, and finally some routine labs. After they'd completed the tour of the last room, the Thin Doctor led Clowes back the way they had come and turned into the corridor down which Dabbs had disappeared earlier. At the end of this corridor was a heavy security door, by which, in a small room to the right, Dabbs was sitting at a workstation, surrounded by monitors. He nodded to the Thin Doctor through the clear partition and reached to activate a switch which caused the door to slide smoothly open.

'Our subject test programme, Ms Clowes – very secure, as you can see.'

The vault which they had now entered rose to twice

the height of the ceilings of the rest of the complex, a good six metres at least. There was a strange smell in the air; Clowes could detect something distinctly animal, not unpleasant, mixing with the clinical ambient lab odour. Beyond the half-moon of the bay in which they now stood was a blank, white, curved wall set with four evenly spaced, numbered doors. The Thin Doctor walked across to the door marked '1' and beckoned to Clowes to follow.

'Let me show you subject number one.' He noticed Clowes' hesitation, adding, 'There's nothing to fear.'

Inside, Clowes found herself with the Thin Doctor in a narrow gallery, one side of which was of transparent material, the screen for what could only be described as an animal cage beyond. The enclosure had an earth floor out of which, in the far corner, grew a good-sized tree rising to the chamber's full height. In the other corner, against the two walls, was a small shelter littered with some kind of bedding material.

'Now just wait, Ms Clowes – he'll see us soon.'

Clowes' first impression was of a flash up in the boughs of the tree, then she saw it: the most bizarre cat she'd ever seen. The large, mottled-silver and fur beast gingerly negotiated the descent of the last two metres of sheer tree-trunk and then trotted over to where the Thin Doctor and Clowes stood behind the screen. The cat pushed itself up against the glazing in a gesture of affection, rubbing itself backwards and forwards.

Clowes was amazed. 'It's a cat, doctor. He's cool, a great big cyborg tomcat. What happened to his coat, though?'

'I knew you were going to ask me that. We have a problem making fur that will stand up to his constant preening activities. The tongue we designed for him keeps shredding and he rips his coat to pieces, Dabbs is constantly patching him up.'

Clowes could picture the bizarre scene, and she smiled.

As the Thin Doctor spoke, the cat stopped to attend to some grooming activity. On finding a bare alloy expanse on his belly, the creature began to hammer its head against the spot, then it leapt up and proceeded to tear round the enclosure, jumping and skidding in a total frenzy.

Clowes glanced at the Thin Doctor.

'We do get this abnormal behaviour, too. It can't work out what's wrong and then it goes into this loop of activity. Because this chassis is so power-efficient, it will now continue to run around until it breaks something. It won't ever tire itself out.'

The cat continued in its rampaging crashing up against the screen with dull thuds on its circuits round the cage.

'We have a big problem with animals, in that it's impossible to communicate to them their new physicality ... Of course we'll not have this problem with our human cyborg.'

Clowes nodded as her gaze was held by the frenzied cyborg cat, now trailing a flailing, shattered hind leg in its interminable laps of the cage.

The Thin Doctor placed a hand on Clowes' shoulder, making her start. 'Come and look at Four, our prototype humanoid.'

As they crossed the bay to cell four, the Thin Doctor cautioned Clowes.

'Now you may well find Four disturbing. He's just like the cyborgs in the *Ouest La Plage*: he has the same humanoid chassis, but Dabbs has given him an ape's coat of hair since he has the brain from a chimpanzee. He looks rather strange and can behave accordingly.'

When they entered the viewing gallery of cell four, the cyborg was sitting on a composite chair at a table constructed of a similar material. The rest of the room was filled with a variety of play apparatus: a large climbing frame, dangling ropes and all kinds of large, heavily made toys, amongst which was a pedal tricycle and some building bricks. The cyborg seemed to be engaged in building an uneven tower of the bricks on the table, when he turned, noticing their presence at the screen.

The first thing Clowes registered were the cyborg's eyes set in the human face. Like the cat cyborg before, this ape-brained machine had scraped much of the hair coating from its body; its head was almost totally bald and the scuffed laminate of its construction was pale and skull-like, unlike the metal alloy of the cat's chassis. The thing looked horrific, but the eyes, remarkably human-like eyes, shone sadly out of the face. She could see straight away that Four was miserable. The ape's attention returned to the bricks.

Reaching up to a small box on the wall behind them, the Thin Doctor produced a stubby microphone and made a clicking sound into it to regain the cyborg's attention. The ape machine halted its activity briefly, then continued to ignore them.

'May I, doctor?' Clowes reached out for the microphone.

'Of course, Ms Clowes, he may respond better to a new voice.'

Clowes took the mike and spoke softly into the device. 'Hello, Four ... Hello ... Are you feeling a bit fed up?' Clowes glanced at the Thin Doctor, raising a quizzical eyebrow as she did so. The Thin Doctor was smiling, nodding for her to continue. 'Hello . . . I've come to see you, Four . . . Say hello . . .'

Now the cyborg turned his whole body, making the chair screech on the floor as it moved with him. He stared at Clowes intently, then sprang up and rushed at the transparent screen. Clowes shrieked and flung herself back against the wall behind her as the cyborg crashed into the screen with a muffled thump. As Clowes composed herself, the cyborg was hunkering down at the foot of the screen and seemed to be attempting to scratch his way under the glazing.

The Thin Doctor had moved along the narrow gallery to recover the microphone where it had gone flying from Clowes' grasp. 'Speak to him again.' The Thin Doctor handed the microphone back to Clowes.

Clowes lowered herself down to where the cyborg was still scrabbling at the foot of the screen. 'You scared the life out of me just then . . . I don't want to hurt you . . . Come on, look at me . . .'

Clowes watched the cyborg stop its scraping and turn its head to look. Just inches apart through the screen, their eyes met and the cyborg slowly raised itself up to its full height, magnetically dragging Clowes with it like a mirror image. The two stood for some time, silently united in their eye-contact through the glass. The Thin Doctor stood back from the pair, admiring this meeting of his two perfect project members.

In the Thin Doctor's office, up in the main Foundation building, Clowes was concluding her enthusiastic assessment of what she'd seen. The Thin Doctor had gambled on just such a turnaround in her attitude: she was clearly behind the project now, her drive in the pursuit of pure scientific advance had been reawak-ened. He knew he could trust her to go the whole distance with the human cyborg. She had indeed been a perfect choice.

'Ms Clowes, thank you for your endorsement of my project. I knew that once you'd seen the advances we've already made, you'd have full confidence in our being able to complete the final stage.'

'It was Four, doctor. He was so well executed, such a real, living creature, after all is said and done. I realized that, if you could produce Four, then the Coton cyborg really was achievable.'

The Thin Doctor switched in the polarizer across the glazing of his office, darkening the room. 'Out to lunch, I think, Ms Clowes . . . a small celebration. Then I'd like you to accompany me to an appointment this afternoon. I have an invitation to visit Electrocorp . . . Of interest to you?'

The Thin Doctor hadn't told Clowes that Electrocorp were sending a Lander to pick them up, although she had thought that Central's Lander-port was an odd choice of a place for lunch. The flight across M4 was an experience. She'd never flown low-level over a city before and she had to keep reminding herself that this wasn't a theme park ride.

Clowes was quite disappointed when the pilot brought them down, after an all-too-short flight, on a landing apron on top of an outrigger building beneath the Electrocorp tower.

Clowes and the Thin Doctor stepped down from the craft, to be greeted by a small welcoming committee of EC personnel who had walked across the apron to meet them. Close up, the tower was more impressive than ever. The enormous trellis frame that bound the one hundred and fifty floors together stretched above the small group's heads like a taut rope securing the blank ceiling of cloud into which the structure disappeared.

'Ms Clowes!' The Thin Doctor had to shout, to capture her attention away from the stunning architecture. She lowered her gaze and trotted to catch up with the group, who were heading towards a buggy on the edge of the landing apron. She apologized as she caught up with the group.

'Tower-struck, Ms Clowes . . .' The speaker identified himself as Rakussen, an executive physicist; he was to be their guide on what could only be a partial tour of the huge Electrocorp plant. 'It's a common affliction of newcomers to M4. The only cure is to work in one of the things – they soon lose their fascination then.' The buggy moved off across the expanse of roof in the direction of a shadowed reception port.

The buggy was abandoned at the reception hall and Rakussen ushered Clowes and the Thin Doctor, now wearing visitor's overalls, on to a power track that took them steadily down into the building below the landing apron.

Rakussen raised his voice above the growing mechanical din. 'This is one of our final assembly halls, Ms Clowes. We have twenty droid lines in this plant altogether. I think that this one is on with utility droids at the moment, but we'll soon see.'

The track levelled out and ran along a gallery overlooking a large, open hall. On the floor below, distinct lines of yellow-coloured droid chassis were ranged in parallel columns, five in all, across the width of the floor. Square-framed, tool-carrying assembly servers arched over the columns of part-finished droids, pausing to perform some task then moving on to the next machine. The overall effect was of a constant staccato ripple of grey servers over the yellow of the droids. At the far end of the building was a sea of yellow where the finished machines were being packed in encapsulating clear wraps, ready for despatch. As Clowes and the Thin Doctor followed Rakussen on a narrow gangway across the hall, they could see smaller monitor droids moving independently up and down the spaces between the production columns.

'As you can see, we're very busy. If I'm not wrong this is a complete shipment of five hundred droids for the new colony on AR Juna at the far end of the Archipelago. Is that right, doctor? You're the galactographer.'

'You're quite right, Rakussen, AR Juna is the furthest Einsam planet at galactic west from TI Creda. PJ Jona is the pole planet, much nearer at galactic south. They're easily confused,' the Thin Doctor replied.

The two shouted loudly above the clatter of the production line below. This exaggerated clarification seemed quite comic to Clowes. The two were clearly trying to impress her – funny, how men could be sometimes – but any delay in this unpleasant environment was not what she needed. She acknowledged the Thin Doctor's display of modest erudition with a suitable expression. 'Can we move on please, gentlemen?' Clowes cut through the din. 'The atmosphere in here is making me feel faint.'

The power track on the far side of the hall carried the group back the way they had come but then continued further under the tower itself. Rakussen led them off on to a flux mat, then checked Clowes and the Thin Doctor through a security gate.

'How do you feel now, Ms Clowes?' Rakussen enquired. 'Our production facilities are often quite humano-hostile. It's a common problem in automated areas, as I'm sure you're aware.'

The Thin Doctor interjected, 'It's my fault, I'm afraid, Ms Clowes is always ill when she goes anywhere with me.'

Rakussen looked non-plussed.

'The doctor is making a joke, Dr Rakussen. Two nights ago, as a generous welcoming gesture, the doctor took me to the *Ouest La Plage* – where the food was a little rich for me.'

'Generous indeed,' Rakussen replied. 'You've never entertained me so well in all these years, doctor.'

'Rakussen . . . you've never entertained me at all!' the Thin Doctor laughed.

'I'm OK now anyway, thank you, Dr Rakussen.' Clowes interrupted the two men's banter with affected politeness.

'I think we'd better continue our tour or we'll be running out of time. I'm now going to take you up to show you some of our cybotics research departments – one of your specialisms, I understand, Ms Clowes. You'd better hold on to your stomach in the elevator, we're going to the hundredth floor.'

The group paused briefly at the entrance to the research floor for Clowes to admire the hazy panorama of Metropolis 4 bathed in diffused wintry sunlight. The Big Mixer tower was just visible in the west, a grey, bland column, its rotating command floors lost in the city's canopy of smog.

Rakussen continued with his commentary as they walked back to the security gates that led on to the open floor beyond. 'This is our Brain Lab. All our central processor units start out here, and we have a number of silicon bubble CPUs in development right now.'

Rakussen took them through the gates and over to a sealed, glazed enclosure that ran the length of the lab. Inside, enviro-suited technicians sat at stations along a large circular tube which curved up from the floor and terminated at the far end of the enclosure. The tube, about a metre in diameter, alternately narrowly pinched and blown up into spheres, was the main bubble production line for the whole of Electrocorp. Clowes expressed surprise that the facility was so small compared to the vast scale of the Electrocorp tower.

'You're not the first to say that, Ms Clowes,' Rakussen answered her comment. 'What very few people know about Electrocorp is that most of the floors in this tower are unoccupied. The tower gives the impression of hundreds of departments, whereas in fact we probably only have around fifty separate research and pre-production facilities.'

'So the tower is there for expansion, and also to make the big statement about the company,' Clowes interjected, scanning the department.

Rakussen continued: 'Partly, of course, Ms Clowes. But the tower is ultimately the size it is because it is the supporting structure for our accelerator. The impressive scale of the building is a handy spin-off from the design, thirty metres taller than the Big Mixer, thirty metres more significant than the Security Service's tower. It puts a big smile on the corporation – we make no secret of it.'

'Educational, Ms Clowes, *n'est-ce pas?*' the Thin Doctor added.

Clowes remembered the smart adjunct from the Thin

Doctor's potted treatise on classical French in the *Ouest La Plage* and smiled at his including her in this intellectual badging.

Rakussen ignored the pretentiousness and continued with his explanation. He pointed to the curve of the tube of the production line. 'This is a duct from one of the accelerator's ports on the floor below. Many of our processes require huge amounts of energy ... the multi-layering of our silicon bubbles here, for example. Each standard processor bubble can use several square metres of silicon film. As you can imagine, to harness the molecular spindrift in order to build the accurate layering, we need to create a very concentrated force-field. And we have all the power we need – on tap from the accelerator loop. We're able to suspend the silicon in a flux-field all the way down the line, adding layers to whatever tolerance we need. The process also naturally charges the leaves of the processor to hold the layers apart, and at the same time gives the structure its great strength. You could smash one of our droids with a light compression pulse – liquidize the chassis – but the processor would be left intact, floating in the mass – like a bubble, no less!' Rakussen smiled at his little joke.

'Are these bubbles in full production?' Clowes asked.

'All our military droids are now being fitted with this CPU, and we're launching an upgrade programme for existing owners. The real benefit that the bubble offers is virtual true parallel processing; a droid can now have almost human-speed spatial awareness and threat-sensing. In a military droid, with its naturally higher than human robustness, this type of processor will make it more than a match for a human opponent. It processes at just over half the speed of the human brain.'

'Sounds frightening, Dr Rakussen.'

'Maybe, Ms Clowes, but we are now well on the way to removing humans completely from any direct combat situation. And, of course, military-type droids don't *have* to be used for combat. Variants of the design can be used for all manner of peaceful applications. You don't have to think too hard about the amazing possibilities this processor offers.'

'So what about the Chromium Programme? It's not a standard droid-type like your military models, is it? Does it use the same processor? The Infonet says that it's the Chromium Programme that's sending Electro-corp share values through the roof.'

'The Chromium Programme ... I noticed that yours and the Thin Doctor's clearance gives you visitor access to the project ...' Rakussen's open attitude had changed noticeably at the mention of the name; he now seemed defensive. 'I hope you'll excuse me, but I really will have to double-check on your access codes. Where's the doctor gone? I need your passes ...'

Clowes handed over the holographic insert from her overall's transparent breast pocket.

The Thin Doctor had drifted away from Clowes and Rakussen at the beginning of the latter's explanation of the accelerator. Now he was across the lab, watching the finished processors emerging from the end of the production line. Rakussen called out to him as he made his way down the side of the glass case.

When Rakussen joined Clowes and the Thin Doctor, who were now both waiting at the department's security gate, he wore a peculiar expression which was made clear as he spoke. 'You're both clear; please excuse my checking. You've clearance from the highest authority, in fact you may care to know that you're classified as

State Trustees ...' The look was one of admiring disbelief.

The Thin Doctor winked at Clowes.

'So you won't be interested in Mechanics, Materials and Testing, I assume?'

'We don't have a lot of time, Rakussen,' the Thin Doctor replied.

'Up we go then ... to the Holy of Holies.'

The elevator ran Rakussen through a sequence of checks after he'd called out floor number one hundred and forty. Clowes and the Thin Doctor had to offer their passes and palms for scanning before the doors closed.

'These mechanical checks are rather laborious, but one-forty and up are heavily restricted. I have only limited security clearance myself,' Rakussen explained. 'It's worth the trouble, though; these floors are something else, there's nothing like this place in the whole Archipelago.'

Floor one-forty was cathedral-like. As they exited the elevator they found themselves on a broad, raised pier of a pure black vitreous material which dropped away on each side in a long series of steps to a curving viewing gallery which obviously ran round the whole circumference of the tower. The glazing of the gallery canted out from the edge of the floor at a shallow angle, on a clear day allowing a view directly down to the city below. Today, however, the entire window offered only the blank, pale-yellow vista of Metropolis 4's smog. Mirroring the causeway which they were now crossing, the ceiling high above possessed the same contours in reverse: it was made of a pale material and reflected the yellow light which, Clowes observed, cast a jaundiced hue on human skin. At the end of the pier was a wall,

110

also sheer black, reaching the full height of the hall, four or five normal storeys high, in Clowes' estimation. What she at first thought was a trick of the light revealed itself to be a shallow, arched recess at the foot of the wall. It was only the sudden presence of a security staffer at the blended black reception desk that gave any impression of depth.

The female security staffer matched the sleek surroundings perfectly: she wore her hair close-cropped, a style that her beautifully even and intelligent features carried effortlessly. Clowes was struck by the woman's self-possession as she ran through the security formalities. She also noted that the Thin Doctor seemed to be quite transfixed by her as well. Unusual for him indeed.

'One more elevator, Ms Clowes,' Rakussen announced. 'Do you feel OK? Only the pier from the main shaft can give some people vertigo. You may also have noticed a slight change in the feel of the tower . . . some do. From this floor upward, the building is gyroscopically balanced. The mechanism runs under the one-fortieth and the raised pier houses the main gyro. The Chromium Programme demanded constant true verticals for its completion, so we had to come up with a way of preventing the tower from swaying about. You'll probably notice the effect more when you leave.

'At last, here we are. Ms Clowes, doctor . . .' Rakussen ushered them through the reception area of the Chromium Programme's floor one.

The heavy black theming of the one-fortieth continued along the corridor in which they now found themselves; there seemed to be no windows or openings to the outside world.

Rakussen stopped at an armoured door at the side of

the corridor and punched a code into a security keypad. 'This is where we start. The Programme's accelerator port.'

In the centre of the chamber they had entered was a large white sphere, some five metres in diameter, from which white insulated tubes radiated, heading off at various angles to other areas of the Chromium Programme's floors. The sphere and its tubing hummed and gave off intermittent dull cracks that were muffled by the insulation.

'This is the Programme's energy distributor,' Rakussen began. 'The Chromium Programme is the most energy-hungry project in the tower.'

The Thin Doctor walked over to the distributor and pressed a hand against the belly of the main sphere, as though checking its vital signs.

'Why's it called the Chromium Programme, Dr Rakussen? And why does it need so much energy?' Clowes wondered.

'The Chromium droid, we call her the Supervisor, is like no other droid in existence,' Rakussen replied. 'The robot is a complete departure from commonly held machine-design philosophy. Although she has all of the standard components of any robot: a CPU, neural systems, server motors etcetera, they have all been engineered from base molecular level.'

'And she's a she, Dr Rakussen,' Clowes smiled. 'She sounds like progress.'

'An understatement, Ms Clowes ... She's the mother of a whole new generation of droids, of a new era of engineering, in fact ... This is no good, I'll see if we can go along and see her – you have to see the Supervisor to really appreciate what I'm saying.'

'Good idea, Rakussen.' The Thin Doctor rejoined

them, back from his inspection of the energy distributor. 'We understand accelerator distributors already.' His tone was dismissive of Rakussen's obvious desire to create a build-up to their seeing the new droid.

'Of course, doctor,' Rakussen laughed. 'I wanted to save you complete surprise at our developments here.'

'Surprise is the preserve of the uninformed, Rakussen. We are now informed. Shall we proceed?'

Clowes logged the Thin Doctor's impatience and suspended her questioning of Rakussen, who now was a little agitated at being rushed in his guided tour. They left the distributor chamber and followed the physicist down the apparently spiralling corridor to the inevitable security control at the entrance to the Chromium Programme's inner sanctum. Clowes received quite a shock when they rounded the final corner and saw two large red sentry droids, one on either side of the barrier. She stepped smartly behind Rakussen as the nearer droid rapidly turned its head to track their advance, its body remaining motionless.

'You have to expect droids in an Electrocorp facility, Ms Clowes,' Rakussen joked over his shoulder. 'As long as you don't jump the barrier, you'll live!'

Clowes had never seen a modern military droid in real life. These things were awesome, they had a silent, powerful presence. She examined the oversize humanoid form of the machine, now a few feet away. The arms, heavily jointed under armour fairings, could pull a man limb from limb in seconds, and these models had mimetic human hands, clenched just now in fists like rocks, more than twice the size of Subject Four's neat extensions.

'Ms Clowes . . .'

She started at finding herself alone with the droid.

The Thin Doctor and Rakussen were already through the security gate. She moved gently away from the sentry, feeling its black sensor eyes following her through the check.

Rakussen settled his guests into comfortable seats in a small, semi-circular viewing theatre. The seating was arranged round a section of a dull dome which pushed out into the room. From the tiered seating they would have a good view of whatever was underneath.

'Drink, anyone, before the show starts? This is an executive suite, so we spare no expense for our guests here.' Rakussen was comfortably back in his host's role, the tension between him and the Thin Doctor having subsided. Clowes and the Thin Doctor each requested water and Rakussen pressed the order into a clicker he had produced from his pocket. 'A few minutes ... Now, Ms Clowes, as to your questions about the Chromium Programme. The Controller is going to switch the polarization on the dome when he's ready and you'll see the Supervisor in all her glory. Then you'll see why the Chromium name-tag is so appropriate.'

'I'm in suspense, Doctor Rakussen.'

'The naming of the Programme actually came from the laser technology that we employed to explore the first principles of the new droid's design. You recall that I said that the droid is constructed from base molecular level; it was a *chromium ion* laser that we used initially to break the basic electronic components and convert them into electro-organic form. I'm sure you'll have read papers on this subject.'

'We developed small electro-ecologies in M2, doctor, while I was studying. We could never build large-scale models that would survive outside a flux-field.'

'Electrocorp had similar problems, I think, around

ten years ago. It was the same for everyone. There was a lot of to-ing and fro-ing between institutions with different ideas, and then the whole research area seemed to die a death.'

'I was involved about six years ago, I suppose. But it was more of a college study exercise than anything.'

'Quite, Ms Clowes, but it was around that time that Electrocorp made their own breakthrough – and kept it very quiet, naturally ... The team here went right back to basics and, again using the chromium ion laser, found that the particular frequency they were using could modify an atom's magnetic axis while retaining all its original properties as a component of a molecule. Do you follow?'

The Thin Doctor cut in at this point. 'You were able to build molecular structures in whatever macro shape you wanted.'

'Absolutely, doctor,' Rakussen continued. 'Simple and complex materials – water or silicon-etched electronics could be atomically bound together in any form we wanted. As long as we could perform the atomic break-down of the material in the first place.'

'I think our refreshments have arrived, gentlemen,' Clowes interrupted Rakussen, watching, fascinated, as a beautifully elegant server droid climbed the stepped gangway between the seating. This chromium droid, clearly a female from its perfectly formed figure, carried in one hand a tray on which stood three tall glasses of water and which never strayed from the perfect horizontal as she moved towards the three scientists.

'Your drinks, madam, sirs.' The droid spoke in smooth, sampled female tones and offered the tray to Clowes sitting in between the two men. They each took a glass, at which the droid politely thanked them and returned to the dark foot of the dome from where she had emerged.

'This viewing theatre is expressly designed for showing the Supervisor and entertaining prospective buyers. The droid you've just seen is a conventionally engineered clone of the Supervisor. I think that they messed up in Control, because you shouldn't really have seen her before you'd seen the original ... I'll have to speak to them about that.' Rakussen chuckled.

'She was *wonderful*, Doctor Rakussen. Can I take her home?'

'A very limited edition, Ms Clowes – she's not for sale. We should see her big sister at any time now.' Rakussen's clicker was emitting a thin beeping sound.

The dome flashed brightly, and it took a little time for them to adjust to the brightness after the subdued lighting of the theatre. Inside the dome they could see a part of what looked like a control terminal. The lighting was cold and very white; the blue surfaces of the monitoring banks seemed soft and held on to the light like sponges. The Supervisor droid stood behind a curving console staring up into the theatre; she was a pure chromium silver, unblemished by any hint of a droid component build. She was sleek, immaculate. Then she moved. Languid and supple, her form displayed an uncanny musculature which flowed with her movement.

'Unreal ...' Clowes uttered her amazement, leaning forward from her seat, scarcely believing what she was seeing. The Thin Doctor's cyborg that she'd seen that morning seemed like a relic from another age. She nearly said so, then checked herself as she caught the scientist looking straight at her. Was he a mind-reader?

'She's real, Ms Clowes ... You're looking at the

116

future of robotics.' Rakussen didn't take his eyes from the beautiful female as he spoke.

'And what is the installation in the dome, Rakussen?' the Thin Doctor asked.

'It's a simulation management console for the production plant. The Supervisor is running her own programme in parallel with ours. We're monitoring her against our own administration. Her decision-making is hyper-rational. Would you believe me if I said she was performing better than our own human system overriders.'

'No, that doesn't surprise me, Rakussen. She obviously doesn't work as a committee like your human staff. If her intelligence is as complete as I've been led to believe, you could have a redundancy schedule on your hands very soon.'

The Supervisor was now ignoring them and had returned to a workstation, which she was operating just like a human.

'How can she be so intelligent, Doctor Rakussen?' Clowes enquired. 'I presume she is using your silicon bubble CPU.'

'CPUs . . . She has a series of processors which, as a result of the electro-organic restructuring, operate just like a human brain – as far as we can tell – frankly her quantum neural functions have taken on some mystery. She has phenomenal memory and learning ability; some of our project technicians believe she's building her own personality. But that's difficult to establish. What we do know is that our team members are falling in love with her. It's quite strange, our psychologist had to remove a technician from the programme due to his inability to relate rationally to her.'

'Incredible – but she is quite beautiful, even with her

blank face. Who decided she should be a female?' Clowes was determined to get her original question answered.

'It was the Supervisor's own decision. She can be any shape she wants to be. She's actually morph capable but has used the attribute only once. The female choice is her molecules' *home* form. We made the company's personnel files available to her as a benchmark for a selection – just physical attributes – and she chose her current shape. She originally had a face, but that seems to have been dispensed with.'

'Maybe she thinks she's more attractive like that, doctor?'

'Now you are sounding like a psychologist, Ms Clowes.' Rakussen wasn't going to see beyond a droid in his view of the Supervisor.

'So let me understand this properly,' Clowes replied. 'The Supervisor is basically a super-fluid construction, where the *fluid* is in fact a conventional set of components re-formed by a flux force-field of some kind?'

'That's more or less correct. She maintains her structure through the enhanced surface tension of the mercury alloy bonding chassis, if you like.'

'And she can operate in any environment? Or do you have to keep her in some sort of special atmosphere, such as there might be in the dome?' Clowes suggested.

Rakussen paused before answering the question. 'That's not free information, Ms Clowes. We do need to keep some aspects of the Programme confidential.' And Rakussen smiled.

The Thin Doctor, who had been studying the droid intently throughout, now leant back slightly sideways in his seat and addressed Rakussen across Clowes. 'This technology, even just the pure metallurgy of the

Chromium Programme, must have massive repercussions for the whole of materials science. Why have you opted to build such a complex machine straight away, when the properties of this – shall we say, *discovery* – can be applied to much simpler structures?'

'We do have an entire materials science project backing the Programme, doctor. This technology renders the complexity of a subject almost irrelevant. But the conversion of any reasonable-sized subject is still a very time-consuming operation, since we are dealing with it literally atom by atom. Electrocorp make droids and, once the successful practice of re-forming atomic systems had been conclusively proven, we went straight for the conversion of one of our products . . . You know Electrocorp's style . . . Why settle for a modified vending machine?'

'So it takes years to create such a machine, Rakussen?'

Rakussen shook his head, smiling. 'I'm not at liberty to discuss every aspect of the Programme, as I said, doctor.'

The Thin Doctor had persuaded the Lander pilot to make the return flight into a tour for Clowes. As the craft cruised over the city, the Thin Doctor pointed out all the landmarks, including the location of the RCA down in a very miserable Industry 2. Clowes hadn't realized that Metropolis 4 was so perfectly sectored. The concentric ring routes and the radial boulevards gave the city a precise geometric topography which served to give the state authorities an absolutely definitive location-addressing system. The Thin Doctor explained that the authorities had completely unambiguous maps of the whole city which were organized in strata of height and depth. Every registered member of the population had a spatial reference coding which could be entered into the Population Control System. The Pop-Con, as it was commonly referred to, could locate any person exactly with some ten metres' accuracy, if that person was wearing a control tag. Tag wearing was not yet compulsory, but on the Census Days (currently one day in every three months) tags had to be worn.

The Thin Doctor hadn't mentioned the Chromium Programme and the Supervisor since they had left Electrocorp. He was enjoying his lecture on Metropolis 4, however, and Clowes was finding it instructional.

'So if you don't wear a tag, the authorities can't locate you?'

'That's right, Ms Clowes.'

'So it's easy to avoid the census checks?'

'You can avoid them up to a point. Every UC in the job-share system has a tag allocated to him or her, so the city-state knows exactly how many tag-wearers there are. You have to remember that a tag is only active when in contact with the individual's skin or when it is receiving a high level of the pheromone of the allocated wearer. Now, if you aren't wearing a tag when there's a census, then this will be picked up by the Pop-Con by default *and* you'll probably receive a Sec-services visit at your accommodation unit.'

'But you might not be in when they call.'

'If you're not there when they check, they know your job-share plan and you'll be classified as *absent with intent*, and then you'll definitely be tracked down.'

Clowes blew out a puff of disbelief. 'They tried to tag people in M2, but it just didn't work. Nobody would wear the things. I hadn't realized that the system actually operated here, doctor.'

'M4 is a very authoritarian state, but it also offers the highest standard of living on the planet, certainly for UCs. People want to live here, and, to do that comfortably, you stick to the rules.'

'So what happens to defaulters if they're caught?'

'For a first offence there's usually just a warning and their coding goes on to a security file. If there's a repeat, then you can have your job-share rescheduled, or sometimes you get detention.'

'And if you avoid detection altogether, you become an official Azzi. Is that right?'

'Yes, you become an officially registered Azzi. Then you're up against it.' The Thin Doctor banged his fist into his palm to reinforce the point.

Clowes considered that she hadn't realized the depth of the state control at all. Metropolis 4 had a fearsome reputation in the whole Archipelago as a production and trading powerhouse; but she had had no idea of the price the mass of the population paid for the status.

'Don't look so concerned, Ms Clowes. It's a natural system for our level of development. You're lucky: you have an education and privileges, you have societal and geographical mobility. You can even become an unregistered Azzi if you want . . .' The Thin Doctor laughed.

'No thanks, doctor.'

The pilot cut into their conversation with a request that they prepare for landing, and the Lander jerked slightly as the ATMs locked to retro blast.

'Electrocorp have eyes and ears everywhere, Uschi. You can't be too careful anywhere on their property.'

The Thin Doctor answered Clowes' question concerning his taciturnity on the Chromium Programme during the flight back from Electrocorp. He was addressing her familiarly again, now they were in the privacy of his mobile, auto-routing gently back to Clowes' apartment block.

'I've great faith in your discretion, but I didn't want to invite even the slightest chance of something slipping out about our own work at the Foundation.'

'I understand, doctor, no offence taken. I suppose we are kind of in competition with the Electrocorp people.'

'Literally, Uschi. Did I not make you aware that our Cyborg Project has a commercial sponsor?'

'I didn't even consider that aspect. I suppose I should have asked.'

'You'll be meeting their representative next week; he wants to be at the transplant. I'll see him before then and I'll be able to vet him. I don't want a fainting or interference of any kind.'

'But what about the Supervisor, doctor. Wasn't she beautiful!'

The Thin Doctor was cool in his appraisal. He still doubted the electronic CPU technology and entered into another lengthy monologue, this time on the limitations of electronic processor architecture.

Clowes was nearly asleep when they reached her block.

CHAPTER SEVEN

'Sorry I was late, doctor ... today of all days. I'd completely forgotten about the census – the A-trains were mobbed.'

Clowes had found herself for the first time in a real rush-hour crush: the whole city's population seemed to be in frantic motion, in total contrast to the normal dull lassitude of the commuting grind. She was a good hour late in reaching the Foundation. She should have remembered the Thin Doctor's lecture on the subject only a week earlier. She said as much to him as she rushed round the tissue lab, collecting the data carts for the cyborg's chemistry synthesizer.

'Can you bring me *floor one*, Uschi? We should double-check its pH, now we have it in Coton's matching fluid.'

Clowes moved around to the Thin Doctor's bench and carefully lifted the transit vessel containing the cranial floor; she positioned it under the Thin Doctor's reference scanner.

'Stand back, Uschi, this kit is a little Heath Robinson-ish. Dabbs made a great job of it, but I don't quite trust the electron screening.' With the vessel in place, the Thin Doctor gingerly dialled in the scan parameters and retired back behind the mobile guard-screen to join Clowes.

'So who's our sponsor, doctor?'

'I don't think they have a name as such; it's a new

company, a venture consortium. Their rep has already arrived. I've left him with Dabbs and the subjects.'

'They're here now?'

'Just the one person: Mr Piaget, a hulk of a man, but with a lovely French name.'

'I didn't see anyone when I came in.'

'He was here early. He came with Coton, very keen ... Wanted to see everything.'

Coton had been brought in that morning by a Security Services detail, before the Sci-Medical Foundation had officially opened its doors. He now lay in the operating theatre of the Cyborg Facility, still sealed in his ICU capsule, which was linked up to the theatre's own support system. The Thin Doctor had already begun the acclimatization run-up: Coton's blood was being transfused and his brain circulation isolated, ready for its endorphin-supported shut-down. Clowes had taken only a quick look at him through the inspection port of the capsule; his colour was then already a deathly grey.

The scanner completed its checks and flashed all clear. Clowes and the Thin Doctor moved back to the bench.

'Is he still wanting to sit in on the transplant? Is he a tecchie, a doctor?'

'Take the stem adapter off the helium plant, I want to start warming the mating plates ... No, he's not really technical at all, a money man I should think ... and yes, he still wants to sit in ... I don't think he quite trusts us.' The Thin Doctor chuckled.

'He's not going to go down on us, is he?'

'We'll see, Uschi ... a fine test for him. Should add a little excitement. Will he, won't he?'

'I admire your cool, doctor ... seems an odd choice not to have someone at least halfway qualified, wouldn't you say?'

'Who are we to question, Uschi? As long as the funding keeps rolling in, then I'm happy. At least with a non-technical, we should be able to keep him as informed as *we* wish. Much more relaxing than having some would-be brain surgeon on the patch.'

'Quite true, doctor. I'm sure you'll be able to handle him just fine.'

'I will, Uschi, I will . . .'

Once they had made a final check on the timings for the electro-chemistry that would support Coton's brain in its new chassis, they left the tissue lab and entered the airlock leading to the sterile zone of Dabbs' chassis workshop.

'Very nice indeed.' The Thin Doctor voiced his approval at Dabbs' fastidious preparation of the cyborg chassis. 'I told you Dabbs was a perfectionist.'

Clowes looked at the chassis lying on a long theatre trolley behind a hissing air screen. The main body and legs were neatly decked in a green shroud of sterile fabric; the head, clearly separated from the body and trailing a thick cord under the shroud, hung supported in a wire frame, allowing free movement and access in any plane. The pale laminate was punctuated by large openings for the optical and auditory systems which would be fitted once the brain and its cranial floor had been located. The lower jaw was completely absent. Clowes also marvelled at the neatness of the presentation, in stark contrast to the clutter of the workshop through the glass partition beyond.

'We can leave it at that, Uschi. I'll have Dabbs bring the chassis through to theatre once we have the climate stabilized.'

Piaget was sitting in the facility's simple mess area,

drinking a cup of the doctor's real coffee, when Clowes and the Thin Doctor entered. Dabbs was fiddling with the coffee machine as they walked in and he turned around, immediately launching into an explanation of the machine's latest ailment. The Thin Doctor listened with rude interest as Clowes hovered to be introduced to Piaget. Piaget, also waiting for an introduction, broke with protocol and rose, offering his hand to Clowes.

'Piaget, from the project sponsors ... You must be Doctor Clowes.'

'Yes, pleased to meet you, Mr Piaget.' Clowes enjoyed Piaget's employment of her professional title. Since she had been spending so much of her time with senior colleagues, she hadn't heard the address for a while.

'You don't share the doctor's love of antiques, then.' Piaget nodded at the contraption on the work top.

'I'm terribly sorry, most rude of me,' the Thin Doctor cut in. 'My poor old machine's on the blink again. I should have introduced you both.'

Dabbs was waving some kind of transformer about and he turned to Piaget. 'It's over a thousand years old, and still working, more or less.' Dabbs gulped particularly over the word *thousand*.

'Thank you, Dabbs, I'll catch up with you later.' The Thin Doctor dismissed the technician and offered his apologies again.

'Your man was telling me about his arm. The episode with the ape-brain cyborg and the chimp. Poor creature, I bet it didn't know what'd hit it.' Piaget laughed, shaking his head. 'He's a bit weird himself, though, your man Dabbs. He wants to be careful, I could see the thing fancying him next!'

Clowes looked hard at the Thin Doctor; he had been avoiding her enquiries about Dabbs' arm.

'Yes, Ms Clowes, we introduced Four to a real ape the week before you arrived here. It was very unpleasant. Dabbs was lucky to get away with the injury he did.'

'Doctor, you should have told me!'

'Oops!' Piaget adopted a sheepish expression, completely unsuitable for his large flat face. 'Have I been letting things out of the bag already?' Piaget found himself enjoying the tecchies' apparent disarray.

'To business, Piaget . . . We have the transplant scheduled for this afternoon, at fourteen hundred. I envisage the main transplant procedure taking at least six hours. There will be some detailed surgical work to be done thereafter, mainly on stabilizing Coton's original body after the CPU removal. I will be transplanting our ape's brain into his cranium to keep his nervous system vital during his dormancy. Do you still wish to sit in with us? You may find part of the work somewhat stomach-turning.'

'I've seen worse before, doctor . . .' Clowes noticed that Piaget seemed to halt himself in giving a wider explanation.

'If you're sure then, Piaget,' the Thin Doctor pressed.

'Quite sure, I was once involved in an Azzi bomb attack – very messy. I've seen blood before.' Piaget made the explanation for Clowes' benefit. The actual images in his mind of the numerous Azzi clean-ups he'd directed could still make him shudder.

Piaget was reticent on the subject of the sponsoring company, and Clowes made little progress in her enquiries as they waited for the cater-net to deliver their lunch. The Thin Doctor had gone off to find Dabbs and continue with the final pre-op routines. Piaget seemed to have no particular qualifications for his role, but it was abundantly clear that he was a true company man and quite dedicated to the project. His references to Coton were oddly familiar. Clowes couldn't put her finger on it, but the man had certainly done his research.

'So you *do* know Coton, Mr Piaget.' Clowes was determined to establish their relationship.

The ex-Floor Commandant met Clowes' assured expression full-on and found some difficulty in avoiding her assertion. He searched for something plausible. 'It was some time ago . . . I worked with him for a while on a communications project.'

'I could tell there was something about you and Coton.' Clowes was smiling with satisfaction. 'What's he like? You do know that I'm going to be responsible for him, post-op. Anything you can tell me about him will be a great help.'

'Well, it was some time ago, doctor.' Piaget was feeling uncomfortable. The mild interrogation of this attractive woman was a world away from his command floor experience. 'Coton was a likeable man, very intelligent, quite an expert in comms transmission.' Piaget knew she had a version of the Service's file, but he still had to be careful.

'Is that your field then, Comms?'

'Well, you could say it's one of my specialisms. My people use me as a project manager in areas they're interested in.'

'And now that's cybotics.'

'Yes . . .'

'How do you feel about Coton, Mr Piaget? Knowing him, I mean . . . It must be a little strange.'

Piaget hesitated. '. . . I wasn't exactly close . . . I only had a professional relationship with the man.'

Piaget was saved by the trilling of the cater-net terminal

announcing lunch. Clowes went over to the machine and produced two flat containers from the delivery drawer. The food had come from the Foundation's own mess facility on the floor above, and when Piaget opened his pack he was pleasantly surprised to find it was still hot and didn't need the re-heat catalyst he always carried. This was a great improvement on the Big Mixer's system. Piaget's mind flashed suddenly to Kraemer, who was now a week overdue on his file search. What the hell was he up to? He'd have to contact him.

Kraemer had tried to tell Piaget about the problems in getting his Lander 6 log together, but the big man had been pretty much tied up with the rest of his leaving formalities. The new job he was going to seemed to be occupying him disproportionately. Some kind of demotion ... The man was into a crisis more like premature senile dementia; every time he'd tried to contact the Floor Commandant directly, he'd been put off – or been given an appointment which had then been postponed. Piaget hadn't realized that the authorization code wouldn't give him access to Flight Control, and that was where all the original comms logs were. He could only read the direct Comms Dept-addressed stuff; there was probably a lot more in Flight's log – stuff that could really screw Piaget's adjustments during a reconciliation. Still, the archive squad had been delayed, which gave him some breathing space. He had one last chance. Piaget wouldn't thank him for it if anyone found out, but probably things couldn't get a lot worse for the paranoid old bastard.

While he'd been checking through Coton's decrypt console, he'd found, among other things – such as a sub-net entry revealing a dodgy real-club, no less – a voice en/decrypt program which could synthesize speech from samples. He read Coton's critical note appended to the software with some amusement: *Not to be used internally – all right for booking hookers for Walker.* There then followed a sample conversation between a synthesized Walker voice and some confused woman at an escort agency. He must have been going to hit Walker with this after he'd set him up, Kraemer thought. Poor devils, the voice wasn't bad though, if you weren't really familiar with the owner. After bringing down a cart containing a Piaget voice log, Kraemer gave it a go: *Piaget, FC Comms Monitoring, I want you to send me all the flight comms log and related materials for recon action . . . blah . . . blah . . .* Kraemer leant back in Coton's old chair with the headset clamped to his ears and laughed quietly to himself.

The thing worked like a dream. He'd spent the whole night putting it together, and now Walker's favourite roster staffer was sending him the works . . . A stream of coded data blittered across his monitoring screen and the auth-code converted it. Kraemer looked up from his console; the afternoon sun had chosen that moment to slide a shaft through the cloud base. So it wasn't a moment of transcendental perfection then . . . He quickly dumped the files on to his back-up terminal and punched in a *compare* command with his original department data. There was a whole string of *no-match* messages . . . Piaget was really going to owe him for this.

Piaget gulped behind the theatre mask which sucked at his breath. He couldn't be sure if it was a reaction to a prolonged exposure to Dabbs' stupid speech, or just the poor adjustment of his equipment. He worried definitely that he was now almost literally being sucked into this tecchie circus. Dabbs had the new cyborg chassis at right-angles to the thing's head-frame, and the Thin Doctor was counting some ancient-looking instruments on the stand beside him. He was a poseur; not for him the spandex suits that the other two and Piaget were wearing – no, he had to wear some fool gown from out of a period hero-doctor flick. Clowes had the top part of Coton's capsule open and was tilting it gently up, raising the poor man's head to the height of the Thin Doctor's chest. Coton's monitoring system dropped a beat as the capsule locked steady. Clowes seemed cool; she waited a second for the next blip. The Intelligence Officer had been really slowed down; it seemed an age before the trace on the monitor picked up again.

'All clear, doctor,' Clowes confirmed Coton's status.

'Then we'll begin ... Set the timer, Dabbs, key the cyborg's chemistry for two hours from now. I'll update you if I want to extend.' The Thin Doctor looked across at Piaget and asked him how he felt.

'I'm fine, doctor.'

'We're just setting our timings for the moment of transfer. It's critical that Coton's brain meets our own fluid's chemistry with minimum trauma.'

The Thin Doctor drew a neat line round Coton's shaven head, addressing Clowes as he did so.

'Drawing skills are critical, Ms Clowes ... Maybe with your holographic plane vector expertise, I should have had you mark out the cranium,' he joked from behind his mask.

'Above the sphenoid and the squamous temporal, doctor, with a curve avoiding the lambdoid suture at the rear of the skull.' Clowes trotted out the textbook cut.

'Very good, doctor.' He had used her proper medical

title for the first time ever, surely a mark of professional respect – this *was* a red-letter day.

'I'm going to hinge the top of the skull above the lambdoid, Ms Clowes, an old dodge – makes a handy dish for holding all the loose bits and resting the knife.' The doctor waved the scalpel he was holding.

The doctor was enjoying himself, Clowes thought, he loves a crowd. Piaget was relieved as he saw the doctor dispense with the knife and lower a laser cutter on to the head. He looked away to the monitor, watching for Coton's reaction to this major attack on his body. There was no change as Clowes worked the control centre, obviously making some kind of compensation.

The rest of the monitoring team were still treating Kraemer like a Section Leader; they knew that he'd been stitched up by the Floor Commandant, and there was still no replacement for him. It was quiet in the department; Azzi transmission activity was pretty much a seasonal thing; at the beginning of winter it always took them some time to adjust. As long as he was circumspect, Kraemer had plenty of opportunity to process the Lander 6 log. He would check out the maintenance confirmation first. May as well start at the beginning of the *no-match* cases.

It took Kraemer an hour or so before he discovered that the peculiar code prefix for the maintenance team referred to two Electrocorp test droids. He had thought it peculiar that there were no voice logs from the pre-flight crew, apart from the console staffer. The timings were extremely rapid; the droids could obviously work faster than any human team and the check list scrolled on over ten screens, all completed in fifty minutes. The ground crews wouldn't like that – the droids had a 100 per cent productivity code.

The flight roster staffer's entry was amusing: there was thinly veiled outrage at Walker's pulling rank to get Coton aboard the Lander. Kraemer moved the entry back to match with Piaget's being already in the exec assembly meeting and therefore unreachable. He saw his own entry as he confirmed the authorization in Piaget's supposed absence and tutted at having to leave it there, granting it a full exec code to match Piaget's own polishing up of the record. 'You really went for it, didn't you, Piaget.' He spoke out loud, since there was nobody around. Piaget's manipulation of the log was bare-faced cheek, and here he was, sorting it out for him. He blew a long sigh at the thought.

The out-flight log stacked up well against the department's version; it was all routine and there were no impolite references to Piaget or the Department. The guys knew how to code that sort of thing up anyway, and *he'd* certainly never find it. The Internals wouldn't bother either; the two subjects were dead – or as good as – and there could be no point in going for them on a disloyalty rap. Coton's first report on the signal fix was clear enough, although the encryption had twisted some of the text – there was no voice from any of the Lorus messages.

It was the total encryption of the first message after a long pause that grabbed Kraemer's attention, though. The code was pure Coton and the message hadn't been unscrambled by Flight's own computers. The same period on Comms Monitoring's own log was completely blank. The inconsistency stood out like a sore thumb, but nobody had turned it up at the enquiry. Kraemer ran a dump to a cart and stuffed it into his number 1 terminal – the entry didn't read. Instead, the log gave some nav-com data where the entry should have been. There was no obvious fault, so someone had not wanted the data to be read, but why?

The Thin Doctor had now completely removed the top half of Coton's skull, exposing his brain's bare sac of protective tissue. Clowes was in close attendance with a flask on a wheeled stand from which trailed a collection of narrow tubes, each fitted with connecting glands of some plastic material. The doctor took each of the tubes in turn and connected them to locations evenly spaced round the sac. Clowes connected a further larger-diameter tube to an existing junction at the top of Coton's spine.

'Just take off ten mil of CSF, Ms Clowes, and introduce it to the cyborg chemistry.' The Thin Doctor looked up at Piaget as he spoke. 'Cerebrospinal fluid, Mr Piaget, makes things a bit messy if we don't drain the stuff off before we begin the removal.'

Piaget nodded his acknowledgement.

'We have a full match with the cyborg, doctor,' Dabbs gulped from behind the console.

'Excellent ... Full drain, Ms Clowes, you can leave me with this for now. Can you float the ape's brain and check its status? I want to do a quick temporary hook-up as soon as we have Coton's brain free.'

The Thin Doctor slowly started to slice into the membrane in a series of radial cuts. Piaget looked away to Dabbs who was now fussing with the cyborg's cranial floor. The thing was floating in fluid within a transparent bag hanging from a frame above the empty robot head. Inside the bag a spider-like machine, remotely controlled by Dabbs, crawled inside the cup of the floor. A miniature monitor screen in a harness on the technician's chest clanked against his aluminium sling as he worked the joystick control.

'Pure surgery, Ms Clowes.' The Thin Doctor spoke as he began to peel back the folds of tissue. 'The brain . . . The one domain that still remains a real challenge to the skills of the knife-man.' He turned briefly to Clowes.

'If you say so, doctor.' She was watching his deft hands intently.

'Clip these folds, please, and hand me the laser speculum. Let's take a look underneath.'

As soon as Clowes had secured the flaps of membrane, the doctor slipped the flat instrument down the side of Coton's now exposed brain.

'I'll need you to do a ten-millimetre laser trepan on the left squamous, Ms Clowes. We need to get a pick-up on Coton's beautifully developed hypothalamus. You'll find that the co-ordinates are already on the console. Use tool template three.'

As Clowes swung the laser cutter from the instrument stand, the flat plastic plate on its flexible extension creased to form a perfect match of the side of Coton's head. Piaget moved a little closer to examine this marvellous device. Clowes located the cutter against Coton's head and triggered the cut. Piaget winced as he caught a whiff of burning flesh.

'Interesting, Mr Piaget?' It was the Thin Doctor who spoke. 'The hypothalamus controls the body's endocrine and autonomic nervous system. We take a close scan pick-up from the organ at the base of the brain, then copy it to Dabbs' console. He can then make a chemistry match and create endorphins and other neuro-chemicals to keep the brain happy in its new home.'

'To prevent rejection, doctor?'

'Yes, more or less. We fool it into thinking it still has a biological chassis to look after.' The Thin Doctor turned back to Clowes. 'Do we have a hole, Ms Clowes?' Clowes was withdrawing the laser cutter. 'Let's have the probe in there then . . .'

Coton's console presented Kraemer with a whole lexicon of codes as he doggedly started the matching routine. While the screen rolled through the checks he reconsidered the possible motives someone might have had for concealing the transmission. Coton would surely not have sent such a densely coded message for a routine TR . . . None of the other stuff was encrypted like this. Had the transmission been inspected at all? Well, it was unquestionably there on the log, and Flight's equipment would have automatically gone into decrypt and have successfully decoded the message. It would even hook to Coton's console if it had to. He'd check the original again . . . Kraemer secured the monitor with Piaget's authorization code and left the computer to continue its checks in a sub-routine.

Back at his own monitoring console, Kraemer opened the file again. Coton's last entry carried a read-date followed by a summary of times the file had been accessed. The summary box held three entries, one of which tallied with the TR's transmission date: Newjune 1st, one twelve hours later, in the small hours of the next day, and one at the end of the month, a week before the enquiry. It was the second that caught Kraemer's attention. 'No one about, Flight would be dead at that time,' Kraemer said into his monitor. He cast his mind back to the events of that day. Of course, the storms were blowing like crazy all through into the next day. Flight and AT would have been heaving with people, there was traffic stacked up all over the place, anyone could have accessed the log . . . Not very conclusive, no link to anyone or anything. Stupid that he felt such a suspicion about a single log entry. Well, if nobody could read it, it couldn't hurt Piaget. It probably *was* some insult about the big man after all.

What *had* happened to Piaget? He was well overdue with his file dupe for him and he'd heard nothing; he couldn't be so desperate any more. It looked like another day was going to be added to the delay and Kraemer was finding that he wasn't bothered at all . . . Piaget was history. . . But Coton's console had now had plenty of time to do its stuff and he was due off shift in half an hour. Kraemer set off again, back down to Coton's old console at the rear of the now nearly empty monitoring floor. When he reached the Decrypt section, he could still see the console down in the sunken pit, ticking quietly in its secure mode. He slumped himself down at the key monitor and lazily stroked in the authorization code, watching the prompted checker feed across the screen. A red highlight dancing around a small line of text in the centre of the screen caused him to swing forward from his reclining position – *Churchill: Enter ID* – the name was familiar, was it some kind of weapons system? Kraemer flopped back in the chair again . . . 'Shit . . . It wants Coton's ID.' He muttered the words under his breath. The machine would now need a palm or an iris match – probably both, knowing Coton. This was the end of the line . . . Kraemer kicked the console's bottom panel in frustration.

*

Piaget reacted to the sudden crash behind him by jerking upright and an object punched into the back of his knees, causing him to leap forward, narrowly avoiding Coton's ICU capsule. Clowes and the Thin Doctor both froze in their work on Coton's skull, staring at the source of the disturbance behind him.

'Dabbs! You blithering idiot!' The Thin Doctor bellowed over his mask voice kit.

Piaget turned to see the technician bent double behind him, now in the process of retrieving his aluminium sling from underneath the cyborg's trolley.

'S . . . sorry, doctor . . .' came the gulpy voice from below the trolley. '. . . I . . . was just removing my sling when it slipped, the articulation had jammed.'

'I told you it was ridiculous device, man! You nearly had Mr Piaget into the subject's capsule . . . Are you all right?' The Thin Doctor addressed his enquiry to Piaget.

Piaget nodded, still in slight shock from the surprise. He himself was in two minds whether to laugh or scream at the patently mad technician.

'May we continue, Dabbs? Has the floor-spider completed its process?' The Thin Doctor turned to Piaget with an explanation. 'The floor-spider is Dabbs' mechanical pet, Mr Piaget. The cranial floor which will locate Coton's brain in the cyborg chassis has several hundred neuron transmitter heads, the small metallic studs visible in the lining. Right up to the time of transplant we keep them sealed to protect them from contamination by our preserving fluid. Now that we have Coton's chemistry matched into the fluid, we can have the spider break the seals and the floor can go live.'

'I call him Henry, Mr Piaget.' Dabbs offered his contribution.

'Very good, Dabbs. Has *Henry* finished his work?' the Thin Doctor enquired with exaggerated politeness.

'All live and hooked to the chassis' centres, doctor. Checks run completely clear,' the technician replied, now back at his wheeled console.

The Thin Doctor busied himself with the settings on a new piece of equipment that Clowes had moved up to Coton's capsule. Clowes took a floppy rubber belt from a hanger on the side of the machine and placed it high under Coton's jaw, fastening it at the back of his neck as the collar slowly inflated.

'The P-cutter's in place, doctor. Can I switch in the sensory support?' Clowes moved two pads from the collar over each of Coton's ears as she spoke.

'Wait a moment, Ms Clowes. I want everyone back out of Coton's field of vision before you do that ... No, not you, Ms Clowes, you stay where you are ...' The Thin Doctor waved his arm at Piaget and Dabbs, who both moved around behind the Thin Doctor. 'When we switch in the sensory support, before we cut the major nerve channels, it's very likely that Coton will become hyper-sentient for a second or even longer.' The Thin Doctor was addressing the whole group. 'Our ape cyborg went through this process, and in this period became aware of Dabbs working over him. I now believe that it was the image of Dabbs he received in these moments of hyper-sensitivity that led to the strong positive association he subsequently displayed during the incident in the cage.'

'Oogh ...' Dabbs let out a gulpy dawning acknowledgement.

'Quiet, Dabbs ... I now want Coton, should he also go through this phase, to see and possibly hear only Ms Clowes, since she will be responsible for him in the post-operative period. Can you remove your mask, Ms Clowes . . . and smile, maybe?'

Clowes followed the doctor's instructions. She felt like an ill-prepared understudy, thrown on stage on the first night.

'A smile, Ms Clowes?' Clowes opened her mouth to speak; she wanted to question the wisdom of this action. 'Don't speak, direct your breath downwards.' The Thin Doctor spoke, directing her from behind Coton's monitoring console. 'Like having a holoportrait.'

Clowes found herself obeying the Thin Doctor's commands and she twisted a peculiar smile across her face. In the same instant, Coton's eyes flashed wide open and rolled to meet Clowes' gaze. She could read only deep terror in the massive pupils. Before Clowes could respond to the look, the eyes flickered shut and a new rhythm joined the chorus of monitoring equipment. The Thin Doctor had switched in the sensory support.

Kraemer pondered how he was going to beat Coton's security system. Somewhere there had to be files containing the palm and iris matches – the Internals probably had something. But even if he could lay his hands on them, which was highly unlikely, Coton would have some other check to be fulfilled, since this was undoubtedly a personal security code. The box flashed again, the words *Enter ID* changed colour, flashing now to purple. Kraemer pulled himself back up to the screen and sensed an insistence in the words as the blink-rate increased. He pressed his palm on the pad and winked at the recognition icon at the top of the screen. The monitor headset at his side emitted a beep. Kraemer grabbed it and brought it to his ear.

The text line was chased across the screen by another, longer message, but the headset remained silent. *Survival is the twin brother of annihilation.* Kraemer read the cryptic message, wondering what was coming next. Coton's unmistakable voice came over the earphone.

'Winston Churchill, leading twentieth-century Mother Earth politician –' There was a slight pause. 'Kraemer.' It was a voice insert, then Coton's voice continued: 'I've included you in my access list. I count you as someone I can trust – replace your palm on the pad and hold it there for the duration of the message.' Kraemer obeyed the instruction. 'This is a special code which backs up all the TRs I consider important and possibly sensitive ... This format survives for ever and cannot be deleted. If I have not been able to access this file, please listen and act on it as you see fit ... Contact Walker if he is not already aware ...' Kraemer looked around to check whether anyone was watching him; he had been quite oblivious to his surroundings during the past few minutes. His eyes fell back on the empty ergo seat that Walker had last occupied four months ago. He suddenly felt very alone.

'TR one ...' The voice had changed to the console's own and there then followed another beep and a noisy, static-laced TR crackled through the set; it was a typical Lorus-corrupted voice transmission which broke and then went into text bits. Kraemer diverted the stream to his data cart: he was better reading this stuff on his own monitor bank, where he could also do a *compare* check with all the other log entries.

Coton's log revealed another string of *no-match* cases, another chapter in what was proving to be something much more complicated than Piaget's stupid cover-up.

*

The particle-cutter had isolated the brain seemingly in seconds, and now Piaget watched aghast as the Thin Doctor lifted the brain from Coton's skull with a vacuum device which held the grey lump in an inverted, hissing cup. The Doctor continued in one flowing movement to lower the brain into a clear fluid-filled tube, at the bottom of which sat the cranial floor, installed by Dabbs some minutes earlier. This whole mating vessel was linked to a hefty umbilical from the cyborg chassis. Dabbs now swung the cyborg monitor console around to where the Thin Doctor could see the panel when the brain docked with the cranial floor. Piaget edged around to the far side of Coton's ICU capsule for a better view, and he held his breath as the brain was released from the vacuum cup and floated gently down the last few centimetres to meet the strange receptacle. At the head of the open tube Clowes guided what Piaget took to be the blood supply-lines and nerve leads into the liquid. They trailed in the oily fluid like sea-grasses.

'Do we have power to the chassis, Dabbs?' The Thin Doctor didn't take his eyes from the brain.

'Minimum supply, doctor.' Dabbs slaughtered the middle word.

'Contact!'

As the Thin Doctor spoke, the cyborg panel lit up like a gambling machine, closely followed by a muffled thud as the cyborg chassis twitched once on the padded mountings of the theatre trolley behind the console.

Piaget let out an involuntary gasp. 'Unbelievable . . .'

'Believe, Mr Piaget.' The Thin Doctor glanced back from the console.

'Congratulations, doctor . . . and you too, Dabbs,' Clowes added, leaning round the console to where Dabbs was fussing with the cyborg chassis.

Dabbs gulped unintelligibly, continuing with his labours.

'Have you traced the dysfunction, Dabbs?' the Thin Doctor enquired. 'The floor's hypothalamus pick-up is giving us an inverted trace. I suspect a wrong circuit termination.'

'I've got the thorax's chemistry sub-processor isolated, doctor. I'll restore it in a moment.'

'We must keep Coton's four Fs in check.'

'Four Fs, doctor?' Piaget peered across at the cyborg's monitor panel as he spoke.

Clowes expanded on the reference. 'You remember that the doctor explained that the hypothalamus looks after the autonomic nervous system – the system that governs our basic functions – and that we have to fool it to keep Coton's brain functioning normally in the new chassis . . .'

'Yes.'

'The four Fs refer to the basic function groups: fighting, feeding, fleeing and er . . . mating, Mr Piaget. If we control these, we have a happy, unconfused cyborg.'

Piaget was already laughing as Clowes finished her sentence. 'Very good, Ms Clowes, I'll remember that.'

'Seriously, Mr Piaget, these are our major concerns, the key to Coton's success.'

'Thank you, Ms Clowes.' The Thin Doctor halted the clarification. 'We can all pat ourselves on the back for having got this far. As soon as Dabbs has the endorphin factorizer properly on line, we can go to the final installation.'

While Dabbs continued with his work, the Thin Doctor directed Clowes to bring over the ape's brain. He would continue stabilizing Coton's remaining body for its storage period.

Clowes questioned this change in order of the procedure, but the doctor was insistent. 'Coton's brain is stable; the trace is only inverted – it's a chassis fault. I don't wish to waste time waiting for Dabbs to fix it.'

The ape's brain carried interfaces for Coton's nervous system, and the hook-up consisted of aligning the mating plates to those now fitted to Coton's body's own nerve terminations. Although the body could be held almost indefinitely in low-level vitality, the maintenance of the nervous system's macro functions demanded the input of a biological neuron generator.

'Can you take care of the cerebration, Ms Clowes? I'll handle the major organs and lower functions.'

Clowes watched in surprise as the Thin Doctor walked around to the lower section of the capsule, leaving her alone with the major interfaces in Coton's skull. He was really putting her to the test – his motives were sometimes unfathomable. Clowes connected the major spinal mating plate to the ape brain's stem connector and programmed the calibrator on the capsule console.

The Thin Doctor had refused point-blank to allow her to examine Coton's injuries. The capsule's open main panel completely obscured her view as he worked silently on the transducer implants. This peculiarly silent work practice continued for an hour or more, during which time the Thin Doctor interrupted the silence only once, to bar Piaget from also peering into the capsule. Piaget eventually retired to a corner of the theatre, where he sat idly scrolling through the physiological reference monitor. It was Dabbs who finally broke the almost morgue-like atmosphere when he announced that he had solved the hypothalamus problem.

'Well done, Dabbs,' the Thin Doctor offered. 'We can

proceed to the final installation just as soon as Ms Clowes and I have completed our stabilization work on the donor body.'

Clowes pondered on the Thin Doctor's use of the words 'donor body'. Coton was now no longer Coton: his whole person, locked in that double handful of grey material, was in transit to a new frame. She looked down at her work on Coton's empty skull: a mass of tubes and cabling ran out to the ape brain's cranial floor adapter floating in its fluid-filled housing. What was happening in *that* grey lump? What kind of personality occupied Coton's body now? She got a feeling that Coton would never return.

The *No-match #1* TR on Coton's file was a frantic demand for information about some light compression sensor heads missing from Lander 6's inventory. There was also a screen dump accompanying the transmission which showed a comms multi-scan, where Kraemer detected a small peak of LC signal under a swath of Azzi VHF. No wonder Coton was going mad: he had this weird trace and no way of checking it out. He'd have to do a check on the tech log when he'd seen the rest of these personal back-ups. The next message had an unreferenced source – he couldn't believe it when he read the attribution – *Kraemer CF4*. Somebody had used his coding to acknowledge Coton's TR ... He cross-checked his own log and found that the transmission was long after his own last entry, and the syntax was unreal; he would never have TR-ed Coton in such a formal fashion. No wonder Coton had specially logged all this stuff – this was dynamite.

There followed a set of repeat messages and answers, all in the same pattern, with Coton not getting anywhere fast. The final message capped the whole thing: *unidentifiable LC or particle TR ... source vector extraterrestrial ... Request immediate BM action ...* Even though Coton was over Lorus, with all its quirky effects, he wouldn't have got that wrong and, appending the *BM – Big Mixer* action, he must have had some serious suspicions about whatever he saw in the transmission.

Kraemer considered his next move. Should he show this to Piaget? Or could this be the stuff the Floor Commandant was really panicking about? If it was, then he must be into something pretty damned heavy. No wonder he was so worried that the archive squad should get into this lot. All of Piaget's freaking out was falling into place.

Kraemer was well over his shift period; the past hours' revelations had completely taken him over – he needed some time to get a handle on all this. He was just shutting down the system and was about to secure the file when he remembered the Lander 6 tech log. He decided to make a quick check on the LC heads – maybe the droids had overlooked something in their super-rapid pre-flight inspection.

The ancillary equipment log registered 100 per cent but, on finding the specific code line, Kraemer, now almost beyond surprise, detected an overwrite – a crude modification, so unambiguous that only a droid-type processor could have performed such a cover-up. Had the heads been missing at the time of the check, or were they removed during it? And would a maintenance droid be able to do that? He had no idea ... Nobody could have done a detailed check on the log, and why should they have checked the ancillary kit? After all, nobody at the enquiry could have known about Coton's coded TR, decrypted to give a load of spurious navcom data. It was getting mighty complicated . . .

Kraemer closed down his console and made ready to go home. He had some thinking to do.

CHAPTER EIGHT

The last week had certainly been stressful for the whole team. The day after the transplant Coton's brain had gone into severe rejection and they had all feared the worst. There had been two occasions when they had lost a live scan completely. The brain was naturally traumatized on a purely physiological level, as they had expected; the ape and the cat cyborgs had already been through the same syndrome. The brain was naked of its original protective contact membrane, and the Thin Doctor's own new, synthetic bio-tissue had to be forced into an accelerated matching process. This was giving problems, as Coton's DNA map seemed to have some major bugs in it. Clowes was amazed at the number of hours the Thin Doctor was able to put in: he never seemed to leave the Cyborg Facility; whenever she took a rest-break, overnight or otherwise, he was unfailingly there at work when she returned. When she entered the theatre on the morning of the seventh day, the doctor was there again, busy hovering over the Coton cyborg's console. He smiled as he greeted her.

'We have a stabilization, Uschi. Our DNA geometry was quite appalling, as you know, but last night I managed to lift some data from Electrocorp's materials science network: a little of their atomic structuring to help us out – what they don't know can't hurt.'

'You hacked into their net, doctor? I thought that was impossible, even for you.'

'I've been trying all week, Uschi. I knew that they had to have what we needed.'

'And the scans are good?'

'Look!' The Thin Doctor pointed at the reference scanner, two pulsing histograms sharing the screen. 'The lower one is Coton's original.'

Clowes was amazed at the similarity between them, and looked back at the cyborg on the sloping trolley, the bared eyes flickering in REM. She turned back to the Thin Doctor. 'He looks great, doctor. What do you think he's thinking? He must be in some kind of dream state.'

'We'll soon be able to wake him,' the doctor replied. 'We can ask him then.'

'How long now? An estimate . . .'

'Well . . .' The Thin Doctor studied the cyborg, seemingly mentally checking off the tasks to be completed. 'He can now be checked for all the motor functions, there are sensory checks, of course, and we must also establish that our masking endorphins are going to hold up.'

'The tests in the bio-lab are looking very good, doctor; I read the projections last night.'

'I agree, but Coton has a rather more complex factorizer than our bench machine, and he's completely live, of course . . . I would say that, if we still have him as stable as this by the end of the week, then we can go ahead and wake him . . . Provided also that Dabbs has been successful dressing him and hooking up the skin's sensor paths.'

'Then the real fun starts, doctor.'

'Exactly . . , You'll be OK, Uschi. If I were a betting man, I'd put money on it.'

'Thank you, I'd better get back to my schedule. I promised Piaget I'd let him have a copy of the rehabilitation plan; he seems to have been getting a little twitchy these last few days.'

'Commercial pressures, Uschi – his people are anxious to get moving. Don't let him bother you though. I'll have a word with him when he appears. He needs to get a grip on the time-scale of this project.'

Clowes left the Thin Doctor and set off for her workstation at the far end of the facility. On the way down the corridor she nearly collided with Dabbs, who came careering out of his tech lab, clearly heading for the cyborg in the theatre.

'S . . . sorry, Clowes!' Dabbs gulped. 'I wasn't looking – I . . . lot on my mind, got to see the doctor.'

'What is it? Something serious, Dabbs?'

The technician seemed terribly preoccupied. 'Can't say . . . Personal matter . . .' With that, he slipped past her and continued on his way.

Clowes looked after him, genuinely worried by his unusual demeanour. When she reached her small office, she closed the door and opened her cyborg rehab file on the workstation. She had a problem concentrating; Dabbs not being himself was a worry. She hoped it was only a temporary thing, as she was really going to need him in the early stages of her work with Coton. She'd check with the doctor later; maybe he'd tell her what was wrong – he'd revealed Dabbs' other little secret, after all . . .

'Ah, Ms Clowes!' It was Piaget who disturbed her, his large face appearing round the door, his exclamation too loud for her in the middle of her documentation. 'I was hoping to catch you away from your lab work.'

'You made me jump, Mr Piaget.'

'You have the rehabilitation plan – excellent . . . Can I see?'

'It's not finished yet, but I can run you a print of the story so far.'

Piaget was slowly getting used to the informality of these tecchies. If one of his staffers had described an incomplete report as a 'story so far', he'd have gone for him straight away. Clowes' undeniable attractiveness also mitigated the suppression of his Sec-services persona – his mind did a quick flick back to Clowes in the tight spandex theatre suit ... 'Yes, good idea. Can you give me a quick run-down on how you see the project progressing? Your post-transplant part, that is.'

Piaget obviously hadn't seen the Thin Doctor that morning; he must have come straight to find her. She stopped herself sending him off to the doctor in the theatre. 'Well, I can give you just that, but it'll cost you some delay in your written report.'

'A quick briefing then, Ms Clowes.'

Piaget sat down on the other seat in the small office and poured himself some water from the dispenser at his shoulder. Clowes could see him settling down for a long sitting; his attentions in her direction were becoming a little too ardent. She really would keep this run-down as sharp as possible.

'OK then, Mr Piaget, I'll try and keep this as brief as I can. We're both busy people with our own priorities just now.'

'True, Ms Clowes.'

'Coton is now, as you'll know from the doctor's own documentation, a unique bio-mechanical. After the prototype subjects, he is the first of his kind and a massive leap forward in human science itself. With his isotope power supply and virtually maintenance-free chassis, he will soon be, to all intents and purposes, as independent as you or I.'

Piaget sipped his water and nodded.

'At the moment Coton is still not sentient; the Thin Doctor's not yet ready to switch in the sensory systems. The process we're in the middle of right now is progressively to increase the periods when we allow him independence from our override system until we're confident that he'll be able to survive completely on his own. The doctor is aiming for the end of this week as the date for Coton to go live.'

'This week? Good, I was getting concerned about the time-factor.'

'It's not going to be simple, though. We have no real idea just how sentient Coton will be when we make the full switch. There are really very many factors which will influence his condition, apart from the obvious psychological trauma that a sentient Coton will encounter at finding himself in a new body ... Think about it ... And there are two other physical factors which we have not yet fully dealt with: the renewal of the biological cells in his brain, and the constant supply and regeneration of the masking endorphins for his autonomic function centres. Remember the four Fs?'

'I liked the four Fs.' Piaget smiled. 'Excellent non-technical briefing material. I've incorporated them into my own report. So how are you dealing with these issues?'

'We're regularly transfusing Coton's brain's blood supply externally at the moment. This is feeding the organ very well, and we do have cell regeneration taking place, but we're still working on his own internal blood factorizer. The endorphin factorizer is in a similar state of development, and we're producing incredibly complex bio-synthetics here. The cat and the ape-brain cyborgs have the same problems: Dabbs takes them in dock every two days and tops up their reservoirs, so to speak.'

'Now your main role, Ms Clowes, apart from your obvious competence as a surgeon and tech back-up person. The Thin Doctor has told me he has full confidence in your being able to handle the post-transplant period.'

'The doctor is very kind, if a little prone to flattery.' Clowes paused, wondering how much to tell Piaget about her particular qualifications. She decided to go for the cut-down version; she couldn't handle going through the whole story again. She also wanted Piaget out of her private space. He had been displaying too great a personal interest in her during the past week; he was beginning to make her feel uncomfortable. She could feel his eyes all over her now.

She was exhausted when Piaget finally left her office. Thank the stars he had some other pressing appointment. However, he seemed to have prolonged the discussion as long as he could, labouring over details she hadn't even thought through herself. Her suspicions about him were certainly correct: the big – it had to be said, ugly – man had a kind of affected concern which really disturbed her; it was as if there was some desperate sub-character beneath, which he was constantly having to hold back. And his humour was unpleasant: he took a neanderthal pleasure in pursuing matters sexual. The incident with Dabbs and the ape was a constant reference for him, and when she answered his enquiry about Coton's masculine drivers, she could see he took a vicarious pleasure from her explanation. Poor Coton, though; it was an important issue: his emasculation as a cyborg was in itself enough to hamper his development severely. But she was getting ahead of herself . . . If they got far enough to worry about that, it would already be a miraculous achievement.

Kraemer felt very uncomfortable and exposed, up on the viewing platform. This gross structure had been built in earlier times, before the city had risen to its present dominance of the planet. The city fathers, two hundred years ago, had had a real pride in their creation and had built the massive arch with no other purpose than to provide a fitting viewpoint from which to survey their domain. Today it was sandwiched between two commercial blocks which dwarfed the arch ridiculously; the only vista now available to those who bothered to make the ascent was of a deep route canyon, slicing north–south through the superstructure of M4's business district.

Even in the fading afternoon light, Kraemer immediately recognized the shape of Piaget as he emerged from the elevator. Anyone else would have spotted him as well. Kraemer panned across the surrounding architecture, sheer glass and composite. He halted his sweep at the reflection of the arch in the building opposite and watched the lumpen image of Piaget ripple its way towards his own distorted shape. As Piaget drew alongside him, their reflections merged into one.

'Kraemer, you've got my data cart?'

'Right here, Commandant.' Kraemer slipped his hand into the pocket of his long winter coat, watching Piaget's eyes follow the movement.

'It's all up to date? Nothing missing . . . Don't give it to me now!' Piaget hissed dramatically as Kraemer withdrew the cart from his pocket. 'Put it on the ledge, below the rail.'

Kraemer followed the instruction, keeping his eyes on Piaget all the while.

The former Floor Commandant turned and met his eye once the cart was lying on the wall. Piaget's face loosened from its concentration and snapped into a smile. 'Well done, Kraemer.' Piaget slipped the cart into his own coat as he spoke. 'You didn't have any problems, then. I did give you more time, as you realize.'

'Nothing I couldn't sort out, sir.' Kraemer pictured the image of Coton's screen. 'I had to chase around for a few things on the system, but I think you'll find that everything's there in perfect order: timings – the lot.'

'Good man ... That's it then. You'll receive some benefit from this, Kraemer. I still have influence, you know ... Good luck.'

That was it, then ... Kraemer watched Piaget disappear into the elevator bay at the far end of the walled platform. No probing questions, still the uncharacteristic nervousness, but a simple hand-over in this stupid public place ... Anyone in the surrounding buildings could have seen them ... The Internals probably had a permanent eye on the arch, it wouldn't surprise him. That thought triggered another. Maybe that was it: Piaget was setting him up in this whole scheme, some kind of deal for him to get his old job back ... Kraemer scanned the buildings again; it was almost dark now, but the white paving of the platform shone brightly, reflecting the light from the surrounding blocks. The place was still as empty as when he had arrived.

Making his way across the paved expanse, Kraemer's mind went back to his strategy for handling the information which he alone still held – well, not quite ... Someone had sent Coton's coded TRs and someone had read them and replied ... Someone in a position to understand their importance, and someone who had the ability to spuriously encode them again. Someone with access to the Sec-services' system. There was still nowhere for him to go ... No Coton, no Walker ... He found himself up the same blind alley as before. Piaget also had to be out of the question ... All he could do was to make further investigations; he might turn up something that would begin to shed light on what was going on. Now he began to feel nervous himself as he entered the empty elevator.

'Well, I suppose it's a relief, doctor. But I should've guessed when Dabbs said it was a personal matter. I mean, the sub-net is virtually his whole personal life, isn't it?'

'That was a very good pun, Uschi ... Shame you weren't aware you were making it ...' The Thin Doctor laughed out loud.

As the humour dawned on her, she sniggered herself. 'I'm sorry, repartee is not my strongest suit. But seriously, I wouldn't intentionally joke about Dabbs' personal life, or anything else about the poor man – unlike our Mr Piaget. Fate's been hard enough on him as it is.'

'I was waiting for you to say something about Piaget. You don't like him much, do you?'

'Frankly, doctor, I find the man both boorish and unintelligent.'

'I think he's rather keen on you, though.'

'You've noticed ...'

'It's clear as day, Uschi. I saw him watching you during the transplant. I think you were the main reason for him staying with it for the whole six hours. I'll speak to him if you like. I can't have him upsetting my team.'

'Oh, I don't think he's directly rude to Dabbs. He just says awful things to me about him. I've made it clear to him once or twice that I don't find it funny.'

'I meant about you, Uschi. If he carries on . . .'

'Then I'll speak to him,' Clowes stated firmly. 'I can look after myself . . .'

'Of course.' The Thin Doctor nodded the phrase.

'. . . But if he ever found out about Dabbs and the sex sub-net – never mind this latest development – then he'd make his life hell, I know he would. Piaget wouldn't be able to resist.' Clowes surprised herself how defensive she felt about Dabbs. 'This new girl on the block that's so upset him, though. How come *Lolita*'s been put in the shade? He . . . or should that be *she* . . . must've had competition before.'

'Now there I'll have to pass, Uschi. The vicissitudes of the virtual sex world are, and will probably remain, a mystery to me.'

'Even in the purely scientific sense, doctor?'

'We'll see; maybe it could be an interesting study area, Ms Clowes.'

'I bet . . . Wouldn't it be funny to discover Piaget on there, though – Now *he* must be a strong contender as a client; I just can't see him as a hooker.'

'The whole beauty of the sub-net is that you can be anything, or anyone, you want to be, Uschi. I would've thought you knew that. What's more, people's real identities are impossible to trace.'

'You're displaying a steadily increasing knowledge, doctor.' Clowes grinned.

'I do believe we have now descended into gossip, Uschi. I wouldn't have believed it, not between you and me, and in working hours as well.' The Thin Doctor let out a short laugh. 'I think we'd better get back to poor old Coton, Dabbs will have the new factorizers working by now.' The Thin Doctor smiled as he gestured dramatically towards the exit from the tissue lab.

The Thin Doctor was right: the new factorizers were performing well. Dabbs switched between the cyborg's own internal system and the theatre's, and there was no change in the monitor trace.

'It looks as if you've done it, Dabbs.' The Thin Doctor placed a hand on the technician's shoulder. 'Well done ... Can you and Clowes begin a soak test? We must first establish the factorizers' reliability. I'm going to leave you both to it. I have a speaking appointment this evening, and I'm quite looking forward to it. I think I've earned some time off.'

'You're leaving the facility, doctor?' Clowes' tone expressed mock horror.

'Yes. I know I can leave Coton in yours and Dabbs' capable hands. If you do need me, I'll have my portable, but I'm sure you'll cope.'

'And after the soak, I can dress him, doctor?' Dabbs asked.

'I think we're nearly ready for that, Dabbs. Give Coton twenty-four hours. I don't want to have to start ripping his skin open to do any more mods.'

Dabbs turned and addressed the bare monocoque cyborg. 'Only another day, Coton, and you'll be a new man.' Dabbs was very proud of his cyborg skin.

The Thin Doctor departed soon after his announcement, leaving Dabbs and Clowes alone in the facility. The pair fussed around for an hour, running checks and taking samples. The Coton cyborg remained steady throughout, only the flickering of the chassis' eyes betraying any outward signs of life.

'I think we should work a shift system, Dabbs,'

Clowes suggested after they had duplicated another task. 'We're beginning to get under each other's feet.'

'G . . . good idea, Clowes,' Dabbs gulped.

'I suggest two-hour sessions. I'll take the first shift, and then you can take over and we'll alternate through the night. Is that OK with you?'

Dabbs agreed and disappeared to his quarters, leaving Clowes sitting at the monitoring console. Coton was performing well: blood and endorphin levels were perfectly constant. Dabbs was quite a genius, she really had doubted that they'd be able to solve the factorizer problem so quickly.

The first shift passed without incident and Clowes handed over to Dabbs and went back to her office, where she folded out the rest couch. It seemed to be no time before she was being woken by Dabbs shaking her roughly, quite agitated.

'All right, Dabbs . . . Sorry, I can't have set my alarm . . . What is it . . .? Is Coton OK?'

Dabbs gulped even more than usual, a sure sign that he was excited about something. 'H . . . he's fine, Clowes . . . I . . . it's just the shift . . . your turn.'

'OK, no panic, I'll sort out the alarm. Here, you set it for my next shift if you like.' She thrust the workstation clicker into Dabbs' hand. This fuss about nothing was annoying her, now she was fully awake.

'N . . . No. It's OK.' Dabbs put the clicker back on the workstation and rushed out of the office. 'I'll be in the theatre!' he called out from down the corridor.

Dabbs rushed through the hand-over at the monitoring console and made his escape back to his quarters. Clowes checked the time: she had stolen only ten minutes of his damned break; Dabbs could be really odd at times. She suddenly remembered her talk with the doctor. 'I wonder, Coton?' She spoke out loud. The cyborg continued his REM.

Coton remained stable through the remaining shift period; she did some manual checks as a safeguard and discovered no discrepancies with the console's own. At the end of the shift, when she had passed the ten minutes she owed Dabbs, he still hadn't showed. She gave him another five then decided to go and look for him. As she walked down the corridor to Dabbs' quarters, she realized she wasn't sure what to expect; she had never been into Dabbs' private domain. She called out as she neared the door but there was no reply. Clowes placed her ear against the composite material; she could hear music – pop trance stuff – then she became aware of talking going on underneath the sound, or was it groaning? No, it couldn't be, Dabbs couldn't be *working* – surely not ... She tried the door release but the door remained closed.

She stood for a minute or two outside the door, wondering about her next move. She thought of hammering on the door but decided it would be more prudent to let Dabbs finish his business – he'd appear back in the theatre soon enough. She'd ask him then, up-front, what he'd been up to. It was about time Dabbs shared his secret with her.

Another fifteen minutes passed, and Dabbs was still absent. Clowes felt a growing irritation at the weird technician's non-appearance. Then an idea occurred to her ... There was a headset in Dabbs' tech lab; he used virtual reality for checking the cyborgs' sensory equipment, so it ought to be possible to use it with the theatre's workstation. All she needed was to get a tap on to Dabb's station's line out, then maybe she would find out what he was really up to.

The sub-net was scarcely hidden on the facility's system and finding the only live line was a cinch. Clowes made a last check on Coton, then slipped on the VR headset and gloves. The system was already live and, once she clicked in the headset, she found herself in a long, broad corridor, the main highway in this virtual world. It was famous, people made jokes about it. She looked around and saw a heavy ornate door, incongruous in the flush lines of the otherwise feature-less passage.

She reached out towards the door and found she had to lean forward to gain motion; she felt the glove harden as she placed her hand on the old-fashioned doorknob. The door swung easily open and Clowes found herself in the foyer of an old building, possibly a hotel, Mother Earth style, perhaps nineteenth or twentieth century. An olfactory message flashed up in front of her: *system not connected – tobacco smoke/perfume* – Clowes didn't know how to enable the server so she left the message hanging. The foyer was deserted; on the reception desk which ran between the foot of two curving staircases there was a large open book – a register, most likely. As Clowes struggled again to move forward, she could hear piano music coming from somewhere above. The pages of the book – it *was* a register – were heavy, and Clowes marvelled at their feel in her hand; if they had duplicated this sensation for Coton, then he really would have full dexterity. The book was full of names and dates: stupid names, sub-net pseudonyms; the last entries were very recent, today's in fact. At the bottom of the list Clowes read the name *Lolita*, and across the page she traced a room number.

Piaget loved a good argument, especially when he was

dealing with some petty official and knew he was in the right. The security monkey at the Sci-Medical Foundation would not accept that his pass was twenty-four-hour authorized.

'I'm sorry, Mr *Paggett*.' The stupid staffer couldn't even pronounce his name properly, reading it from the screen. 'Your pass doesn't have the necessary coding to let you in at this time.'

'PE-AH-JAY...! Can't you read! Look, I'm authorized by the Honorary Director, the Thin Doctor himself ... Read the code again.'

The staffer passed the holocard through the reader and waited for another inevitable negative. Piaget had now gone through the stage of losing patience. He'd been working at home on Kraemer's data cart, but his domestic workstation wouldn't open the log; he needed to use some more powerful kit with a decrypt server — like the machines in the Cyborg Facility.

'Sorry, sir, it's negative again.' The security monkey turned the screen for Piaget's inspection.

'Voice Sub-Basement Two, ask for the Thin Doctor.'

'The Thin Doctor's logged out, sir.' The staffer obviously didn't trust himself to risk another mispronunciation of Piaget's name.

'Clowes, then, Ms CL-OUSE!'

'She's still there, sir.'

'Well, do it then! Voice her up!'

The staffer picked up the voice set and passed a call down to the mysterious facility.

'There's no answer, sir. Maybe they're busy. It's not unusual.'

'I know that, Staffer, I spend a lot of time there myself. I want to spend more time there now!'

Piaget wasn't going to let this stupid duty monkey

deny him access to the machines that would let him read Kraemer's cart. He'd grind this pathetic staffer into the ground if it took him all night. Piaget was well versed in attritional techniques.

Clowes struggled to move back from the hotel's reception desk. She waved her arms and leant back in the seat – she was obviously missing some other piece of the VR set. Eventually she managed to move away by pushing the workstation's chair backwards while holding her head in a near-horizontal plane; the room swung about her and then slewed suddenly sideways ... she had fallen over. The right-hand staircase was now directly in front of her, sweeping away to her left, exaggerated by the slightly over-wide view of the headset's sensors. She was stuck, and none of her increasingly wild movements seemed to be able to raise her back up. She pulled the equipment off her head and checked back to Coton – he was perfectly stable – no Dabbs either, thank goodness.

Clowes didn't hear the voice message from Security as she put the headset back on. When she had readjusted to the VR world again, she was surprised to find that she was upright – the headset must have reset itself when she took it off. She was still fighting to get some forward movement towards the staircase when she registered two figures rushing down the steps. A male and a female, both partially dressed, leapt from the final step and came rushing straight at her, both looking back up the stairs. The male shouted something as he pushed his female companion straight through Clowes; they were making a bee-line for the door behind her. She heard it crash shut, then there was silence. A new olfactory message flashed up in front of her:

burning: electrical/bio-tissue – Clowes looked back to the door; she could see a trail of filigree ash littering the path which the two VR characters had left in their wake. A rasping hiss behind her caused her to swing around.

Dabbs came flying out of his corridor and cannoned straight into the burly mass of Piaget, knocking him against an empty theatre trolley. Dabbs fell, rolling on for a couple of metres, and came to a halt in the middle of the corridor junction, where he remained, sitting, blubbering unintelligibly. Piaget pushed himself to his feet from his own bizarre, supplicatory position against the trolley and walked over to the crazed technician. He crouched down at the man's side.

'What the hell's going on, Dabbs?'

Dabbs let out more unintelligible gulpiness.

'I've been upstairs, trying to voice you for the last hour. Where's Clowes?'

'Oogh . . . O . . . On shift with Coton, M . . . Mr Piaget.'

'Is she all right, man? Get up . . .'

Piaget put his arms round Dabbs' chest, lifting him from behind; he winced at the man's feeble boniness.

'I'm going to find Clowes . . . Sort yourself out, man . . .' Dabbs was obviously OK, Piaget thought. But what about Clowes? Was the damned cyborg on the loose? He set off cautiously down the corridor towards the theatre.

The headset's view filled with a beautiful silver female face. It was strangely familiar to Clowes; she found herself transfixed as the blank eyes seemed to hold her. There was a softer, rasping noise and the face pulled back on an elegantly horrible, long – very long – arching neck. The whole parent figure was now two metres away from her, an exquisite, pure, silver female. *The Supervisor* marched round Clowes' virtual space. Clowes was a ghost in this virtual world: she had not logged on and ID-ed herself, but this *creature* knew she was there. Clowes followed the Supervisor, tracking round her; more olfactory messages flashed across her vision but she looked right through them. Then, quite suddenly, the face melted and the Supervisor launched herself through Clowes in a molten bolt of fluid. Before Clowes could swing around, the door to the strange foyer had slammed shut and there was silence again.

'Ms Clowes . . .' A voice and a hand on her shoulder brought her zooming back to the Cyborg Facility. Piaget spoke again as she slipped off the headset. 'What's been going on? The Facility's been incommunicado for over an hour and Dabbs seems to have flipped out.'

Clowes gathered her senses and swivelled around to address Piaget. 'Dabbs . . . Is he all right?'

'Kind of, Ms Clowes . . . He ran into me, literally, in the corridor just now. I thought he'd been attacked by one of his subjects, or that maybe our friend here –' Piaget turned towards the cyborg '– had gone crazy. What's the VR set for?'

Clowes became aware of Dabbs at this moment – he was standing some way behind Piaget, waiting for Clowes to explain the presence of the headset. She read a look of dread in his eyes.

'Coton's sensory systems, Mr Piaget. I was running checks on our latest mods, we're running a soak test on the chassis.' She was keen to get Piaget off his investigatory tack. 'Dabbs and I have been taking shifts, sleeping in between . . . What's wrong, Dabbs? You look like you've been having a *nightmare*.' She leant round Piaget to address the technician. Would he take up her cue?

Dabbs gulped into an explanation. 'A-A-A-An awful nightmare . . . I was being chased by *Four* . . . I . . . I'm sorry, Mr Piaget, for crashing into you like that. I must've been sleep-walking.'

'You were going crazy, Dabbs . . . Some serious kind of sleep-walking, you were neonized!'

'Sorry you couldn't reach us on the voice system, Mr Piaget, with Dabbs asleep and me in a world of my own on the VR kit.'

'You've just reminded me.' Piaget glanced up at the ceiling. 'Can you voice Security and tell them I'm here in the facility. I had the devil's own job getting in here tonight. I had to do a deal with them.'

CHAPTER NINE

The cyborg looked amazing ... He simply *was* Coton — the holograms from his file scarcely did him justice. He now stood upright in a maintenance frame, fully clad in his synthetic skin covering and supported by elasticated straps. The rolling track on which he was now walking hummed softly. Alongside him, Dabbs trotted on an identical track, fully hooked up to the VR station. It was one hell of a contrast. Clowes couldn't help but laugh as Dabbs looked away from the cyborg only to see Coton's head follow the movement as though wondering who this odd little shadow-person was. The Thin Doctor was sharing her amusement at the spectacle.

'Right, Dabbs, that's enough. You can stop now.' He communicated down the voice link to the panting technician. 'Try some more expressional articulation. Coton is no longer responding to your exhausted look.'

Dabbs stopped and began some facial exercises, but only his twitching ears were visible at either side of the pick-up mask. Coton's face twisted and changed in sympathy with the Dabbs ear motion.

'Wonderful. Now blow and suck for me, please.'

Coton's face followed in response.

'The compressor was a very neat idea, Dabbs; he looks nearly as tired as you must do behind that mask.'

Dabbs gulped an approving muffled response.

'Kill the VR kit, Uschi, I think we've seen enough. That's it, Dabbs, Ms Clowes is shutting down the station. Thank you.' The Thin Doctor looked around at Clowes then across to the theatre door. 'Still no Piaget, Uschi?'

'No, no sign of him.'

'Well, he's going to have to miss the big moment. I'm going to switch Coton live. He's as ready as he'll ever be.'

'I want him dressed properly, doctor. Has Dabbs got those lab fatigues handy?'

'Ask him yourself, he's just about free of the VR kit.'

Clowes looked over at Dabbs shedding the sensor encasement from his body; only a set of facial pick-ups remained. He was grimacing as he peeled them off his skin.

'We're on, Dabbs, we're going to wake Coton. Have you got the fatigues handy? I don't want him naked when he comes round. He needs to be controlled as he learns about his new body. What he's got and what he hasn't ... You understand.' Clowes smiled knowingly at Dabbs. Their mutual understanding had deepened considerably since the sub-net episode.

Everything's in your rehab suite, Clowes. I'll dress him once we've moved him through.'

The Cyborg Rehabilitation Suite was a secure set of rooms adjoining the Facility's subjects' cells. The suite contained a full support console and was equipped with an inventory of aids to help Coton readjust to his new being. Clowes had even selected prints and holographs to hang on the walls; she wanted the environment to reflect, as closely as possible, a comfortable accommodation unit such as Coton had had before his accident. She'd been barred from visiting Coton's actual AU by the Security Services, but she was pleased with the overall atmosphere she had created in these few facility rooms. She flopped down on one of the sofas while she nervously watched Dabbs clothe Coton then move him into the recliner where he would lie during the wake-up process. The Thin Doctor entered, carrying a tray with a glass of water on it.

'A blocker, Ms Clowes. I think you should take it, you need to relax.'

'No thanks, doctor, give it to Dabbs. I think I need all the nervous energy I can get.'

'If you're sure?'

Dabbs refused the blocker as well and continued his task of locating the cyborg's pick-ups. Finally he secured the restraining straps over Coton's limbs and torso, then made a few last checks on the monitoring console.

'C . . . Calibrations match, doctor. I think we're ready,' Dabbs gulped. *Calibration* was one of those words.

'Do you know what day it is, Pepper?' Piaget was not happy at this summons to the new Metro Cybotics HQ. 'They're going to wake Coton. He'll be live.'

'I know.' Pepper walked back across the empty office space, leaving the window and its panorama of eastern Industry 1. He sat down at the bare table and picked up Piaget's most recent data cart from a stack of similar ones. 'I've read your last report, Piaget, most comprehensive. We're fully aware of the significance of today.'

'So why don't you want me there?'

'We want you there all right. I trust you'll be heading straight back there after this meeting.'

'Immediately, Pepper.'

'Electrocorp has a problem, Piaget . . .' Piaget waited as Pepper paused and fingered the data cart thoughtfully. 'Their production has stopped entirely. We received a leak yesterday afternoon.'

'Huh ... That can only be good news for us, then.' But Piaget saw no satisfaction on Pepper's face as he made the comment.

'In some ways, yes – but we're concerned about the specific nature of the problem. Our report was from an unconfirmed source and linked the shut-down directly to their Chromium Programme droid, the *Supervisor*. The machine has been running a parallel plant management system for the past few months. Our report suggested that the droid had cut out Electrocorp's own computing and control centre.'

'Wow, that's some achievement. They must have every back-up system under the sun.'

'So they have, Piaget. But if our report is to be believed – and we're working on a confirmation right now – then all of EC's systems were bypassed. Imagine: something with the capability of doing that represents a serious threat to every system in the city.'

'And beyond, I presume,' Piaget added.

'You get the picture, Piaget. We're not panicking, but we intend to put out a city-wide low-level virus warning. This'll be happening sometime today, depending on our intelligence gathering. I wanted you to be aware: this could be very dangerous for the security of our Cyborg Project. I'd like you to brief the Thin Doctor personally so that he can take his own precautions. He'll understand the ramifications.'

'Of course, Pepper.'

'One other thing, Piaget. Just something of interest to you, given recent events. Comms Monitoring has picked up some weird Light Compression signals out in Lorus, source unknown. We've also got some Azzi TRs out there again. Strange, eh? Especially at this time of year, there's already snow lying in the Wastelands.'

'Very strange . . .' Piaget paused, vainly trying to look past Pepper to the city's fringe, which was lost in a grey haze. 'Can you keep me informed?'

'Yes, I thought you'd be interested. The Archive Squad is checking out the first recorded Azzi TRs from Lorus . . . Lander 6 . . . Coton . . . Mind you, we may get a full debrief yet . . . You'd better get back to Coton, Piaget. We need a full report, asap, but make sure you brief the doctor before anything else.'

This was the last thing he needed: the Archive Squad all over Kraemer's new files. Piaget stroked the natural wood of the executive block's reception as he logged out. At least he hoped it was natural; he wasn't superstitious, but any additional fail-safe was a bonus. 'Kraemer – better check back with him.'

'Sorry, sir?' The security staffer looked up from his console.

'Er, nothing . . . Just thinking out loud.' Piaget's mind flashed back to his pious damned stress counsellor.

'The tomography has positively bloomed, doctor. Look at the monitor!' Clowes beckoned to the Thin Doctor to join her at the console. 'The sensors have sent the whole thing crazy.'

Coton followed the shape across the room. It was a logical occurrence; those figures moved like that. The long thin one joined the other over at the pale board which was set with bright squares, which he recognized, but no more. There was also the noise: a bright, familiar pattern of sound, up and down, warm and comforting. He looked back round the space surrounding him: it too had a logic, the right shape. He perceived another of those moving shapes, this one smaller, moving at his side. Coton heard a chaotic crash as his field of vision filled with this other shape.

'He's moved his head.' Clowes was excitedly stating the obvious. Dabbs started as his attention was distracted from his palm monitor.

'Wonderful,' the Thin Doctor murmured.

A bright light swung about in relation to this figure next to him. It was attached. The light steadied and Coton saw another familiar, rippling shape start to dance in the brightness.

'The hands, doctor, watch Coton's hands.' Clowes moved closer to Coton as she spoke. 'He's mimicking Dabbs. Hold your hand still, Dabbs; keep it on the monitor so Coton can see it.'

Coton's hand movements stopped.

'Now start again – carry on with what you were doing.'

Coton's fingers moved, tapping on the padding of the recliner.

'He's away, doctor, he's already making progress.' Clowes looked back towards the Thin Doctor, now standing beside her.

'So you'd say we have potential here, Uschi?'

'If I didn't know how he was built, I'd say it was a miracle. I'm serious. Coton is fully sentient, the connections he's just made to move his hand . . . It's amazing. Congratulations, this is a historic moment . . . And to you, Dabbs!'

Dabbs looked up from his monitor checks.

'Congratulations, Dabbs . . . You're going to be famous!'

Coton had found something else. A warmth and lightness heightened his comfortable state, and something in the noises round him communicated this feeling.

'Can we release his right arm, Dabbs?' Clowes asked.

'Drop the power first,' the Thin Doctor interrupted. 'Take care, Uschi.'

'Just give him enough to lift the arm's own weight, Dabbs . . . I want to see if he'll raise his hand to look at it.'

Coton kind of knew it was there. He was in the middle of a boundless, heavy bulk, but now a part of his consciousness was working away at a distance. A separation from the main sense of his wholeness. He had only a tenuous control; it took all his strength and concentration to make this movement of his own. He could hear more of the higher-pitched noise round him; it filled him with well-being. The rippling shape fell away from him and he was back in the sunken, heavy mass again. One of the taller shapes moved towards him and he suddenly thought he could be like that.

Coton's arm had dropped back and Clowes moved over to the cyborg. The Thin Doctor looked on with satisfaction: his assistant had now effortlessly moved into her key role. Clowes was displaying a natural approach to this new phase of the project. He smiled across at Dabbs as the technician also paused to watch Clowes' next move.

'Raise Coton up a little, please, Dabbs.'

The technician complied, using the recliner clicker from his overall's breast pocket.

Clowes took Coton's free arm. Raising it from the elbow with her left hand, she grasped Coton's hand with her right and shook it gently. The cyborg twitched and its legs kicked out straight, then fell back. Clowes maintained her grip. 'Hi, Coton, my name's Ursula Clowes, I'll be looking after you for the next few months – or maybe weeks at this rate.'

Coton felt a current run through his entire mass. The part of him that had been free a moment ago was now being compressed, not unpleasantly, by some soft, warm contact. As he concentrated on seeing again, he had a different view: higher now, and the tall figure was close to him, still slightly above, linking with the distant sensation-generating extension of his bulk. He felt himself return the gentle pressure from the tall shape. Coupled with the soft sound the shape made, this was good, really good. He felt some profound flash of recollection at the process.

Clowes stood for some time holding the cyborg's hand. Coton had closed his eyes, and slowly his grip weakened. She found her thoughts drifting back to the memory of her brother. How many days and nights had she spent doing just this: holding a hand, sensing its temperature and every tiny movement? When she looked back at Coton's face, at this cyborg's synthetic face, she felt an emotion stronger than sympathy. She placed her hand on his brow, she didn't really know why ... maybe to get a little nearer to the human that was Coton? His brain and personality just below her palm, the only real life in this chassis ... She wished she didn't understand his technology so well.

Clowes looked around to find that she was alone in the Rehab Suite. The subdued lighting and the soft green of the picture-hung walls consolidated the calmness she now felt. She quietly secured Coton's arm back to the recliner and moved back out of the pool of light.

Clowes made sure that the armoured door had secured itself, then she turned to head for the mess area. Dabbs' tiny workstation office was lit and, as she drew level with the glass partition, she could see the back of

Piaget; he was with the Thin Doctor, Piaget's jerky movements suggesting an animated discussion was in progress; the Doctor looked serious as he listened to whatever Piaget was saying. The office was sealed, so she couldn't hear a thing. If it was important, she'd hear soon enough.

When she entered the mess area, Dabbs was fiddling yet again with the Thin Doctor's antique coffee maker.

'More problems, Dabbs?'

'Thermostat, Clowes; the hot plate's boiling the coffee.'

Clowes came over to look for herself; it seemed a good opportunity for her to ask another question.

'Dabbs, after our experience with the sub-net. Did you speak to the doctor about it? I didn't say a word, as you requested.'

'Er, no ... I decided I wouldn't bother him again. I was in the wrong, working on the net when I should've been with Coton. Thanks for keeping your promise.'

'Have you been back since?'

'Just once. The net was deserted, it's never been like that before. That thing had gone, too. She's killed the whole world, I'm worried that it'll fold with no one using it, it's not good for the software. A system like that has to be used all the time.'

'And that time when I was there was the first time you'd seen the er ... your *competitor*?'

'She attacked us. My client and me. U ... Up until that point I hadn't seen her. She's killed others, people who'd spent years developing their characters. They'll have to start all over, if they dare to get on the net again.' Dabbs began to get more gulpy as he grew emotional.

'So what are you going to do?'

'I've started a bulletin board. I'm trying to get people back together again. I've had some response. That monster character smashed all the protocols, but I think we can set up a design group to prevent someone doing that again.'

'You think so, Dabbs?'

'Mm . . . It's achievable.'

'Could I see your software design, Dabbs? I may be able to help.'

Dabbs had been fussing with the coffee machine throughout all this conversation. He now stopped and looked straight at Clowes. 'Do you know something, Clowes?'

'I have an idea I just might.'

'Dabbs . . . Ms Clowes, I want you to isolate all the workstations immediately . . . all the network connections, Dabbs. I want them physically disconnected, not just switched out.' The Thin Doctor made the announcement as he swept into the room with Piaget just behind him.

'What's going on, doctor?' Clowes spun around from the worktop.

'A city-wide virus alert, Ms Clowes. Low level, but I'm taking no chances.'

On hearing the dreaded word 'virus', Dabbs scuttled past the Thin Doctor and Piaget.

The Thin Doctor called after him. 'When you've done that, I want you to cable us an internal system. Start with a direct link from the rehab console to the theatre!'

'Good evening, Mr Piaget. Are you the bringer of these bad tidings?'

'Sorry to say so, Ms Clowes. There'll be an Infonet announcement within the hour. My people are a little ahead of the game.'

'Metro Cybotics, Ms Clowes,' the Thin Doctor added grandly. 'Mr Piaget's company was floated yesterday. We'll be watching the markets intently from now on, Piaget – if they don't shut down the Infonet, that is.'

'We've gone public only with the company, doctor. Our product line is still a secret.'

'I should hope so too. I think we took that as understood. *N'est-ce pas*, Ms Clowes?'

Clowes smiled at the doctor. 'I'm going to spend the night in the Rehab Suite; I'll be monitoring the cortex stimulation programme. I think Coton may be responding faster than we imagined.'

'And you can do a manual override Ms Clowes; very good. You see what good people we have here, Mr Piaget?'

'That was never in doubt,' Piaget lied.

The Thin Doctor refused Piaget's request to see Coton. The sentient cyborg needed to develop a rest pattern, particularly in these early stages. He told Piaget that he would be able to see the cyborg in the morning, that their priority now was to conduct their progress meeting. The doctor seemed to be telling Piaget his own job; there were shareholders to think about. Clowes excused herself and returned to the Rehab Suite.

Coton was peaceful; he lay in the dim pool of light in the centre of the room, occasionally moving a finger or twitching an expression across his face; he was remarkably humanoid. Clowes logged the facial movements against the neuron firings on the encephalograph. The twitches were brought about by wild synaptic activity, a sure sign that an assimilation process was taking place in Coton's mind. One of Clowes' neurobiology graduation papers had explored the phenomenon of perception. She had demonstrated that the creation of new ideas stemmed from this apparently chaotic nervous activity, the very activity Coton was displaying now. It was most common in sleep; the new ideas would then be stored somehow – that was still a mystery to her – and could then be summoned up by the brain on waking. But it was Coton's linking to the facial nerve cortex that especially excited her. For Coton to think and then to transmit these abstractions to his expressional centres was a sophistication that she had only dared dream of. The multi-neuron transmitters of the cranial floor were so impressive, the Thin Doctor's design was almost of another technology. Where did his genius come from? Coton was set to be a superhuman, barring a massive technical disaster. But now that kind of eventuality seemed to be receding; Coton's design, dare she think it . . . seemed perfect.

Somewhere in the middle of the night, when Clowes was dozing in between her checks, she heard the climate control panel pop with the opening of the airlock door.

It was Dabbs; his odd, short form bobbed across the gloom to her, and he waved some object in his hand as he spoke in a comical gulpy whisper. 'Clowes, I was thinking about what you said. I've got the sub-net protocols.' The object in his hand was a data cart.

'What time is it?' Clowes rubbed her eyes.

'Three-thirty. The facility's empty, the doctor and Piaget left an hour ago. I thought . . .'

'We could look at the sub-net data.' Clowes completed Dabbs' sentence.

'Yes, it's a good time. I'm worried about leaving it too long, and after what you said . . .'

'Don't you want to know about Coton?'

Dabbs glanced across to the silent cyborg. 'I trust

him with you, Clowes. The doctor said that I was to go to you first from now on; he seems to be handing over the project.'

'I thought that as well – though he's not said anything officially. He's spending more and more time with Piaget now, have you noticed? Take a look at Coton for me though, will you. I'd like your opinion.'

Dabbs handed Clowes the data cart and she rose and walked over to the workstation. Dabbs trotted across to the cyborg while Clowes accessed the sub-net data.

She was surprised to see the scale of the files.

'Dabbs? Have you got the whole thing on here, the whole virtual world?'

'Hmm.' Dabbs was thoughtful, watching Coton's mobile face. 'Pretty well ... Y'know, Coton reminds me of someone.'

'Come and enter the access code for me,' Clowes called out from the console.

Dabbs palmed in his ID and the front menu appeared on the screen. Dabbs had accessed the Net Manager privilege tables.

Clowes looked at Dabbs. 'This is all yours, isn't it? You created the whole damn sub-net ...'

'Well, er ...' Dabbs gulped nervously. 'Yes, I suppose I did.'

'You crafty so-and-so, Dabbs. The doctor said you made a tidy income from your activities ... Does he know it's all yours?'

'I never told him that; he only knows that I work the net as *Lolita*. He caught me once – I told you – but I don't think he realizes the whole thing's mine.'

'Show me the log-on files, Dabbs; let's see who created the monster.'

Dabbs brushed a code into the blank palm pad. 'I've

already looked through the codes, Clowes. They're all familiar to me: nobody new, no new sources.'

'Can you identify actual people from this?' Clowes surveyed the lists of numbers.

'*I* can, but nobody else. It's purely a recognition thing. I started the net, and my knowledge has just grown from there.'

'Does the monster show at all? Is there any reference here?'

Dabbs scrolled through the columns and pointed to the final log-on entries on the screen. 'Here's *Lolita*, my location code, double encrypted to hide the facility.' Dabbs sniggered oddly. 'And here's my last client; his ID code and the prefix lets me know where he's from, the source ID.'

'The log-on location?'

'Yes, he's a regular. You can see more of his entries above.'

'And the monster? To have a form in the world, not to be a ghost like I was ... there has to be a log-on point, surely?'

'Look.' Dabbs held the workstation's cursor over a code line. 'This has to be the monster. No log-on code, but there's a double location entry – it is in fact mine decrypted. This place, the Cyborg Facility.'

'Here? Can you identify a terminal?'

'That's why I'm stuck. The terminal's mine. No one else can access the sub-net from my terminal, the security won't let that happen. It's got to be an echo code, it bounces back the recognition terminal's address to the thing's own source address and overwrites it. That's the only explanation. It's a perfect cover-up.'

Clowes studied the codes again and mulled over Dabbs' interpretation of the data. The Supervisor was an impressive processing machine, perhaps she could have accessed the sub-net from her consoles at Electrocorp. It was perfectly possible that somebody there was already hooked into Dabbs' virtual world. Could she also have come up with this cover-up device? Possible . . . but why should she?

'Do you have any Electrocorp addresses there, Dabbs?'

Dabbs laughed. 'Plenty . . . The sub-net is used from nearly every department . . . The long night shifts, y'know.'

'And the, er, monster definitely didn't carry an Electrocorp address?'

'It's like I said. The source is completely covered. It could originally've come from an EC location, but there's no way of knowing that.'

Clowes looked away to Coton lying silently on the recliner.

'What d'you think, Clowes? What is it about Electrocorp?'

'You've heard of the Chromium Programme, Dabbs. The Infonet has been carrying all sorts of stories about it.'

Dabbs gulped hard. 'The Chromium Programme, their silver droid . . . I'm stupid: it was their droid, or a manifestation of it. Some joker at Electrocorp stuck it on the network – the crazy bastards! Oogh! Excuse me, Clowes . . .'

Clowes left Dabbs with his own interpretation of the Supervisor's sub-net intrusion. The Thin Doctor had sworn her to secrecy about their visit to Electrocorp – another of his curious motivations backing the policy. Dabbs seemed to know very little about the Chromium Programme; she considered breaking the Doctor's trust, but decided to wait until she could gather some intelligence to back up her suspicions.

'So, Dabbs, it doesn't look as if we can go much further. I'm sorry I wasn't any help with the software.'

'You were a help, Clowes.' Dabbs seemed sincerely grateful. '*Electrocorp* ... At least I can do some vetting on my new user list.' The technician began shutting down the data files.

'There was something else you said, though, Dabbs, when you were over by Coton. About him reminding you of someone ...'

'Yes. Could be someone on the sub-net. I don't know ... Maybe it'll click when he's fully conscious. I'll let you know.'

Clowes stopped herself from seizing on a suggestion.

'Does he look familiar to you too, Clowes?' Dabbs remarked, registering Clowes' hesitation.

'Maybe ... Let's wait till he wakes up, like you said. We'll see if it's the same person ... Good night, Dabbs.'

Clowes spent the rest of the night dozing between fits of wakefulness when she couldn't help but churn through her mind the association she had made between Coton and the virtual world Supervisor. Why should it be? Why should Coton remind her of the virtual world's Supervisor?

Clowes was no wiser the next morning. The cyborg was back sitting upright on the recliner, his face carrying a pained expression not unlike the one the malevolent droid displayed prior to her morphing. Clowes was still looking for the connection ... If Coton really was feeling pain, they needed to sort it out before they went any further. It seemed to be linked to the movement of his head. Clowes directed Dabbs to trace the nerve tracking back from the facial cortex.

'Good morning, Ms Clowes, Dabbs ...' The Thin Doctor entered the Rehab Suite, ushering Piaget past him out of the airlock.

'My God!' Piaget's exclamation was loaded with incredulity. Clowes looked around to the big man then back to Coton; she could see the cyborg's jaw working as if to speak.

'You've certainly got a way with cyborgs, Mr Piaget. What a response ...' Clowes redirected Dabbs to monitor Coton's reaction to Piaget's speech.

'It's really Coton, Ms Clowes. You've done a superb job, doctor.'

'My team, Piaget,' the Thin Doctor replied. 'This has only been possible through teamwork.'

Piaget's voice opened a flood of memory in Coton's mind. He saw a screed of familiar images: the command floor, a monitor bank, a set of faces, a whole scramble of information. All was clear as day, he recognized every element but couldn't put a name or an understandable label to any of it. His eyes focused on the large figure who had just spoken. Piaget ... he tried hard to join the visual image to this familiar attribution; both were so abstract, but he felt that, if he could somehow link them, that would be a key to something. A massive sense of potential threatened to burst him apart.

'Ms Clowes, we have a new centre blooming on the encephalograph,' Dabbs said as he turned the screen towards the group standing in front of Coton.

'Memory, Ms Clowes?' The Thin Doctor turned back from Coton and his eyes flashed to Piaget, who also seemed to be waiting for her reply.

'Most probably, doctor. . . Mr Piaget, how long did you

spend working with Coton? You seem to have triggered some profound cerebral activity.'

'Some months.' Piaget mumbled a little, seemingly unwilling to say more; he almost seemed scared that Coton would overhear.

'Can you speak directly to Coton, Mr Piaget. When the doctor introduced me to the prototype subjects, they responded very well to a new voice ... Just ask him how he's feeling, as you would to someone recovering from an operation.' Clowes observed Piaget's hesitation. 'Please, Mr Piaget ... Can you go up to Coton's side?'

Piaget moved slowly to the side of the recliner, Coton's eyes tracking him all the way. The cyborg grimaced again as he turned his head towards Piaget, now standing next to him.

The Thin Doctor commented on Coton's possible pain signal. 'Check the auditory sensitivity, Dabbs. I suspect he may be being deafened by our chassis' servos.'

Piaget spoke. 'Good morning, Coton. How are you feeling?'

'More, please, Mr Piaget. Repeat the phrase if you will. I'm interested in the recognition response,' Clowes called over from the console.

Piaget repeated the phrase.

Coton's neuron vortex evened out into a regular doughnut shape. 'Doctor, look, we have a lovely neuron torus,' Clowes called excitedly.

It was Piaget. The shape and its sound was called *Piaget*. It was unpleasant though, what had happened to the softer shape? The warm sounds *she* made. Yes *she*, she was a different combination of things ... He could just sense her in the background, behind the noises coming from this *Piaget* up close to him. Coton felt one of his extensions lift.

Piaget leapt back from the cyborg as the arm snapped the retaining strap taut. 'I didn't know he could move!' Piaget fought to compose himself before the tecchie crew. He could see they were all amused at his fright.

'Power down, Dabbs!' The Thin Doctor walked over to Piaget from the monitoring console. 'Are you all right, Piaget?'

Piaget grunted and shook his shoulders. 'I ... I'm fine, doctor.'

Clowes looked at Dabbs. It was obvious that Piaget was quite rattled by the encounter. Dabbs returned her quizzical expression. The Doctor meanwhile had escorted Piaget to the back of the room.

'Working with droids is a bit like working with animals, Piaget: there's plenty of opportunity for them to make fools of us. I'm sorry about that, Coton's a little unpredictable at this stage.'

Piaget muttered an acknowledgement to the Thin Doctor, and the pair left the Rehab Suite at Piaget's instigation. They continued their low-voiced dialogue as they entered the airlock.

'We'd better carry on, Dabbs.' Clowes watched the door slide shut. 'Management stuff ... Bring Coton's power back up to standard.' Clowes walked back over to the cyborg... 'So, you're not too keen on Piaget either ...' Clowes was speaking to Coton, but loudly enough for Dabbs to hear. '... Join the club.' She could have sworn there was flicker of recognition across the cyborg's face.

CHAPTER TEN

The Lorus light compression signals ended as abruptly as they had begun. Kraemer had logged that they had coincided almost exactly with the beginning and end of the virus alert from the week before. It seemed clear to him that there was definite link, but the new management didn't appear to be interested. Kraemer had to confess to himself that, if Piaget had still been around, some action would have been taken. As it was, the command floor still lacked a full commandant; the acting officers they had in place were a poor substitute.

The information was leaked on the Infonet that all Electrocorp's production had been halted throughout the virus scare. That was interesting, but there was always malicious gossip about the mighty corporation. Kraemer felt inclined to believe this latest story, though, and there were ways he could check. He knew a couple of people he could contact to confirm the rumour. They were a bit *azzi*, vague acquaintances who had job-share slots somewhere in Electrocorp ... The sort of people he had to be careful about knowing, as he knew full well that he was on the Internals' monitoring lists. The interest concerning the new Lorus signals had died down, the Internals had done their archive check on the Lander 6 log, and he'd heard nothing. Life was getting steadily back to normal, but it was much more dull these days. With the loss of Coton and Walker he'd lost his close contact with the Mobiles teams – and Piaget,

God bless him, wherever he was – he was actually missing the Old Man.

Kraemer's investigations into the whole Lander 6 affair had drawn a blank. He'd had to keep a low profile while the Internals were in doing the archive check. The only thing left was Coton's console; the Churchill code was still there, and the only other thing he could check out was the odd reference to the real-club, a notorious place in Industry 2. However, it could be dangerous to go there – even an innocent visit would attract the attention of the Internals. His last avenue of enquiry was Coton's and Walker's personnel files. He had put in a request to view them, using Piaget's authorization code, which still seemed to work. The only drawback would be that he'd have to access them on Piaget's old workstation; they were probably there now, he just needed an excuse to go up there.

Coton was now able to walk and appeared to have complete motor functionality across his whole chassis. Clowes had him moving round the room secured to a frame which Dabbs had originally made for the ape-brained cyborg. The scaffold structure rotated round its own axis, fixed between the floor and the ceiling of the Rehab Suite's main room. Coton trudged interminably around in circles like some animal pumping water from a well in ancient times. The cyborg had displayed no unwelcome behavioural characteristics in the week that he'd been free from the recliner, and his sensory systems appeared to be functioning well. Every so often Clowes would instruct Dabbs to put some object in Coton's way, a chair or some smaller item, and Coton would negotiate the obstacle employing a flawless, apparently human level of judgement. Today there was an interesting development, however: the cyborg was now stopping to remove objects from his path rather than just swinging round them.

'The ape never did that at this stage, C ... Clowes.' Dabbs gulped approvingly.

'He didn't respond to simple spoken commands either, Dabbs ... I was reading your notes last night – very comprehensive, by the way. We're actually getting quite a lot of divergence from the ape's progress now. I just wish that Coton would speak or initiate communication.'

'There's still lots of activity on the EEG, lots of assimilation taking place; he's probably just thinking of some fitting first words.' Dabbs smiled.

Even as Dabbs spoke, Clowes could see the monitor's neuron vortex distort in registration of the sound. Coton's face also seemed to be becoming more subtle in its articulation, taking on a look of concentration as he paused to pursue a removing task.

Coton was doing what they expected him to do: he was walking around, hooked up to this frame thing, and now he was moving a chair out of the way. It was all perfectly clear to him: there was the funny little man Dabbs and the lovely female Clowes who were observing all of this and making approving comments, but using a level of communication strangely beyond him. He heard all their words and felt their tone, yet they meant nothing to him. He could even repeat them inside to himself – perfectly ... Still, this was quite a pleasant activity, and his guardians seemed happy. He might as well carry on until they asked him to stop; it was nice when they asked him to stop and start, they both seemed very pleased when he obeyed.

'I'm really worried about some possibly profound

damage, Dabbs. Now we're over the first stage, no more euphoria. D'you know what I mean?'

'I know what you mean.' Dabbs gulped. 'But the cat and the ape subjects have been perfect in the extended period – even with the endorphin problem, their behaviour is still entirely natural.'

'It's just that, looking at Coton, his expression, the simplicity of the man, his brain could easily be damaged and it could take us months to realize it, years even.'

'Clowes, you're looking at him in much too human terms, you even called him a man just then.'

'I know – but look at his face, look at his docility. It's so unnatural. It worries me.'

'He is unnatural though, isn't he – he's the most unnatural person on the planet!'

'What about his speech centres, Dabbs? He's not made a sound yet.'

'He's functioning perfectly. In the run we did last week, we had a balance on both sides of the brain and we had a neuron response at Coton's synthesizer.'

'Aphasia, though, Dabbs, left-lobe dysfunction; we did have a weaker trace, you remember.'

'It's better now, though. Look at the scans – we put that down to the trauma phase. Why don't you move on to the comprehension tests? All his motor and sensory paths are well up to expectation ... You'll feel better moving on.'

'And ahead of time.' As she spoke, Clowes watched Coton's deft handling of the latest object, a spindly theatre stand. The cyborg was carefully wheeling the frame out of his path.

'Do it ... The doctor's given you control now,' Dabbs urged.

'I'll look at the notes again, Dabbs. I want to use

some more personal-association stuff; you saw the reaction Coton had to Piaget. Maybe if we drag more out of his personnel file we can strike a real connection.'

Clowes retired to the suite's reference station and opened the Coton file again.

Clowes had studied the file many times before; once again she grew frustrated at its brevity where it dealt with Coton's personal background, the very detail she wanted. Coton's service record was well documented: he had had a wide experience in the Security Services: field operations, mobile units; he'd been a leading officer in breaking Azzi networks. There were several commendations for bravery and loyal service. His last role, where he was leading a decryption team on Azzi transmissions, was rated several increments above the norm, almost a Staff position ... the Service certainly rated their man. It did seem a little odd to her that Coton should have been out on active mobile duties at all, but there was no reference to the Lander crash, since the file had been terminated before that incident.

Coton came from an influential family; his father was a politician, ex-Security Services and a member of the lower chamber of Metropolis 4's General Council of Fathers – probably a *Trad*, bearing in mind his background. Clowes pondered on the older man's possible reaction to his son's present predicament. The Thin Doctor had been extremely vague, evasive even, when she enquired about Coton's family. He had referred her back to this file whenever she made reference to the subject. If Jon Coton Senior was aware of his son's status – though she doubted whether he was in full possession of the facts – then he was probably stupidly proud that his son was still being of service to the state. Clowes imagined the Thin Doctor explaining to Coton's father that his son was involved in some wonderful, top-secret, sci-medical programme. The city's politicos, especially the Trads, were a fairly awful breed of people. If they could scratch a little bit of honour, reflected or otherwise, along the way as they squeezed and manipulated society, then that was a real bonus for them.

Coton's mother was dead; she had died shortly after he was born. The record commented on Coton's natural conception, not a gene-genie like so many of his class, a point in his favour. He also had a half-sister, Renata: his father had remarried and had produced this offspring, this time using a gene-bank. The second wife and Coton's father had not stuck together though, and they had been separated for twenty years; the file here was again very patchy, the personal background having been heavily edited. There was no reference to any further family.

Clowes looked for further elements to select for her association tests with Coton. There were some holographs and audio samples on the file. The audio files seemed to consist exclusively of Jon Coton Senior spouting pompously in the Council Chamber. She suddenly remembered how she'd received her negative impression of this man: these had been the first files she'd accessed on receiving the document, all those weeks back. Clowes already had some of these samples on a cart she'd prepared for the test, which she was now bringing forward. 'Not much hope here.' She spoke out loud to herself. 'Probably send Coton to sleep . . . and us too.'

'Pardon, Clowes?' Dabbs crossed to her from Coton as she vocalized her frustration at the thin amount of material.

'Oogh!' Dabbs gulped in shock at the monitor screen. 'It's her!' Dabbs was suddenly animated, pointing at the first hologram on the next file she'd just lazily accessed.

'Who?' Clowes swung back around to see what he was fussing about. The screen carried a hologram of a family group: Coton, his father and stepmother ... and a little girl, five or six years old. Renata? The likeness was immediate, even in this little girl's face ... It was the Supervisor and someone else ... Clowes' mind did a quick somersault ... The beautiful security staffer in Electrocorp!

'Woww!' Clowes let the word trail away to nothing. 'It is her ... unmistakable.' Renata Coton had the perfect features of the Supervisor. All the features that the Supervisor must have copied for herself from Electrocorp's personnel files.

Dabbs looked back to Clowes from the screen. 'Is that Coton's family ... His sister?'

'Renata, Dabbs ... Coton's freaking half-sister ... I've looked at this file so many times as well ... I think we've got our match.'

Dabbs' eyes were bulging with surprise and bewilderment. Clowes could see him going through the mental cross-checking to see how this could possibly be. Without her knowledge of Renata being on the Electrocorp personnel files and the rest, Dabbs would certainly not be able to explain this to himself. Clowes played with the idea of letting him into her knowledge, but something held her back; there seemed to be more to all of this. She wasn't a hundred per cent sure of Dabbs' discretion as far as the Thin Doctor was concerned. It might even be dangerous for Dabbs to know. It was also the Thin Doctor, surely in some way at the root of all this, which set up a further, deeper concern.

'I can see it in Coton now. Bizarre ... the silver monster and Coton ... all linked through this picture of a little girl.' Clowes chose her words carefully.

'But that's only answered our first question, Clowes. H ... How could it happen?' Dabbs was beginning to gulp again in his bafflement.

Clowes blew a puff of feigned incomprehension. 'A data-net leak, our system here?'

'You mean you had this file open when you accessed the sub-net?'

'Maybe ...'

'Nah.' Dabbs was dismissive. 'You would've known and made the link before now ... Technically almost impossible as well.'

'What else then?'

'I dunno ... I really don't know.'

'We'll have to work on it, Dabbs. Keep it between ourselves for now, though.'

'Hmm ...' Dabbs was still lost in thought.

'I think we'll have to add this to our collection of confidences.'

'Yes, Clowes. I need time to think about this before we go any further.'

'I'm not happy about this, Pepper.'

'Can it, Piaget!' Pepper hissed. 'This is the memorial service of one of your best officers. Be mournful.'

'It's your freaking speech!'

'Just read it when the time comes.'

Kraemer caught sight of Piaget at the head of the gathering in the Big Mixer's lower exec assembly room. He was sitting with a staff officer, engaged in a typically Piaget exchange: probably arguing about some kind of protocol. He'd never seen Piaget out of uniform before – funny how he looked so impotent.

There was good turnout for Coton's tribute. Everybody on the command floor had been shocked when the notice came up on the e-mail. When Coton had been recovered from the Lander smash alive, it was tacitly understood that they'd get him back eventually. There were many familiar faces; Decrypt must have shut down altogether for them to present themselves here; and all of the mobile crews not on ops had made an appearance. Kraemer also noticed that even the Met. Mapping staffer from the night of the crash had made it. Coton had been a popular guy, no mistake. The murmuring in the crowd hushed as Coton's father appeared and took his seat on the platform at the front of the hall. Piaget was now up there, too; he shook Coton's father's hand as they exchanged some quiet words. It was Piaget who opened the proceedings. Kraemer noted the big man's nervousness – strange how he'd changed since leaving the Comms Floor command.

Piaget rose to begin his speech. Even taking into account the former Floor Commandant's nervousness, it was a pretty poor performance. Piaget seemed to be reading most of what he was saying from the podium's prompting equipment. It was almost as if he'd done a quick trawl through Coton's record and had got some piece of software to write the damned speech. Only at the end, when he was obviously ad-libbing the last few sentences, did a little humanity creep into the oration. There was still something missing, though; Kraemer caught Piaget's eye for a second and read something like panic.

Coton's father followed smartly on from Piaget. He wasn't much better as he launched into a great eulogy on the Security Services and what a valuable role they played in keeping society together. He loosened quite noticeably, however, when he finally got around to talking about his son. Then something strange happened ... Coton's father was into the bit about duty and how a part of his own family had made the ultimate sacrifice, when he suddenly faltered and stopped in mid-sentence, his eyes fixed on the back of the hall, as if he'd seen a ghost. Nearly everyone turned around to see what had taken such a powerful hold on his attention. At that moment Kraemer had seriously expected to see Coton, and he wasn't alone, he found out later. As the crowd turned, one female figure was left in the group at the back of the hall who did not. This woman, tall and perfectly poised, stood for a moment as all eyes fell on her. Although wearing a short, crisp, black veil beneath a small pill-box hat, it was clear to all that this merely shadowed the features of a quite beautiful face. The woman's look fell away from Coton's speechless father, then she excused herself to those standing near her, the thin group parted, and she turned and was gone.

Coton's father seemed to want to call out, but he restrained himself. Without uttering another word to complete his speech, he left the platform, disappearing through a door behind the side drapes.

Talk flew around in the Big Mixer for days after the event. Kraemer whittled down the rumours to his own personal favourite: an estranged daughter, the majority of the suggestions being just too ridiculous. The speculation also rekindled his determination to get a look at Coton's personnel file. The time factor was now even more critical, since the files of the deceased Coton would soon be archived, and then access would be more or less impossible. Kraemer took his chance a week later as another virus scare upset the routine of the Comms Floor.

It was late on a Friday afternoon, almost dark outside, and the whole of the Comms Monitoring floor was in a flurry as technicians broke out all the network connections. Kraemer had just finished the back-up of his week's monitoring when one of the relief officers stepped down into the monitor bank trench.

'Er, Kraemer.' It was Brennan, one of the more personable of the so-called Sub-Commandants. 'Can you take a look at the key station on the Management Mezz?'

'Certainly, sir. Is there a problem?' Kraemer couldn't believe he was being given legitimate access to Piaget's old terminal.

'I'm not sure. It's this virus scare, I'd like you to double-check my security in the isolation mode.' Brennan was frankly clueless on the Comms Floor's systems.

'I'll come straight away, sir.'

The Sub-Commandant smiled gratefully and Kraemer followed him out of the trench and along the main walkway towards the Management Mezz. When they arrived at the workstation, Kraemer could see that it was still running in open access. Brennan hadn't trusted himself even to switch to disconnect-standby.

Kraemer thought quickly. 'I'll need to check all the auto-backups before I switch, sir.'

'Do whatever you have to, Kraemer. Do you need me here?'

'No, sir.' Kraemer limited his would-be grin to a slight smile. 'I can carry on on my own – it may take a while, though. Depends how much you've got on here, sir.'

'I'll leave you to it then. I'll be at Bank Three if you need me.'

'Very good, sir.' This was perfect.

Coton's file code was there, clear as day on the unopened list. The relief officers couldn't have understood what it was; Kraemer wasn't even going to need Piaget's authorization code to open it. 'Heaven-sent,' he muttered as he clicked open the file.

Kraemer took some satisfaction from discovering Renata. There was a wonderful hologram of a happy family group, a much slimmer Jon Coton Senior and a little girl – striking-looking, even at that young age. There was all kinds of information on the file; speech samples, holograms, personal addresses. Kraemer checked on Renata again; could be interesting to know where a woman like that actually lived. He was disappointed to find a 'not known' against the address query he'd entered, but there was a link code to another part of the file. Kraemer clicked it up to see what it was. There followed a short explanation of Coton's parents' separation and J. Coton Senior's second wife, Kraemer noted. Then it got interesting as Renata earned herself an Internals reference number; she had disappeared from the system with her mother, by the look of it. She was 'no-reference' everywhere else. She had to be an official Azzi ... No wonder Coton's old man had nearly had a heart attack when he saw her at the tribute. He probably hadn't seen her for years prior to that afternoon. Kraemer sat back for a short while while he pondered the implications. Coton's father must be absolutely paranoid about her: a man in his position with an Azzi daughter and ex-wife. Hell, that was some kind of personal stuff for a Trad politician. He must be going frantic, now that she'd surfaced again – but what a woman . . . incredible, whichever way you looked at her. Then he thought back to Coton and the reason he had this file on the system. Kraemer smiled to himself at being distracted by this beautiful woman and he scrolled through Coton's service record right up to the Newjune date of the crash.

The Lander 6 Enquiry file had been appended, and Kraemer wound through it until he found the hospital ICU reference behind. Coton had been in Central's own military intensive care unit and nobody had known, just round the corner from the Sci-Medical Foundation in Central 1. Nobody on the Command Floor had known he was so close; would-be visitors, himself included, had been told all sorts of stuff: that he was across the city, in M2 even, somebody had said.

Kraemer went on to the medical report; but it was all impenetrable jargon, then there was an entry that he'd been moved to the Sci-Medical Foundation – for some kind of advanced surgery, Kraemer surmised. Then he flicked ahead to check on the date of Coton's death, for his own personal reasons, to know exactly, he could remember every year, he could do that much for Coton . . . When he looked, there was no date; the file couldn't have been updated – but then there *were* other check dates right up to today. The main system had been addressing the copy file as it sat on Piaget's old workstation. There was one other check he could do.

Kraemer looked around to see if anyone else was about. He'd been completely engrossed for the past however long – thirty-two minutes, it said on the file matrix – but the mezzanine was still empty. The key terminal was still hooked to the Big Mixer's main server network; stupid Brennan, he thought, then rapped in Piaget's authorization code and found himself on

Coton's personnel file's main network tree. Kraemer chased the command syntax down the branches and found something that woke up all his suspicions of the weeks before. Coton's deep system file was still live ... it had a peculiar dual reference attached ... A bizarre thought entered his head ... 'Two Cotons, a double ID?' He mouthed the words back to the console, then his mind flashed back to Piaget, his complete character change, the new and mysterious demotion. Kraemer felt a strange brightness as he exited back to the open file on the workstation; an idea had taken root and he was going to pursue it ... He dumped some useful bits on to a data cart: Jon Coton Senior's address, and a few other details. He deleted his access record and made the file secure. It took another minute to carry out Brennan's original isolation and back-up request, then he shut down the station and went off to report back to the Sub-Commandant.

Coton won another trick and growled his satisfaction to Clowes as she scanned her remaining hand of nines and sevens – not a single trump among them.

'Use the synthesizer, Coton.' She spoke carefully to the cyborg; his comprehension was still slow.

Coton laboriously worked the table-top machine's control pad, eventually succeeding in transmitting his message. 'A whitewash, Clowes?' The speech synthesizer delivered the statement fluently in Coton's own file-sampled voice.

'Very good, Coton. You'll be doing that yourself soon, when Dabbs has done his mods.'

'Mmm . . .' Coton hummed in response.

Coton's progress since the comprehension exercises

had been astonishing. As Dabbs had assured her, there was no sign of any brain damage; it was clear that all Coton had needed was some time to assimilate all the new signals in his nervous system. She should have had more confidence. If there had been serious brain damage, Coton would never have got beyond a vegetative state. The progression the cyborg was displaying was exponential. Almost by the hour Clowes could read more and more understanding entering into the cyborg's consciousness. Coton the decrypt specialist's impressive logic was obviously a great bonus to him; he seemed able to build on quite small amounts of re-acquired knowledge and to extrapolate the information into his growing understanding. The competent card playing was a clear demonstration of the steady restoration of his faculties; he was already up to Clowes' own standard of play. Now if Dabbs could only succeed in tuning Coton's speech centre, then full functionality would be achieved.

Clowes' thoughts strayed to what would happen after that. In the whole of the project documentation there was no reference to what would happen to a successful cyborg after the testing period. It was a topic the Thin Doctor avoided. The doctor was becoming more and more remote, and Piaget had reduced his visits to brief appearances, and then always in the company of the doctor. Coton was still registering peculiar responses to Piaget but was unable to expand on this. His long-term memory was fragmented and he could summon only simple recognition responses, which he couldn't back up with any more information. The relationship with Piaget was definitely disturbing for him, though; that much was clear to Piaget, too. Piaget could be such a help to Coton, but he was reluctant to face up to the cyborg. The whole Coton–Piaget thing was occupying her more and more.

'You're thinking, Clowes . . . What about?' The speech synthesizer summoned her back to Coton and the card game.

'Sorry, Coton, I was in a dream again. I was actually thinking about Piaget. Have you had any more thoughts?'

Coton used the key pad again. 'Security Services.' The machine blipped and repeated the words.

'Any more?' Clowes looked into Coton's cyborg eyes, and the irises snapped open to a deep black as he met her gaze.

'No, but a definite link – feels very positive.'

Clowes noticed that Coton hadn't even looked at the control pad to make this last statement . . . more progress. 'That's very interesting . . . Can you work on it? Think back to your old job, the Big Mixer, picture the command floor.'

Coton bowed his head and picked up the scatter of cards on the low table, flicking them into a neat stack in his left hand; his fine motor control was immaculate, better than a human's. In this task his friction reactive finger covering gave him a degree of precision a magician would gladly kill for. The cyborg fanned and compressed the full pack in a single, easy action.

'You could consider a stage career with that technique, Coton.'

The cyborg looked up at her and transferred the cards to his left hand. With his right he activated the synthesizer again. 'In what kind of stages, Clowes?'

Incomprehension again . . . Clowes realized that there was much more work to be done.

*

Renata Coton watched the Electrocorp executive board members file back across the pier to the tower's main elevator. They were subdued and there was little discussion among them after their meeting up in the Chromium Programme's exec suite. This was the second time in three weeks they had all gathered for an extraordinary meeting – their extraordinary droid was giving them problems. She held the check-in log open and reconciled it with the exit listings: there were still three execs up in the suite. Renata dumped the names on to a small portable data manager which she had hooked into the workstation; it was all valuable information. The latest developments with the new droid, she was sure it had to be the Supervisor, were presenting her people with a perfect window of opportunity for their activities. Electrocorp had effectively managed to freeze the whole of M4's data systems on two occasions now. Her brief was to pinpoint the source of the disturbance and identify the individuals in control – or not, as it now seemed to be turning out.

Electrocorp was a lumbering giant of an organization; such was its size and influence in Metropolis 4 that, no matter what policy it pursued, it could achieve its aims. The only limiting factor on the corporation was time. It was abundantly clear to Renata and her people – the Sec-services classified them as just another Azzi faction – that Electrocorp was echoing exactly the behaviour of the Mother Earth commercial organizations which had wrecked the ecology of their own planet a thousand years before. Electrocorp was only the leader in this suicidal rush to destroy TI Creda and all the other planets of the Archipelago. Just as had happened on Mother Earth, there was now ridiculous competition among rival corporations to see who could do the most damage in the name of progress.

Renata carefully slid the tiny data manager into its hiding place inside the frame of her seat and fixed back the loose fold in the upholstery. She fed the tiny stick of silicon which held her day's download into an empty stimulant capsule, which she then clipped into her tab-case. Her shift was over and the relief staffer would be along in a few minutes.

Renata had little problem with the security checks at Electrocorp. She always carried the same few personal items which the scanners recognized unfailingly. Her one-fortieth-floor coding gave her virtual immunity from the physical pilferage checks regularly instituted by the bored security staffers on Level Zero. She was a high-grade trustworthy staffer within Electrocorp, a cover she felt justly proud of . . .

Her trip on the A-train back to South Two was as uneventful as usual; it was only when she alighted that she realized something was going on: the station was crawling with Sec-services personnel. Renata became aware of someone walking close alongside her as she moved with the crowd pouring from the train.

'Stick right by me, Renna, they're doing a Sector check,' a familiar voice hissed. It was Leach, her some-time lover and the group's leader. 'Clarky and Naden are going to set up a diversion. Keep together with me, and we'll walk straight through.'

As they neared the barriers at the station exit, Renata caught sight of the two crazy hackers in the parallel queue. Clarky looked straight at her but made no sign of recognition. He was probably as stoned as usual. Just as she and Leach offered their IDs to the security staffer at the checkpoint, all hell broke loose at the other gate. She glanced across to the disturbance and just caught sight of the demented face of Naden as he launched himself at Clarky in a highly realistic, total-freak-out attack. She felt Leach tugging at her and they were through and out on to the street.

Leach refused to discuss anything on the walk to the wohnblock. It was only when they had got themselves into her apartment that he decided to open up. Renata retired into the kitchen alcove and Leach followed her like some snapping dog, firing off a string of expletives.

'You freakin' idiot, Renna!' he bawled at her back as she hammered the aged nutro-converter into action. 'What the hell did you think you were doing, going to the Big Mixer!'

Renata remained silent, still fiddling with the now-humming food processor.

Leach continued his remonstration. 'Let's see if I can get recognized? I know, I'll go and see my pa who I haven't seen for twenty years ... I know a great public place!' Leach's tone was stupid-girlie-sarcastic. Then he let fly again. 'What the freak's up with you? You've gotta be cra-zee!'

'OK, OK ...' Renata turned around to face Leach. 'It was stupid, I know ... It was my brother's tribute, my freaking *dead brother*, Leach.'

'Yeah, the half-brother you despised ... The one who made his living blasting the shit out of all our teamsters!'

'He'd changed, Leach. You know I saw him last year.'

'Another freak-ass stupidity.'

'No, Leach ... Nothing happened after that. You know he did nothing to trace me.'

'For all you know, Renna ... There's probably a beautiful fat file on the tracking process right now. *I*

204

*met my azzi sister at the Congo real-club . . . on Wednes-
day the . . .'*

'You can freak yourself, Leach . . . Jon was on Decryption, non-combatant stuff, he'd had enough of all of that
action-man bit.'

'He was a Sec-services intelligence officer, Renna . . .
ambitious, committed . . . I can't go with you on this
new-character stuff.' Leach paused. 'Anyway, he's dead
now . . . you've been to his tribute and you've blown
your ID . . . That's what's at issue now. You were so
freaking stupid to do that.'

'I dispute that.' Renata spoke quietly. 'My father
recognized me, no one else. My face was covered and I'd
checked into the Big Mixer with my number two ID,
not my Electrocorp set.'

'Oh great, Renna, so you've got no number two ID
now.'

'Not necessarily.'

'Yes necessarily . . . Your old man will have had all
of the tribute attendees' IDs through every data bank
on the planet by now . . . Your number two is dead . . .
And even if it isn't, I'm gonna kill it anyway . . . Do
you realize what kind of a danger this is for all of
us?'

'Yeah, yeah. It was mad, but I had to go. You can
understand that on the one level, can't you, Leach?'

'Almost, Renna, if he hadn't been a freaking Sec-
services . . .' Leach abandoned the sentence. 'So what
are you going to do about your Electrocorp position?'

'Carry on, of course . . . I'm getting some good stuff
and you know things are getting pretty wild in there . . .
I've got to carry on.'

'I don't like to keep saying this, Renna – it's bad for
your ego – but you are actually quite strikingly good-

looking, kind of noticeable . . . It's only a matter of time before somebody finds you.'

'Cut that crap again, Leach . . . I'm a regular Electrocorp staffer . . . Nobody special in that place, a face in three thousand employees, not including job-sharers . . .'

'Yeah, and the whole freaking board of directors files past you every other day . . . They're all politicos . . . connected . . . probably your old man's party cronies.'

'My father's a Trad, in case you'd forgotten . . . He hates those Electrocorp bastards.'

The nutro-converter had finished its business and was flashing a 'Ready' message. Clowes placed her hand on the delivery drawer.

'D'you want to eat? I've got a salmon en croûte here . . . Twenty per cent natural . . . there's enough for two.'

'Sure! How can I resist?' Despite the sarcastic tone, Leach wanted to stay. He looked his partner up and down. Renata was an incredible woman despite her appalling taste in food.

As she cut the pancake of fused glutamate, Renata made her final statement in the debate. 'I'm going to carry on. I mean it . . . I've got a great big z-powder in my tab case. If anyone comes for me, I'll drop it . . . No more brain, no more Renata Coton . . . The group'll be safe, I put my life on it.'

CHAPTER ELEVEN

The Thin Doctor invited Piaget to sit down at the antique table in his office.

'I thought the memorial service was a rather rash idea, Piaget.' The understatement was clear in the Doctor's tone.

'It was Pepper's.'

'I wasn't accusing you, Piaget.'

'Coton's father was becoming too interested in his son's progress in the ICU. His visits were putting pressure on our people in the hospital.'

'And they couldn't handle that?'

'He was wanting to see more and more, and we only had one officer who fully understood the situation. Coton's father is an influential and persuasive individual, doctor ... he was wanting to have Coton moved.'

'Hmpf ...' the Thin Doctor snorted contemptuously. 'So Pepper decided to kill him off. This is going to complicate things ... I should have been consulted.'

'I thought you'd want a say in the matter.'

'And then to have a public event to draw attention to the whole thing. Crass stupidity.' The Thin Doctor raised his hands, reinforcing the point.

'The hospital released the news of Coton's death on to the net ... standard practice. Once that had happened, Pepper decided we had to go the whole distance. Coton's old man would've forced something anyway.'

'It's done now, Piaget ... We'll have to manage things

more closely from now on. Whatever further bright ideas Pepper might have, brief me first before he actions any of them.'

'That may be difficult.'

'If you want this project to continue, Piaget, I have to have complete control. You can tell that to Pepper ... But I'll go over your head if I have to.'

'I'll pass on your concerns, doctor.' Piaget held himself impassive at the Thin Doctor's arrogance. This damned tecchie interfering with the command chain. What was happening to his own role in this mad scheme ... He was now nothing more than a messenger boy between a pair of smart-ass egos.

'Possibly a silly question, Piaget. But is there a Coton obituary on the Infonet? Another *standard practice*?' The Thin Doctor paused briefly as Piaget searched for an answer. 'If there is, can I suggest that it's deleted as soon as possible ... I don't think Clowes and Dabbs need to know that Coton's dead ... Do you agree, Piaget?'

Piaget cursed himself for not having checked. The Thin Doctor was twisting the knife.

It was getting his speech ability that had somehow changed Coton. Clowes watched him now in the gymnasium they had installed in an empty subject cell. The cyborg was pumping furiously on a horizontal bar, he could do ninety chin-ups in a minute and would hold the pace for as long as he liked. Since his first outpourings of enthusiasm for his new physical state, he had now gone into a deep depression; he'd hardly said a word to her that morning. The gymnasium was a retreat for him, but it only served to compound the reality of his non-human-ness. She had always known that there were going to be problems as Coton became more aware of his situation, but she hadn't been sure how these were going to manifest themselves.

When he had suddenly developed the power of speech with the successful installation of the new synthesizer, it had been remarkable how Coton only used a vocabulary of positive words and phrases. His whole persona also appeared to become much more simple; the reflectiveness he had displayed when using the external speech machine had disappeared. It had been great to see him so pleased with himself at that point, but his morale went into a steady decline as the days passed. The closest analogy Clowes could come up with was that he had become like one of those dumb gene-genie athletics stars, lacking any interest in matters beyond the physical here-and-now. His almost complete lack of deep memory recall also had to be a hindrance to any further personality development. She suspected that his memory was returning but couldn't understand why he had become so uncommunicative. A typical depression symptom, yes; but the problem with Coton was that he wasn't typical of anything – there was no accepted model for someone like Coton.

There was a click behind her as the viewing gallery door slid open. The Thin Doctor entered and walked over to Clowes' side.

'It's the chemistry, Uschi.'

'Sorry, doctor?'

'Coton, I've just read your latest bulletin on the console. We're not refreshing him fast enough. His brain is becoming confused.'

'But all our tests are positive, Dabbs' factorizers are generating a perfect chemistry.'

'I know, Uschi. It's his brain's metabolism, it's too

slow. We've been very successful in fooling Coton's brain into thinking it still has a biological body to support, but we're paying the price for all that endorphin blanking. We're dulling other centres, memory and routine responses.'

'So you don't think it's purely psychological?'

'That's the end result: symptoms of depression and this type of pointless energy-burning that he's demonstrating here.'

Coton was now running at a rapid pace on the gymnasium's rolling track.

'You say pointless-energy burning, doctor . . . because he can't actually burn off any energy from his chassis?'

'Yes. His mind tells him to lose some of the anxiety he's feeling by making himself tired . . . And, of course, physical tiredness is an alien sensation to him. I'm worried that the activity may turn into aggression when he realizes that he's deriving no benefit. Have you spoken to him today?'

'No, he was really moody this morning.'

'Would you mind trying again? I think you should sit down quietly with him and tell him about the problem. He ought to be able to grasp the idea if you're careful in your explanation. Wait till he's had enough of the gym.'

'What about the aggression you mentioned, doctor? You've got me worried now.'

'He won't harm you, Uschi . . . I'm convinced of that.'

'What makes you so sure?' Clowes' trust in the doctor had lessened in the last weeks.

'His response traces to you. I've been watching them on the monitor right from the start. You're his best friend, Uschi, his mother, possibly more . . .'

The Thin Doctor finished the statement smiling knowingly. Before Clowes could ask him to explain exactly how he meant it, he had ducked out through the gallery door. Clowes turned back to watch Coton, who was still dashing along on the rolling track.

Renata concentrated hard through the screen of the mobile as she held the machine an exact ten metres behind the vehicle in front. It was the real skill in stealing mobiles, you had to avoid immediate detection by matching the auto-route-governed traffic flow exactly. Naden the hacker could crack a vehicle's ID code, but he was hopeless when it came to driving the things. Renata swung the mobile off the western ring and headed north out of Central 5 towards the Farm Park, where they had a rendezvous with their supplier.

'Phew, another successful lift job.' Naden glanced behind him at the solid stream of traffic they'd just left.

'Nice and easy, Naden, that's how you have to do it ... Stick the trafficom on for a minute, let's see if they've logged us yet.'

'I'll give it thirty secs, Renna. They'll pick us up for definite if we run it for longer.'

Naden zapped to the bulletin menu, where dangerously faulty or stolen mobiles were listed as soon as the central computers interpreted an alarm from a routeway sensor.

'Nah ...' Naden scanned the small screen. 'Oops, there we go, we've just joined the list. Not bad ... about ten minutes.' He snapped off the console.

Renata increased the mobile's speed down the boulevard, bringing them up close behind a commercial.

'We'll shadow this baby through the next intersection then dump out on the edge of the Farms.'

'OK, driver.' Naden crouched down in the passenger seat, trying to steal a look beyond the large vehicle in front. He squinted through the gap between the commercial's chassis struts above the lift pad. As they tailed the commercial through the intersection, their presence triggered the beacons.

'Oh shit, that's blown it! Dump now, or go for the farm?' Renata threw a look at Naden as she pulled the mobile out from behind the fat rear of the commercial.

'The farm . . . Go for it!' Naden definitely had his mad head on today.

They abandoned the mobile on a run-off margin, just before the boulevard ran into the agribusiness district, and slid down the concrete banking on to the lip of an iced-over drainage channel, halfway down the steep slope. They dropped down into the channel and Naden led the way along to where the Farm Park's perimeter fence cut across it up to the routeway. Renata looked out at the Farm Park, stretching out below them on the vast plain that ran out from the raised boulevard banking. It was a huge acreage of long flat sheds that housed Metropolis 4's agricultural industry, quite pleasingly chequered now with a dusting of snow. This was the first time she'd ever been out here. Naden normally went to score with his buddy Clarky, but he was too out of it when their man Griff, The Farmer, had contacted them to say the crop was ready.

Naden slipped under the fence and Renata followed. They hugged the inside of the perimeter, keeping low in the scrubby vegetation down the sweep of the banking. It was a trek of a kilometre or so down past the first shed to where Naden began to dive out of the bushes looking for his Farmer. When they finally spotted him, they were both surprised to see Griff standing out in the open at the corner of the second massive block. He beckoned to them to come over, seemingly completely unconcerned at their being observed.

'All the droids are US, I tried to tell Clarky on the TR, but I don't think he was happening.' Griff laughed. 'You must be Renna, the driver.'

'Hi, Griff, a hell of a farm you've got here.' Renata grasped the Farmer's outstretched hand.

'Wait till you see inside.'

As Griff took them through a small door in the side of the shed, Renna was immediately struck by the warm, wholesome smell that met her nostrils. They seemed to be in an airlock. Naden closed the outer door and Griff brushed past Renata to let them through into the building proper. The atmosphere was tropical compared to the winter chill outside.

They stepped out into a dimly lit, narrow canyon — narrow in the sense that it was a thin strip in the scale of the vast shed; it was about ten metres wide. The whole of the central part of the shed was occupied by a huge concrete-and-steel structure, which supported the tiers of growing belts, textile bands planted with grain and other crops, Griff's specials among them. The whole construction ran the entire length and width of the building; the individually UV-lit belts gave the field frame, as Griff named it, the impression of a building within a building, ten or more storeys high.

'Here, take off your coats, we keep a regular twenty degrees in here.' Griff pointed to some hanging rails by the airlock door. He continued: 'Yeah, all the droids are out, the second time this week. There's no one in the place 'cept us.'

Once Naden and Renata had deposited their coats, Griff marched them off down the gangway to an open elevator platform on the side of the field frame. As the elevator set off, he launched into an explanation of the system to Renna, who was marvelling at the scale of the machinery.

'Each belt is a controlled environment; as it creeps along, we can hit it with anything we want: light, heat, water, fertilizer, you name it. And we can speed it up or whatever. This shed is running on a regular twenty-four-hour cycle, one revolution a day. Daytime on the top belt run, night underneath. This is all high-grade produce, not the forced, manipulated stuff that goes into most of the crap we eat.'

The elevator reached the top level where the rich, fecund smell up in the roof of the building was almost overpowering. Naden led them off the platform and set off along a slender walkway bridging the top belt. He'd been here before.

'After you, Renna. Follow Naden, he knows where my little garden is.'

'This atmosphere's a bit rich, isn't it.' Renna wrinkled her nose at the Farmer.

'You want to do a job-share in a fish farm, now that's something else. This is good wholesome farming air, m'girl!'

Naden was well ahead of them. When Renata and Griff caught up with him over the centre of the belt, where the narrow walkway spread into a workstation area, he was busy at a control terminal.

'It's what's known as a symbiotic relationship, Renna.' Naden spoke without looking up from the screen. 'I do the programming and the Farmer works the land.'

Griff laughed. 'Naden allocates certain plots on the belts for a little extra-intensive agriculture of those

214

special, hard-to-manage crops: opium, tobacco, y'know, proper cash crops.'

Renata looked down on to the barely moving belt. All she could see through the criss-cross of luminaires was a sea of nearly ripened wheat.

'You won't spot 'em just like that, Renna. Naden's got 'em organized into little strips and pockets where only the control system knows where they are. We've classed 'em as undesirable surplus vegetation; once they're ripened up, the harvester weeds them out.'

'Very neat, Griff. I knew Naden had to be good for something or other.'

'It's beautiful, Renna – nature and machine in perfect harmony. All I have to do is sort through the compost baler at the right time and pack the stuff for my wholesalers to take to the market.'

Naden finished his adjustments on the workstation and sauntered over to Griff and Renata at the platform rail. He spoke matter-of-factly to the Farmer.

'You'll be OK for another month now, Griff. All of the B-crops are set to ripen. We can do some seeding once we've got that lot harvested.'

'Cool. We can get your stuff now.' Griff motioned for them to continue across the walkway.

On the far side of the field frame there was an elevator identical to the one they had used on the other side. Griff took them down to ground level and led them to a bank of silos, midway down the structure. He halted by the third towering cylinder and disappeared amongst the support columns. When his bent-up figure re-emerged, he was dragging four flat vacuum-packed sacks.

'Who's dope, who's smoke?' Griff asked the question holding a pair of sacks on each arm. Each pair was strapped together at one end so that they could be slipped over a carrier's shoulders and worn like a vest.

Naden shrugged at Renata, took the sacks from Griff's left arm and hung them over his body.

'That's the dope, Naden. Yours is the smoke then, Renna.' Griff separated the two sacks and helped her on with the valuable load. 'You'll be a lot warmer on the trip home. A good insulator, is vegetable matter . . .'

As they made their way back to the airlock at which they had entered, Renata asked Griff how he managed when the droids were on patrol.

'It's all down to timing then. They're pretty stupid machines, they have set routines which you have to know how to dodge. It's more fun with the droids actually. Y'know, if I didn't have this extra little job in here, I think I'd go mad.'

Renata was keen to research a little further and asked another question. 'Are they all Electrocorp models?'

'Yep, every one. They're normally very reliable and good at what they do — except for security, that is.' Griff laughed.

'So what do you think's been making them go US?'

'It's the upgrade . . . There was a whole team of EC tecchies in here a couple of months ago, fitting new processors or something. Not long after, the droids all started to do weird things and now they're on strike — every other day, more or less. Why the interest?'

Naden shot a look at Renata.

'Oh, nothing really, just worried in case they wake up, I suppose.'

In the airlock Griff gave them both cards for the Farm Park's A-train line; they would be able to mingle with the job-sharers off the last shift. The load they both carried had them having to stand and sweat all the way across Metropolis 4. It was worth it, though: pure, natural, non-state-controlled stimulants were highly valuable commodities. Their sale in the real-clubs would support their entire group for a month.

Clowes was sitting at the facility's main admin workstation; she gasped as she read the news on the Infonet screen.

'Doctor, have you seen this? He's dead . . .' She pointed at the headline above the crush of text. The Thin Doctor was rapidly at her side. '. . . Pechard's been killed by the restaurant droids . . .'

As Clowes turned to look at his reaction, the Thin Doctor almost seemed to smile – a strange expression, she thought.

'Er, yes, Uschi. I was going to tell you. I heard from the Cybotics Circle this morning and it slipped my mind completely, what with the new Coton installation.'

Clowes had been disappointed that they had had to put Coton on to the same controlled-release endorphin programme as the cat and ape cyborgs. He had lost his total independence; now he would have to have the chemical cartridges replaced every two days to prevent him going into rejection trauma. It placed a lot of pressure on the team, but Coton was responding well to the new system: his attitude had changed overnight. Clowes was expecting his deep memory to return any day.

'That's horrible news though, isn't it? But how can they blame an Azzi faction for it?'

'The state has its reasons, I'm sure, Uschi. The Azzis could well be into the robots' update systems. You know that the restaurant droids were permanently hooked to a data net, that's why they were such good conversationalists.'

'Seems far-fetched to me, doctor. And all the other droid-based disturbances ... it's like a virus. You'd need to be very well linked into a droid control net to cause the havoc that's sweeping the city ... You don't think that Coton could be affected, do you?'

'No, Uschi, I think we're very well isolated here.'

'He has a proprietary base-chassis, though. Lots of his sub-processors are pure Electrocorp, programmed by them.'

'No fear, it has to be a CPU problem, and I think our CPU's a little non-standard, *n'est-ce pas?*'

The Thin Doctor's increasing use of this French adjunct was getting on her nerves.

'Speaking of French, doctor ... Where's Piaget? He's not been near the facility in ages.'

'I think it's his company. There's lots going on for him at the moment, events that are keeping him out of our hair. I thought you'd be pleased he wasn't around, Uschi. You're not exactly the best of pals with him.'

'He's been so odd, the last few times he was here. His reaction to Coton has been really peculiar, almost like he's avoiding him on purpose.'

'Who am I to judge Piaget? He's a busy man ... But he'll turn up soon enough, I guarantee ...' The Thin Doctor rattled the stack of data carts he'd been holding all through the conversation. 'I must get to my lecture, Uschi ... more students thirsting for knowledge ...' He smiled and turned for the door. 'One last thing ... keep a close eye on Coton, I want to know immediately when his memory functions begin to come on stream. I have some tests that have to be done.'

*

'The Doctor knows something about Piaget, but he's not telling us a thing.' These were Clowes' first words to Dabbs when she met him at the Rehab Suite's security door.

'I know about Piaget, Clowes.' Dabbs gulped hard. 'Coton's just told me this morning.'

'What? What did he say? Has he got his memory back?'

'C . . . completely . . . He wants to talk to you . . . I was on my way to find you.'

'Let me through then . . . What did he say?'

'Is the Thin Doctor still here?' Dabbs was obstructing her path now as he spoke.

'No, he's gone off to a lecture . . . Now let me past!'

Dabbs moved to one side and Clowes seized the heavy manual lock of the security door.

'I'm going to stay in the front. I'll voice you if the doctor comes back,' Dabbs said to Clowes as she tripped slightly on the bottom lip of the airlock. When she got through into the Rehab Suite, Coton was sitting on one of the large sofas round the edge of the main room.

'Coton, what have you said to Dabbs? What is it about Piaget?'

'Sit down, Clowes . . . This may come as a surprise to you.'

Clowes joined the remarkably cool humanoid sitting on the sofa. She prepared herself for the revelation from Coton's deep memory, the information that had so fazed Dabbs.

The security receptionist eyed Kraemer suspiciously. The young Sec-services staffer stood shuffling nervously in the foyer of Coton's father's magnificent residential block. Every time he moved his feet on the polished stone his shoes screeched as if in harmony with the part of him that was screaming to abandon this crazy notion and get out fast. Was this really a good idea? It was only a hunch after all, a hunch that seemed more and more implausible by the second. Well, Coton's old man had agreed to see him, and he considered that he hadn't really over-sold himself on the voice link two days before ... He'd said that it was personal stuff about his son. It could be something or nothing so far as Coton's father was concerned. Kraemer looked away to the sealed door of the building, then back to the security staffer. He couldn't chicken out now, even if he wanted to.

The sharp clacking of expensive shoes on marble made him turn around. Jon Coton Senior was walking down the steps to meet him personally.

'Mr Kraemer,' Coton's father called out to him from halfway down the sweep of the broad staircase. 'Would you like to come up?' The voice of a political orator filled the classical but bleak hall. When Kraemer gave his affirmative, the weakness of his own voice, swallowed up in the space, made him cringe.

Coton's father ushered Kraemer into his apartment, at the same instant mercifully relieving him of the embarrassment caused by his squeaking shoes on the sleek flooring. Now he felt that he almost had to wade through the deep pile of the carpeting of the luxuriously appointed suite of rooms. Jon Coton Senior took his heavy coat from him and bade him sit down in a commodious, genuine leather armchair. Kraemer squeezed at the irresistible tactility of the natural material.

Coton's father sat down opposite him in a matching chair. 'Please relax, Kraemer; you're very welcome here.

It's good to meet one of Jon's old colleagues. You're the only person from the Service to have visited me since Jon's death. Apart from that peculiar fellow, Piaget, the Floor Commandant ... Your ex-Floor Commandant, should I say.'

'Yes, sir ...' Kraemer was finding it hard to fulfil Coton's father's request.

'Good riddance, I say, Kraemer. The man was a blithering wreck ... Here, have a drink – a proper one.' Coton's father picked up a decanter containing what Kraemer could only assume was whisky and poured a generous measure into a sculpted glass. 'That'll put you on your feet, Kraemer.'

Taking the glass, Kraemer logged Coton's father's dismissal of Piaget as a 'blithering wreck'. Interesting that he viewed the man in the same way; he took some comfort from the thought. He took a sip of the costly liquid, which tasted strong and pure.

'Now then, Kraemer,' Coton's father led off again, 'when you spoke to me the other day – and I don't know how you got my link number, but that's by the bye – you suggested to me that you knew something about my son. I got the impression that this was some sensitive information ... Am I right, or is your hesitation a natural nervous state?' The older man leant back, waiting for Kraemer's reply.

'Well, Mr Coton, sir, I'm not quite sure how to start explaining the story ...'

'*Just as you feel, Kraemer* ... Tell me about my son,' Jon Coton Senior interrupted, urging him to proceed.

'You may find what I have to say rather shocking – there are all sorts of implications.' Kraemer paused as he registered the interest in Coton's father's face.

The older man spoke again. 'It's a mistake to look too

far ahead. Only one link in the chain of destiny can be handled at a time ... Winston Churchill said that, Kraemer. A very wise man, a politician's politician.' He finished the statement smiling at having shared this great wisdom.

Kraemer's mind leapt at the mention of the name *Churchill*: the *Churchill* in Coton's indestructible code. He thought of Coton being hammered with such wise axioms throughout his childhood and smiled to himself.

'That's struck a chord, eh! Begin at the beginning.'

Kraemer took the politician's advice and went right back to his role in the mission that had started the whole chain of events. Coton's father listened carefully, interrupting Kraemer only once for a short lecture on the great twentieth-century politician when he mentioned Coton's *Churchill* code. As Kraemer progressed, he could see astonishment growing in Coton's father's face as it dawned on him that this lowly Security Services staffer was suggesting that his son was still alive. When he had finished the tale, Kraemer took a large slug of whisky and dropped back in the armchair to await Coton's father's response.

Jon Coton Senior remained silent for what felt like an age to Kraemer. We're all wise men until the moment we open our mouths, somebody had told him once. But this was Coton Senior's politician persona working now and the delay was calculated.

Eventually the older man spoke. 'If anyone else had come to me with this, Kraemer ... I'd probably have booted him out before he'd got even halfway through. I believe your story ... I can see absolutely no other reason for you to put yourself through all this other than out of loyalty to a comrade and a desire to seek the truth. Two of the noblest of motives, Kraemer.'

'Thank you, sir. It's a relief for me to share this with someone.' Kraemer surprised himself with the understatement.

Coton's father poured them both another whisky. 'So where do we go from here, Kraemer? That's the question, isn't it? And the reason you came to me. For which I'm deeply grateful, I assure you.'

'I have to repeat that all this is only a hunch, sir.'

'Don't worry, Kraemer. I'm not quite going to believe that my son is back from the dead just yet. But your description of Piaget and the way he's gone through such a change and has disappeared from the scene, that's what struck me ... And then, when I linked it with my own recent dealings with the man ... He's more involved in this thing than you'd imagined. I'd put money on that.'

'It's funny how you've altered my perception of him too, sir. I just hadn't been able to make a strong enough connection.'

'It's called sharing intelligence, Kraemer. We both have a bigger picture now. Mine much bigger ...'

'The prospect of what might be going on is quite frightening to me, sir.'

'Take heart, Kraemer; you have an ally. Now we should pool some more of our intelligence. Do you have all these file reference codes? I can make enquiries where even you cannot.'

When he left the block Kraemer wasn't sure which was having the greater effect: Coton's father's acceptance of his story or the alcohol. He wandered down the street in a daze. Coton's father was going to pursue Coton's dual file reference and had asked him to put a notice out on the Infonet for his daughter to contact him. Kraemer, for the first time in his life . . . felt deeply sorry for a politician.

Coton's facial expression was uncanny. Clowes could see nervousness written right across it. Once again she marvelled at the engineering behind the face, then she thought briefly of poor Pechard.

Coton spoke quietly. 'Piaget is not who you think he is, Clowes. He's Sec-services . . . my old boss from the Comms Department.'

'What?' Clowes' jaw dropped in disbelief. 'Sec-services? You sure?' She realized it was stupid to ask, looking at Coton's face, but Coton's memory could still be playing tricks on him.

'It's no system fault, Clowes.' Coton brought a hand to his head. 'I know him . . . very well . . . You've seen his reaction to me.'

'Hold on, Coton . . . Let me get this straight . . . We have your old Commandant on the project, masquerading as a cybotics company rep?'

'That's about it,' Coton replied, nodding.

'What the hell's he doing, then? What's the Sec-services' involvement in all this?'

'That's the big question, Clowes. Dabbs is on to it now, I think . . . He said he'd check the project files, if he could get access.'

Clowes remembered the Thin Doctor mentioning the new tests he wanted to do as Coton's memory returned. Could he have been intending to do a screening check to obliterate this Piaget information from Coton's mind?

'The doctor's in on this too, Coton . . . I know he is. What did Dabbs say when you told him? That might have been silly to tell him.'

'I felt real silly at the time.' Coton shook his lowered

head. 'I had this incredible rush and everything just fell into place. I blurted the whole thing out to Dabbs – he was the only one there.'

Clowes sprang up from the sofa as a thought rushed into her head, and she grabbed the voice set from the workstation.

'Dabbs, please voice me up immediately.' Within a few seconds she heard the technician's gulpy response and breathed out a sigh of relief – he was still there. 'It's OK, Dabbs, only me. Can you come down to the Rehab Suite for a minute?'

In the discussion that followed his arrival, Dabbs convinced Clowes where his loyalties lay. Dabbs too was unable to shed any light on the special tests the Thin Doctor wanted to perform as Coton's memory returned. She could only voice her suspicions to the cyborg and Dabbs. He was no fan of Piaget though; he gulped off on a long discourse about how the man had been unpleasant to him on more than one occasion. Clowes had to stop him as he grew more and more heated on the subject.

'OK, OK, Dabbs ... We're all slugging for the same team here. Now we have to get ourselves organized on how we're going to deal with this ... Coton, you're going to have to act dumb – no real memory recall when the Thin Doctor shows again, and definitely nothing if Piaget makes an appearance ... Can you do that?'

'I suppose so, Clowes. If you're sure the doctor wants to z-out my memory ... that's a powerful incentive.'

'Can you get back on the files, Dabbs? You could spot something you wouldn't have thought significant before.'

'That's just what I was doing, Clowes.'

'Sorry, Dabbs, I'm getting a little wound up.'

Dabbs trotted back towards the airlock, and Clowes turned to Coton again

'Why would a high-ranking Comms Officer be involved in this project, Coton? What could he possibly contribute?'

'I've had a thought on that, Clowes ... Piaget's been angling for a Staff Officer position for the past year, well up until the time I was taken out ... Now maybe he's got his promotion and he isn't a Comms Officer any more.'

'I don't get it.' Clowes was genuinely bemused.

'I don't get it fully either, Clowes, but a Sec-services Staff Officer can have any kind of project responsibility. He could be just a link man for whatever real motive his people have behind the Cyborg Project ...' Coton fell silent, then began to utter a strange noise that his synthesizer couldn't quite handle. 'Hell, it's me, Clowes, this is all about freakin' me. I'm a live test bed ... You've got to get me out of here ...' Coton let out more of the strange, subdued barking.

Clowes instinctively put her arm round the cyborg. Was this Coton crying? It was as close as he could get, but his body was completely still, harder and cooler than a human's. She thought about his final plea to her. It was impossible ... right now, anyway ... The Thin Doctor alone had control of the endorphins that were the key to his survival.

CHAPTER TWELVE

Clowes remained with Coton for the whole night; they both needed some peace. Coton drifted into head-rest mode: his brain still required rest, even though his chassis had no need of a rejuvenative biological process. Clowes was fitful through the night, the cyborg steadily pushed against her making her more and more uncomfortable. Coton's upper body weighed twice that of a human, packed with his heavily clad central power supply and distributor servos. Eventually she moved away from him, letting Coton sink gently sideways, until only his head remained in her lap.

As she dozed, her thoughts turned once again back to her brother, Georg, the innumerable similar nights she'd spent with him as he slept, unsure what developments the following day would bring. At least Coton's general physical stability now seemed assured; he was as capable of surviving as the prototype subjects which had now had almost a year of their new physicality. The real similarity between Coton and Georg was the anxiety that went with the process. Coton's complete sentience had brought with it a realization of his powerlessness in the hands of the technical support team. She wondered whether Dabbs was still awake, busy combing the project files; she took comfort in having him as a confidant. But she would have to bring him fully into her confidence and tell him about the Supervisor, now that she was sure he shared her feelings concerning the Thin Doctor and Piaget. It was vital that they come up with a real strategy for handling the situation, now that the Cyborg Project seemed to be sliding into a confusion of intrigue and uncertainty.

Clowes stroked her hand across Coton's head and considered his desperate plea to be helped out of his situation. How could they possibly get him out of the facility and keep him surviving? The Thin Doctor now had the cyborg on the external endorphin replacement programme, which completely bound him into a dependence on the facility's bio-chemistry lab. She had checked the factorizer line and had noticed that the doctor had encrypted the production code, making it highly unlikely that she or Dabbs would be able to run any batches of the vital fluids. They had to be freshly produced before transfer anyway, critically matched to the changing chemistry of the last charge in the cyborg's chassis. The Thin Doctor certainly had control: Coton would not survive beyond forty-eight hours without endorphin replacement.

The full board of Metro Cybotics was assembling for the meeting. Piaget sat in silence, halfway along the grand oval table, and watched with increasing surprise the number of people filling the twenty or so places. Pepper was at the head of the table, and Piaget also recognized the chairman from the Staff selection board, a couple of places down on his right. The mood was subdued, tense even. Piaget felt nervous as he arranged the bulletins from the Cyborg Project in front of him; he felt seriously unprepared for what was to follow.

'Morning, Piaget.' The Thin Doctor's voice first surprised and then warmed him. Thank the stars he wasn't going to be alone to handle the presentation; he would be able to hand over to the doctor as soon as things got sticky.

He spoke in the Thin Doctor's ear as the latter sat down beside him. 'What the hell are you doing here?'

The doctor turned to Piaget, apparently amused at Piaget's conspiratorial manner. 'Couldn't leave you to cope with this on your own, Piaget ... This is important.'

Piaget wasn't quite sure how to react to the remark: a damning of his competence, but reassuring at the same time.

'Good morning, gentlemen ... ladies.' Pepper spoke up clearly above the hum of conversation. Piaget scanned for females in the assembly and spotted two uniformed Security Services officers at the far end of the table.

Pepper began with the formalities, thanking everyone for attending at such short notice. He introduced various key personnel, naming Piaget and the Thin Doctor as the security and technical directors of the Metro Cybotics company.

Piaget was surprised at the other persons present: two techies from Electrocorp and a fair complement of Sec-services personnel, including Internals.

Pepper outlined the agenda. 'I will ask Staff Superintendent Navarro of the Security Services to give us a briefing on the city-wide situation. His intelligence is, needless to say, the most accurate information we have at the present time. Please discount any reports you may have received from the Infonet. Security has demanded that stringent censoring be imposed on all disturbance reports of the last weeks ... I will then be asking Messrs Gillespie and Roach from Electrocorp to give us a technical run-down on our present difficulties ... Our solution action will be presented by myself, supported by my colleagues, the Thin Doctor and Mr Piaget.'

SS Navarro, a great hulk of a man known as *the Battleship* in security service circles, asked Pepper to illuminate the large screen hanging behind the head of the table where he stood. The screen lit, showing a plan view of Metropolis 4. Navarro produced a laser pointer and began his briefing.

The virus scares of the previous weeks, which had resulted in the periodic shut-down of all of the city's major information networks, had spawned a rash of criminal activity. The whole of Metropolis 4's communications network had turned into a free-for-all, with Azzi hackers tapping into various, normally secure systems, committing monetary fraud and software piracy. In itself this was a significant threat to the stability of society: untold damage was being done, and repairing the hacked-out nets was proving difficult for the supervising authorities. Navarro switched the screen to a topograph of the information networks which overlay the city. He highlighted the scale of the intrusions, illuminating the considerable number of known break-in points.

Navarro continued for some time with detailed explanations of some specific network collapses. 'This is only one aspect of the trouble which we now have on our hands, ladies and gentlemen ... Some of you, I know, are also aware of the new negative developments taking place within our automated industries and droid-run establishments.' Thus Navarro led into the second part of his lecture.

Serious malfunctions were taking place in all of Metropolis 4's industries: automatic management processes were going haywire. All the city's industries were being affected, even power-generation and food-production. The threat was profound. Where droids were employed, these were beginning to fail or were running in their own routines, uncontrollable by any override system. A general policy was now being implemented to disable all robots, using whatever means were available. The Security Services had set up armed take-out squads, which were being summoned to more and more locations as malfunction alarms streamed in from all over the city. The Security Services were being stretched to the limit. Navarro clicked up more overlays on the city map to highlight the point, then began his conclusion.

'You will all have read the Infonet reports that Azzi groupings are at the root of all of this trouble ... We were confused ourselves at the outset, what with all the parasitic Azzi activity riding on the disturbances. I regret to have to tell you that Azzi groups are *not* the source of the problem ... I say I regret, since the real source of the disturbances is rather more threatening than mere Azzi activity. The source of this crisis ... and I use that word in its fullest sense ... is Electrocorp ... specifically their new *Supervisor* droid.'

Low exclamations rippled round the table.

Piaget turned to the Thin Doctor, who seemed quite unmoved by the revelation. 'You knew, doctor ...'

'I had my suspicions, Piaget.'

Navarro continued: 'I know that this comes as a surprise to many of you – but please, if we may proceed ... You will gain more of an understanding of the situation from the Electrocorp representatives here today.' Navarro summoned the tecchies to the head of the table. Just one of the Electrocorp people raised himself in response and walked around to the large lecture screen.

Roach, introducing himself as a project manager, re-lit the screen so that it showed an animated flick of the Supervisor droid at the robot plant's duplicate control centre. A buzz rose from the assembly: clearly everyone was impressed. Pepper called for quiet, and Roach went on to explain the Supervisor's technology and her test role, that of running the robot production facility.

'We grew suspicious when our production first came to a halt. There was no trace of a major system failure; all our equipment was clear, but then we discovered some complete impositions on our control network. There was a blanket diversion of all data routeings to the Supervisor's terminal. On this first occasion we cut the power to the duplicate terminal and regained control. The data-net disturbances that took place at the same time, the virus scares, we took to be just a coincidence; we hadn't had a city-wide shut-down for a long time. Then, not long after that, we noticed an increase in production faults: finished droids weren't checking out, and we started to get reports from our user-base that upgraded droids were going into malfunction. We decided to undertake a complete quality survey, which took some time.'

Roach called up some more animations of Electrocorp droid types on the screen: curiously constructed insect-oids and more conventional machines closely resembling the human form.

'These are our main production droids: custom-built loaders, construction robots and the humanoid military models. All of them were giving us problems. We were baffled that we couldn't find any hard answers in our survey. When we then started to receive call-outs from users of our automated production equipment, we realized that there had to be something profoundly wrong, so we went back to the Supervisor.'

The second Electrocorp tecchie, Gillespie, had now joined Roach and he took over the briefing at this point. 'I've been involved with the Chromium Programme right from its inception, six years ago. As you can see from just looking at the machine, this droid represents a major breakthrough in robotics technology. It also takes innovations from materials science, logic development and nearly every other scientific discipline you care to mention. This pooling of technologies has combined to make a humanoid machine that is the closest thing yet to the fully sentient android of science fiction stories. In fact, the Supervisor now seems to be in the process of proving that very statement.' There was a sense of rueful triumph in his words.

Piaget smiled knowingly at Gillespie, catching the tecchie's eye. Despite the seriousness of the intelligence he was hearing, he was beginning to enjoy this meeting. There was a strong chance of a surprise coming to these smart-ass Electrocorp people. He stole a glance at the Thin Doctor, who was making some notes on a write-pad.

Gillespie continued: 'The Supervisor has been in tests for six months in our duplicate control centre. Until recently she has exceeded all our expectations as a virtually autonomous droid ... well, she is still exceeding our expectations, but the consequences of her doing that have proved negative in the extreme.'

'Please clarify the point, Doctor Gillespie,' Navarro interrupted.

'Such is the Supervisor's intelligence, the robot appears, to all intents and purposes, to have developed her own personality. Even while we were in the early stages of testing, we were finding that our tech-team was developing a strangely strong allegiance to her — most strange, we thought at the time. We even brought in psychologists to assess the situation, but they put this phenomenon down to a healthy team spirit. We had to leave it at that, but we still dismissed some members, for what we in the project management saw as non-objectivity.'

'Again, doctor . . .' Navarro was betraying annoyance at the tecchie's vagueness.

'It was as though certain project staffers were becoming emotionally involved, almost in love with her, superintendent.'

Navarro raised his eyebrows and asked Gillespie to continue.

'So we find we've created a machine with an amazing intelligence, remarkable physical characteristics and a virtual personality which even seems to transcend the human/machine divide. The Supervisor appears to have employed all of her growing power to spread an influence across all our company's installations and in-the-field robotic products. Our project staffers have named this influence the Supervisor's *Ego Virus*.'

Gillespie paused at this point, apparently checking that the group were keeping up with his explanation. Piaget considered that it *was* sounding rather far-fetched, but nobody offered any questions to the tecchie, so he continued.

'As you have already heard from Superintendent Navarro, there has been an increasing incidence of serious disturbances in the city, and, in the case of our robots, in locations beyond. These have all been traced back to our Supervisor droid . . . I know that may sound ridicu-

lous to you all, but we have indisputable evidence ...
Two days ago we evacuated all personnel and shut
down all power to our Electrocorp tower. We cut ...
physically disconnected all data-net links, only to find
that the droid had tapped into the tower's energy accelerator for its power source and had created its own
transmission links, using equipment available on the
development programme's sealed floors. We are unable
to shut down the accelerator in the short term; we need
a period of some months to render the machine safe ...'

'I understand that this is being instituted right now,
Doctor Gillespie,' Navarro interrupted again.

'I was getting to that, superintendent ... This morning
our decommissioning team received a transmission from
the tower threatening instant shut-down if they per-
sisted in their work. The transmission came from the
Supervisor – it was no Azzi TR, the Supervisor has her
own unique code ... We have now suspended the
decom-operation.'

Navarro raised his hand to Gillespie to stop him.
'And what would be the consequences of a rapid shut-
down, Doctor Gillespie? How much of a threat is this?'

'The type of shut-down that the Supervisor could
impose would initiate a nuclear explosion, superintendent ... probably one big enough to wipe out the heart
of M4 ...'

Pepper glanced across at the Thin Doctor as though
seeking confirmation of this prognosis. The Thin Doctor
nodded in affirmation of Gillespie's statement. Pepper
spoke up. 'I'd like to stop you there, Doctor Gillespie. I
think that everyone here now understands the gravity
of the situation. I believe that a detailed threat analysis
at this point is unnecessary. Although I'm sure ...
Superintendent Navarro ...' Pepper turned to address

the Security Services chief directly. '... I'm sure that such activity is taking place as we speak.' Navarro nodded silent confirmation. 'Now I would like to introduce you to my colleague, the Thin Doctor, no stranger to many of you, I'm sure. We would like to explain a project that we at Metro Cybotics have been working on and how it has a direct bearing on this grave circumstance which threatens our city.'

The Thin Doctor rose from his seat and walked over to the workstation that drove the briefing screen. He loaded a data cart into the feed port and sat down in a chair just behind Pepper, who was beginning his presentation of the fictitious Metro Cybotics company. Piaget ran his eyes over the meeting's visitors; they were all closely following Pepper's introduction. So he was going to stick to the whole company scam. Piaget considered the group round the table: they were a broad mix, some obviously in the know, some not. He silently cursed Pepper and the Thin Doctor for not letting him in on the real nature of this board meeting.

Pepper continued, expanding on the problems of dealing with the Supervisor. She had now issued the threat to destroy the Robotics Tower and therefore half the city in the ensuing explosion of the energy accelerator. She would carry out this threat if she detected any interference with her activities. These activities were also becoming more and more unpredictable. Pepper referred back to Navarro's mention of the threat to basic services, such as power-generation and food-production. A virtual checkmate was Pepper's analysis. All conventional interdiction methods were precluded by the ease with which they would be detected and the resultant unthinkable retaliatory action the psychotic droid could take. Pepper handed over to the Thin Doctor to explain just how the Metro Cybotics project offered the only hope of a successful termination of the Supervisor's reign.

It was patently clear that the Thin Doctor knew exactly what was happening at Electrocorp – he seemed to be better briefed than the Electrocorp people themselves. His threat assessment of the Supervisor was comprehensive: she was completely in control of the Robotics Tower and had enlisted the services of Electrocorp's latest droid types in the defence of her new realm; it seemed that she was quite in a position to dictate terms to the City Fathers. In short, she had control of the city. The Thin Doctor chose to illustrate the Supervisor as a psychotic super-human with the power to infiltrate whatever system she liked. She had used the Electrocorp plant as a mere training ground for the action she was now pursuing.

When asked by Navarro as to her possible motives, the Thin Doctor offered little reasoned analysis. 'Psychosis is entirely possible in advanced droid intelligence systems, Mr Navarro.'

The Thin Doctor avoided the man's Service title, Piaget observed. He always did it to maintain his own sense of superiority; the arch-techchie was obviously loving having this audience for his smart-ass arrogant lecture. But Piaget had to concede that the content was impressive.

The Thin Doctor now turned from Navarro to bestow another pearl of wisdom on the meeting: 'We can summarize the condition by saying simply that the psychotic takes his or her own erroneous perceptions and then proceeds to act, using a reasoning system based on these ... Thus the psychotic's base motives are often impossible to fathom, if they exist at all.'

'That doesn't get us very far, doctor,' Navarro commented.

'At present our policy should be only to understand the *threat* that the Supervisor poses and then to come up with a solution action ... As Mr Pepper hinted in his introduction, we at Metro Cybotics have a discreet interdiction vehicle: a machine which will be immune to the Supervisor's influence, the pernicious Ego system-virus, as Mr Gillespie neatly described it.'

The Thin Doctor waved a palm-clicker at the lecture screen and brought up a representation of the human brain. Piaget sat back in his chair. He recognized the screen from the very first presentation the Doctor had given him, all those weeks back ... He was going to go for the whole thing; he couldn't resist giving this crowd the big build-up. Piaget listened, watching the group round the table as the Thin Doctor warmed to his task.

Piaget noted with considerable pleasure the Electro-corp tecchies' expressions of scepticism when the Thin Doctor suggested to them that a robot with a biological brain could exist. The Doctor's presentation was calculated to generate the maximum of surprise. First of all he showed some flicks of the cat cyborg, edited with sequences from the actual transplant operation. Then he progressed to the ape-brained machine. Piaget watched as the two Electrocorp tecchies steadily became transfixed.

The Thin Doctor spent some time dwelling on the ape cyborg, almost suggesting that this was the machine which he planned to use to destroy the Supervisor. He explained that the employment of a biologically driven droid to infiltrate the Electrocorp Tower was the only way in which the Supervisor could be taken out. A cyborg's trump card was that such a machine would not be perceived as a threat by the defending droids. On the contrary, a cyborg would be interpreted by the military droids' sensors as an ally.

The Electrocorp tecchies conceded that this would probably be the case. There was a further bonus in that a biological intelligence system would be immune to the Supervisor's Ego virus. The Electrocorp people nodded their agreement again.

The Thin Doctor flipped back to his original task of explaining the development of a human-brained cyborg. He paused after he reintroduced the concept, then let the lecture screen run with a history of Coton's creation. The Thin Doctor stepped back from the screen and moved to halfway along the table, clasping his hands together in his own precious way as he watched the animation flick begin.

When the evacuation had taken place, Renata Coton had found herself rather compromised. The very moment the announcement came to the one hundred and forty-fifth floor, she was in the conference suite unloading the auto-saved notes from the write-pads of the executive management committee. To have presented herself at the floor's assembly point at that moment would almost certainly have led to a break of her cover. Instead of joining the organized exodus, she had decided to hole up in the suite's compact mess area. As things turned out, it had been a fortunate choice of location.

Not long after the tower had been cleared, Renata had monitored everything on the mess area's security console; the power was shut down: heating, lighting, air-con and the comms system, everything went dead, and she found herself in a pitch-black prison. Unsure of her surroundings, she decided to stay put and see whether the power would return. As she sat in the darkness, she remembered the stack of write-pads she'd collected. They were all self-powered and would offer her at least a little light, if only she could find them.

She steeled herself to make a move after what seemed like several hours of indecision. She was nervous about the glowing, emergency-powered motion sensor in the far corner of the ceiling. It remained steady as she managed to find her way across to the doors that led on to the exec suite quite easily. On reaching the spot, she found to her dismay that they had closed on auto when the power had gone down. She felt along the smoothness to where the two leaves interlocked; there was a small gap which she was able to work on. She had just about got the doors a hand's width apart when she heard a noise in the room beyond. She froze, locking her right fist into the gap she had created, and peered into the blackness. Something was out there, moving almost silently down the length of the narrow room. She thought about pulling her hand from between the door leaves but stopped herself when she realized that the source of the gentle humming noise had to be a droid of some kind. If it was on this floor it had to be a security droid, a droid equipped with motion *and* heat sensors. A cold sweat came over her: she knew that if the machine scanned the doors, it would immediately register her fist. She thought fast and shook her free arm out of her jacket then gingerly stuffed the material through the gap over her other fist, now dripping with the sweat running down her arm. She sat silently and awkwardly with her back against the door, blowing her no doubt blazingly hot breath away down the wall. She waited for the smash of the droid against the door; she could imagine its sensors going wild at the stream of hot air that had to be flowing out through the gap. No smash came . . . At one point she thought she detected a slight vibration in the floor as the droid went past, but she couldn't be sure. Her right hand and forearm had gone into a cramp, the only genuine sensation an effervescent tingling of trapped blood and nerves.

Renata grew tired but was too uncomfortable and too scared to sleep. Once she had made the decision to move, it took her some time to work her hand free and regain its use. The doors had remained open and, when she stood, after convincing herself that the droid had gone, she found she was able to force them apart, gripping one leaf with her hands and pushing the other with her foot. As she moved to the place where she knew she had left the write-pads on the table, she realized that the temperature of the suite had risen considerably. It must have been that which had saved her from detection.

She took the stack of tablets back into the mess area and managed to get the doors to shut back as far as the fist's width that the droid might have registered. She settled herself down with the first pad and flicked on the power. She was right; it gave her enough light to make out her immediate surroundings. Once she flicked to the last saved document, though, its contents filled her with horror. She forgot her original intention of checking out the mess area using its light and read the high security memo on the Supervisor's current status . . . and the droid's demands. She was effectively a prisoner – maybe the lights would never come on again. She found she had no idea what to do next, she could only wait. Renata noted from the pad's time matrix that she'd been stuck in the tower for fourteen hours; it was now well into the next morning. Her thoughts turned to Leach: he'd be going crazy wondering what had happened to her ... He'd be convinced that she'd been picked up and was about to blow the group's cover.

Later that morning the power returned to the suite and its mess area. Renata had heard no further noises and felt slightly better, now that she could at least see. She also needed to eat so she went to check out the mess store cabinet. She wasn't going to starve, all the racks were full of food packs; she selected an invitingly labelled sachet and dumped it into the converter. Renata waited at the gap in the doors while the machine went through its processes, but the exec suite beyond remained empty and silent.

She consumed the ready-meal, crouching by an extractor vent in the wall skirting. She was no expert on Electrocorp's droids but was taking no chances on their not having olfactory sensors. Once she had finished, she walked up and down sniffing the air in a double check, though she certainly couldn't detect any residual odour. She considered her predicament again: she had no real idea of what was going on, only that the crazy Supervisor droid had seemingly taken over the entire plant. It really was a wild situation; she was probably the only human left in the tower. She looked at the security console and wondered whether she dared boot it up. Would the central control pick up the terminal if it went on-line? She went back to the doors and squinted across the room to the suite's main workstation console; it was lit but was hellishly exposed. If anyone, or anything, came into the room while she was using that, then it would be all over. She tried to think back to her own console on the security reception; she'd looked at the network routeings many times in the past, and this mess area terminal had to be a slave-console of the suite's key station. She made the decision and returned to the small console desk.

It was excellent . . . The console booted using a proto-col through the suite's main workstation. Renata scrolled through the menu listings and summoned the City Infonet. It seemed a good idea to see the state's version of events. The lead story gave a laughable report about a major systems failure at Electrocorp: the plant had been shut down and technicians were work-ing on the fault. The whole of Industry 1 had been turned into a restricted area, due to the danger of a toxic gas release from the disrupted production pro-cesses. Well, it was plausible, she thought, not a bad effort from the Sec-services propaganda machine. There were other pieces concerning droid disturbances and more virus alerts, but anyone with half a brain could see that the city was in a state of chaos. She flicked the pages down to the personal columns; maybe Leach had inserted one of his cryptic group-messages.

The message she found wasn't cryptic at all . . . Clear as day was a plea from her freaking father for her to contact him. Renata read the announcement several times . . . No, it was for real, definitely not a Leach message . . . no dumb key-words. She read the link number; it was Central, but not her father's private address zone. She went through the columns again, but there was nothing that could be from Leach. She felt badly let down, then she thought that he could well have something to do with this request from her father. It was his latest obsession, after all . . . Could she answer it, though? That was the big question . . . Was the console hooked to transmit? And who else was going to log the outgoing message?

Renata wrestled with the options before her. To get in touch with her father, let him know where she was and completely blow all she'd worked for for the last few years, or to keep quiet and hope that she'd be able to get out of here. If she made a transmission, she also knew it would be logged and associated to this very terminal; that would immediately shorten the odds on her survival. She'd wait. Maybe there'd be a pure Leach message that would show up. He might even have worked out where she was, and perhaps he could even come up with some kind of a rescue plan. She realized she needed to sleep; she wouldn't do anything until she had a clearer head, but for now she needed to find somewhere secure. Renata looked back at the mess long food cabinet.

Clowes hadn't reckoned with the Thin Doctor's forcefulness and the real control he still exerted over the Cyborg Project. When he returned that afternoon from the Metro Cybotics meeting, he summoned her into his small study in the main facility.

'Uschi.' He was adopting his familiar tone again, and Clowes knew something was up. 'You're looking quite dreadful . . . so tired. I think you need to take some time off.'

The statement – a veiled command, it seemed – took her by surprise. 'You . . . you really think so, doctor?'

'Yes. I'm worried about you, you haven't been home in days.'

Clowes gathered her senses, her suspicions rebuilding themselves rapidly in her head. 'It's not possible, doctor. We have Coton at such a critical stage . . . I don't mean to sound vain, but I believe it's only my input right now that'll have Coton really performing up to expectations.'

The Thin Doctor toyed with Clowes' latest bulletin cart on his desk. 'I'm well aware of Coton's progress, Uschi, and naturally I value your unique talents, but you also have to take care of yourself.' The Doctor's paternal tone was also becoming strict. Before she could utter another sentence in her argument for staying with Coton, the Thin Doctor continued: 'I wasn't going to mention this, Uschi, but I have been noticing some errors and over-writes in your reports, sure signs of exhaustion. The last thing I want is for you to make a serious mistake now, just out of tiredness.'

So the doctor had noticed her adjustments to the records concerning Coton's sentience. She'd been foolish to think he wouldn't have detected the changes. Clowes sensed that she was losing the battle. She wondered whether she dared express her real concerns over the project. 'Doctor, I'm very concerned about the management of the project.' The words just spilled out, and Clowes thought she'd better continue. 'It's just that you and Piaget have hardly been around . . .'

The Thin Doctor interrupted her. 'I know I've been rather lax of late, Uschi, you're quite right . . . and our Mr Piaget, he has a lot of wider concerns that he has to busy himself with . . . It's my intention to take up the reins again now, Uschi . . . I will confide in you that there have been some new developments – you know about the city disturbances . . . We have to take the project on to a new tack.'

'Can't you tell me more, doctor?'

The Thin Doctor took a sharp intake of breath and made a pained expression. 'It's frankly rather sensitive just now . . . I'd rather brief you, once you've had some time off . . . A couple of days, Uschi, that's all I'm suggesting.'

Clowes realized that there was nothing she could do but comply with the Thin Doctor's command, short of really blowing all of her concerns into the open, and she wasn't ready for that; that had to be done on her own terms. She worried deeply at what the Thin Doctor's real motives were, but she trusted that, at base, Coton would be safe without her for two days. The doctor couldn't possibly threaten Coton's actual survival.

As she left the facility, Clowes met Piaget in the Foundation's main reception.

'On your way home, Ms Clowes?' Piaget's tone was strangely light-hearted, almost as if he knew exactly what her movements were. Clowes noted that he was carrying an Electrocorp document under his arm. He carried on past her, heading for the elevator, and there was a definite spring in his step.

Kraemer smacked his hands down on the console's control surface in frustration. The virus alert precautions had completely messed the Big Mixer's systems. There was a message waiting for him from his Infonet announcement and he couldn't access it . . . It had to be from Renata.

Coton's old man had been as good as his word, and he now had a contact name which the politician had unearthed via the Coton file reference he'd given him. This *Ursula Clowes* sounded promising, a sci-med tecchie; but she was proving difficult to contact. He had her link number, but she was constantly unavailable; she wasn't even answering the e-mail messages he'd been leaving every day. Perhaps he'd been too cryptic with the wording, and she couldn't understand what he was driving at. As Coton's father had said, he had to be sure that this woman was safe to let into his confidence. Neither he nor Coton's old man knew what her connection to Coton could be. *Tread carefully*, Jon Coton Senior had told him.

Kraemer's screen beeped again, he was back on-line. 'Right, you freakin' silicon idiot, give us the net!' Kraemer smiled at his neighbouring screen staffer who had turned to see what he was cursing at. 'Freakin' virus alert, Tawney, I can't hold a lock for two minutes . . .'

Tawney shrugged in sympathy and turned back to his own screen.

Kraemer's answer box finally appeared on the screen. He entered his personal reply box code and the text flowed in. *Here I am – Rapunzel* . . . That was it, nothing more. Kraemer looked for a reference, but there was only a blank code line. Renata, if it was Renata, had not wanted her message to be traceable. The Infonet central computer would have to have something though, Kraemer thought. He could probably get the department's Decrypt people to do him a trace – he could tell them it was a suspected Azzi TR code. He shut down his console and headed off to Decryption.

'I've got a weird one . . . I'm trying to link some possible Azzi TRs to an Infonet announcement.' Kraemer had approached Stoddart, the Intelligence Officer who now occupied Coton's old decrypt pit.

'Oh yeah? Have you got a cart?' Stoddart was still concentrating on some photo-codes on his screen.

'Er, well no, not here . . . It's just a short text line, four words. I was wondering if you could do me a quick check on the key-word . . . Run it against your Infonet check list?'

Stoddart turned and looked Kraemer up and down suspiciously. 'This *is* Sec-services business –' The Intelligence Officer read Kraemer's breast ID '– er, Kraemer? Only I've detected that this terminal's been hacked recently ... You wouldn't know anything about that, would you?'

'No, Mr Stoddart. It's been shut down ever since we lost Coton, as far as I know.'

Stoddart winked at his screen and shut down his pictures. 'OK, Kraemer, what's the key-word?' He spoke resignedly.

'Rapunzel ... Romeo Alpha ...'

'I know, I know: *Rapunzel* ... like the woman stuck in a tower ...' Stoddart clicked the word into his console.

'A woman, Mr Stoddart?'

'Yeah, a fairy-tale character ... You knew Coton well, didn't you?' Stoddart kept his eye on the scrolling checker as he spoke.

'Yes, quite well,' Kraemer answered vacantly, his thoughts on Renata.

'Hmm ... You could be in business, Kraemer. I've got two references ... *Here I am* – *Rapunzel* ... that's a box answer ... and then an announcement ... *Leach* – *Rapunzel can't let her hair down* ... That's Azzi stuff all right ... Crazy.'

'Two references, Mr Stoddart?'

'That's what I just gave you ... Two ... Hang on ...' Stoddart ran a security check on the names and pointed to the listings on the screen. 'There, look at Leach ... A screen-full of records, but your *Rapunzel* doesn't give us anything. She could be a new operator, another hacker cashing in on the disturbances.'

'And you've got no sender codes for any of the messages?'

'No, Kraemer, they're all secure.'

'Who was Rapunzel again?' Kraemer felt he needed to clarify the reference.

'Some princess locked in a tower by a wicked witch. She had really long hair that a knight could climb up and rescue her . . . Happy?'

'Yeah, I think so . . . Locked in a tower . . .' Kraemer mumbled wistfully.

'Take a break, Kraemer . . . If you need any more, come and see me. You can tell me about Coton next time; he was some kind of a hero, wasn't he?'

CHAPTER THIRTEEN

Renata emptied her bag on to the work surface next to a water flask she'd found and the pile of ready-meal sachets she'd just run through the processor. She had to move fast now that she'd sent the messages to the Infonet. It wasn't much of a survival kit: the data-manager, the tab-cartridge, her small portable voice set and the home-made cigarette lighter Leach had given her. She selected the items which she could still fit in the bag; the food sachets and the water flask took priority – she couldn't know how long she'd be on the run from the droids. The bag bulged and she was able to slip in only the lighter and the portable from among her personal effects.

She decided that her immediate target had to be to reach somewhere where she could get the portable to work, a window or a maintenance hatch. Once she'd got a message out, then she could concentrate on descending through the tower. She thought back to her cryptic – hopefully droid-fooling – messages on the Infonet. They *had* been a little silly, but Leach would suss it out. Heaven only knew what her father would make of his message ... So what, the old bastard couldn't really be bothered about her, but he had seemed to freak out when he saw her at the memorial service.

Renata moved quickly into the exec suite and reached the exit leading to the corridor. She was now faced with choosing her moment to open the blank doors. She went for it straight away; there could be droids along at any minute. The double doors parted silently and she eased her head out into the corridor – it was clear, no signs of life. Only a small swirl of rubbery dust on the polished floor betrayed the fact that a robot had recently turned outside the room – the droid from last night, Renata guessed. The whole of this floor was exec management, there was little reason for any machine to be active, Renata told herself – if any droid was around, it could only be one looking to investigate the mess area console. She cursed as she reasoned away in her search for some comfort, then slipped out of the door and moved carefully down the short corridor towards a blind T-junction.

It had taken Clowes three hours to get home; the A-trains had been completely disrupted by the disturbances and she'd had to take a circular diversion to reach her local station. One of her fellow commuters told her that the system was being run manually. Not reassuring, as the driverless cars bulleted along at two hundred clicks per minute. The whole of the city was markedly darker than usual; more than half the blocks were in total shut-down, as there was a power conservation programme in operation. Following events on the Infonet had not prepared her for the real scale of the disruption that Metropolis 4 was suffering. Clowes felt she had probably been spending too much time in the Cyborg Facility.

As she entered her dim apartment she could see immediately the glow of the e-mail indicator on her workstation. Who could that be? The Thin Doctor calling her back, or Dabbs even ... She hoped not, but she couldn't imagine anyone else; after all, she still had no social contacts in M4. She opened the menu to find a whole file jammed with repeat messages going back four days. 'Urgent, or what?' She spoke out loud as she winked at the security icon. *Ursula Clowes please contact E. Kraemer – re – ex-tile – not a ceramic material – geddit?* There was a Central link number following, unusual for nuisance mail, Clowes thought. But this couldn't be nuisance mail – it was too weird; maybe she just ought to contact E. Kraemer straight away, Clearly this person desperately wanted to get in touch, but he or she wanted her to know something else too ... She read the word puzzle again; it was probably one of those competitions: you had to come up with a linking word and then you won yourself a thousand credits or something. 'Ex-tile, not ceramic, but some kind of material.' She spoke at the screen. Then realization dawned on her ... 'T-extile ... Cotton ... Minus a T ...' Co-ton, stupid, but which one ...? J. D. or Renata? And who the hell was Kraemer?

Clowes tried the number, but there was no live link, so she decided to leave a message. 'Right then, E. Kraemer, try this for size ...' She tapped her own code into the machine. *A little crude, your puzzle – Best regards from a certain interested UC.* Clowes looked at the text line and decided that it was definitely worse than E. Kraemer's. Still, the code was discreet enough to exclude anyone who couldn't think beyond the use of 'UC' as the short name for *underclass*; she was sure that E. Kraemer would understand. She clicked *send*, and in a few seconds a receipt message confirmed back.

The following morning, as she stood in the shower letting the water soothe her body, Clowes considered that the Thin Doctor had been right: she *had* been pretty well stressed out. She stretched her arms above her head and felt the tension across her shoulders. As she repeated the action she found herself able to reach higher and higher, until she could just touch the ceiling-mounted shower-head. Never before had her body been so tight, and she pledged to herself that she would take proper exercise: a walk or even a run in the snow outside, perhaps. It was wonderful. Here she was at eleven in the morning on a weekday, and all she had planned was getting some fresh air. But before that she'd have a proper café breakfast in the small real-club she'd noticed on her block. She had to eat, and today she could enjoy something better than the facility's flavourless fare.

She was at the door, just on the point of leaving for her breakfast when the workstation trilled an incoming e-mail message. She nearly ignored it, but her curiosity about E. Kraemer got the better of her – it had to be Kraemer. She walked across the apartment to the machine. The text line built along the top of the screen: *Thanks UC – we must meet – important – name place and time – This evening? After 9 – Confirm ASAP – EK.* Clowes thought for a second then logged-on to E. Kraemer's live link. She rapped out a quick reply: *Real-Club Azzocial 9.30 – How will I know you?* Clowes waited for the return, which came in a few seconds: *I'll know you – Till later – EK.* The link went dead. 'Creepy ...' Clowes uttered the word aloud. 'And me in the RCA on my own – I must be going mad.' Clowes reckoned she didn't really know any other location where she could be at that time of night, and she certainly didn't want E. Kraemer to visit her apartment. She felt her holiday mood dissolving and her thoughts ran back to Coton. There was something about the

Kraemer messages that made her feel that he or she was sympathetic. It was intuition, she trusted her intuition.

The real-club at the end of the block was closed. A notice running on the display on the security blind explained that, due to the disturbances, they had to operate within city-directed opening times. Clowes pondered the information and predicted that this was going to be a problem in all the clubs in her neighbourhood. The street was certainly quiet. When she looked down the gentle slope to the distant boulevard, the traffic flow was thin and intermittent. She decided to walk down to Central 1; there was bound to be more activity down there, and the real-clubs would certainly be open. On her way, Clowes read more and more notices and they all said the same thing: restrictions imposed due to the disturbances. She wondered if the RCA would still be operating; after all, the Thin Doctor had told her that it was only *tolerated* by the authorities. Perhaps her choice of rendezvous had not been so clever with hindsight – but she'd find out soon enough. She'd cruise the place first in a hire-mobile.

Even though she'd promised herself that she wouldn't use the power-tracks in Central, she needn't have bothered, as they were all stationary. There were more notices explaining the power conservation measures that were in force; the city had really been transformed. Every minute she saw new Sec-services mobiles winding their way independently through the stagnant, auto-routed, civilian vehicles.

Clowes found it wryly amusing that, when eventually she found an operating real-club, it was only just round the corner from the Sci-Medical Foundation. She took a seat in the window and ordered breakfast. While she ate, she browsed through the table-top Infonet console; it was full of reports of shortages and transport divert information. There was a big feature on the complete shut-down of Electrocorp, and this made Clowes think back to the Supervisor. What would they be doing with her? How could she survive without her support team? It was probably all propaganda anyway; there were often digs at Electrocorp on the Infonet, the city-run information service had a bit of a complex about the company. There was concern in political circles over the sheer trading power of the massive corporation.

A small disturbance at the counter at the back of the real-club caused Clowes to turn around from her reading. The bar was empty and the sound of two voices in dispute carried across to her, sitting in the corner of the window bay. The manager seemed to be refusing to supply a customer with whatever it was that had been ordered. It was the odd gulpy protestations of the customer which really grabbed Clowes' attention, though; it was Dabbs ... What the hell was he doing outside the facility? And in such a public place? Clowes held back from going over to him and concentrated on the exchange. Dabbs seemed to be collecting some genuine coffee for the Thin Doctor but the credit float on whatever card he was using was insufficient to cover the bill. Clowes was surprised as she overheard the value of the commodity. Dabbs gulped on about disruptions in the credit system and reminded the bar manager as to the identity of the actual end-user, the famous and undeniably wealthy Thin Doctor. The manager finally relented and handed over the goods.

Dabbs was making a bee-line for the exit when Clowes called out to him. 'Dabbs! Dabbs ... Over here!'

The technician froze when he saw Clowes sitting there. A look of confused panic wrote itself across his face.

'Dabbs ... What's wrong? Come over here.' Clowes spoke solicitously, seeing the technician's desperate nervousness in this public space.

'C ... Clowes ... Why are you here?' There was heavy suspicion in his voice.

'Just getting something to eat.' Clowes balanced Dabbs' tone with exaggerated innocence. 'Everywhere's shut at home.'

'Th ... Then you don't know?'

'Don't know what, Dabbs? Sit down ... Tell me.'

Dabbs moved awkwardly. Clowes thought for a moment that he was going to make a run for it, then he sat down on the chair opposite her. What was it he had to tell her?

'Oogh ... Er, it's C ... Coton, w ... we ... we've moved him.'

'Where? What've you done? Tell me exactly ...' Clowes felt all of her morning's relaxation activity wind itself back in. 'Settle down, Dabbs. You've got to tell me what the Thin Doctor's been doing.'

Dabbs looked around as though the Thin Doctor were going to leap out from under a table at any minute.

'It's all right, Dabbs ... If the Doctor's sent you out, he won't be coming out himself, OK? Come on, tell me what's been going on.'

Dabbs concentrated hard then blurted out: 'W ... We've had to put Coton into a new chassis!'

Clowes saw the bar manager pause in his activities and look over at the odd couple. She waved her hands at Dabbs, urging him to quieten down; she couldn't believe what she was hearing. 'A new chassis? What new chassis?' she half hissed.

'The c ... combat chassis, Clowes, the one we made for the ape cyborg.' Dabbs looked afraid of his interrogator.

'Wait ... Wait ... Dabbs ... *There's another chassis? There's always been another chassis?* Why the hell didn't you tell me!'

'I thought we'd junked it, Clowes ... The new proper chassis is so good, I didn't think we could ever go back to the metal one.'

'Coton is now in a *metal combat chassis?* Did you do this last night? No wonder the doctor wanted me out of the way.' It was getting worse by the second.

'Oogh ... The doctor said you wouldn't understand,' Dabbs gulped.

'Too freaking right, Dabbs! How could you go along with all this, did you assist in the transfer?'

'I ... I had no choice ... The doctor took Coton into theatre on his own. When he called me in, he already had Coton's cranial floor on bypass and the combat chassis waiting.'

Clowes halted her interrogation as it all sank in. She'd betrayed Coton, left him to the *Mad Professor* just when she knew in her bones that the man had some secret agenda. She'd walked out on him, the poor devil. What kind of state would he be in? She remembered Coton's voice begging her to help him two nights ago.

'How's Coton then, Dabbs? Is he sentient?'

'Hmm ... Yes, he is. H ... He's still on monitoring umbilicals, but he's all there. Piaget's in with him now. There's some kind of briefing going on. Then the doctor sent me out here.'

'So Coton's fine? Is he talking and everything?'

'Yes, Clowes, he seems as good as he was in the humanoid chassis. He can talk ... walk ... everything ... He's just still hooked up, that's all.'

'How do *you* feel, Dabbs?' Clowes realized that she'd just given the poor technician a real battering.

'I ... I'm not sure. But Coton's OK ... really, he is ... What are you going to do?'

Clowes snorted, non-plussed at Dabbs' question. She hadn't a clue at that moment ... Should she rush around to the facility right away? No, that wouldn't be sensible; both she and Dabbs would be dismissed at once ... She paused even longer, remembering her appointment with the mysterious E. Kraemer.

'Clowes ... I'll have to go back,' Dabbs said, as though he was expecting her to suggest otherwise.

'I know you do, Dabbs ... Look ... Give me some time. You'll have to try and carry on as normally as you can. I'll be back in the facility tomorrow night, maybe earlier ... and if anything else happens ... if they physically move Coton ... let me know, use the e-mail to my apartment.'

'OK, Clowes. I'll be off then ... S ... Sorry ...'

Dabbs shuffled out from the tight space at the table and left the real-club. Clowes watched the progress of the funny little man through the window. She noticed him stumble as he caught his thick-soled shoes on the dead power-sidewalk.

Renata had had a long day in the tower; so far she had managed to avoid detection, as far as she knew. It had taken her an age to wind her way through the exec floor's passages. Every junction she'd reached presented a heart-stopping choice: exactly when to make her move round its blind corner. She cursed herself for not having brought her make-up set's mirror; it could have helped her get some kind of a look before having to risk poking her head out, round into she knew not what. She had finally made it to the management floor's reception area; she knew that across the open space, by the elevator shaft, there was a services access hatch. All she had to do was turn the next corner and jump the security gates. Renata eased her head round the smooth curve of the corner; the broad radius forced her to be more exposed than she would have liked. She flattened herself against the cool wall, which pressed her sweat-dampened suit across her shoulder-blades. She shuddered at the sensation and edged out a little, still inching her way forward.

The droid took her completely by surprise; it stepped backwards, its foot gently pressing hers against the wall-skirting as its head panned the elevator bay opposite. Renata had no option but to remain where she was. The mad thought entered her head that the only way she could avoid detection was to shadow the three-metre giant. She waited for the robot to move, praying that its head couldn't do a three-sixty. The bright-red sentry droid held its position for some long minutes then stepped forward from the wall towards the security gates. Renata trod hedgingly in its footsteps as it advanced towards her desired destination.

Two levels above, on the Chromium Programme's Floor One, the Supervisor completed another circuit of monitoring banks in the nil-static zone. She paused as a double blip interrupted the rhythm of the single-pass signals from the security console. She morph-turned, her form sucking in on itself then pushing back out as she now faced in the opposite direction. The process sent blue zags of static ripping from her feet across to the collector nodes at the edge of the insulated floor. There was an intruder: none of her droids passed through the security gates in pairs.

Renata melted away sideways as the droid stepped into the elevator, and she leapt for the access hatch, The cover opened mercifully easily and she tumbled into the unknown space. As her eyes accustomed themselves to the dimness, she found that she was in a small cube of a room, its scant illumination coming from an indicator panel on the wall above. She noticed a ladder in the corner, leading up to a circular trap. She had just stepped across to the foot of the ladder when she heard a clunk against the access hatch. She was halfway up it when the security droid's fist piled through the composite material, sending leaves of shattered laminate slicing towards her. Renata kicked herself up the last few rungs and spun the trap's locking ring open. The droid's arm had extended well into the room and was flailing around viciously as she clamped the cover shut again.

She was now standing on the roof of the box; dull thumps shuddered through the structure and she knew she had to keep moving, since the droid was probably powerful enough to rip its way into the cube below. It was freezing in the services shaft. Renata peered over the edge but could see only a dwindling series of light haloes in both directions, up and down. There was a deafening crash and the platform lurched across the void – the heavy robot had entered the box. She leapt for the cable trunking now zooming towards her and thrust her hands into an open slat of the carrier panelling. She hung on, breathless, and looked down to see the box break from the side of the shaft and tumble away in a cloud of dust and sparks. The stink of burning insulation swept past her, borne on fresher air. There had to be some access to the outside from here – a vent maybe, where she could switch her voice set to transmit and get a message to Leach. She began to climb upwards.

Clowes felt stupid, she hadn't even considered that the RCA people wouldn't take her credit card. She was just about to manoeuvre herself back out of the cramped entrance when a fresh-faced young man reached across her.

'I'll get that . . .' The young man slid two cash tokens under the scratched perspex screen. 'Come on, Urs . . .'

Kraemer took Clowes' elbow and guided her gently along the dingy passageway to the head of the stairs that led down into the club.

'Not a good choice, Urs.' Kraemer kept his voice low. 'This place is crawling with every kind of filth.'

'Kraemer, if you insist on using my first name, call me Uschi . . .' Clowes didn't quite know what to make of this strange individual; she had no real clue to his motives here tonight. They descended the precipitous staircase together without further words as the bright sound of natural music rose in clipped bubbles of noise up the slanting shaft.

Clowes led the way from the stairs and headed for the alcoves where she had sat with the Thin Doctor on her first visit; she knew they would be able to talk there. Clowes settled herself in the centre of the curve of the seating, from where she commanded a clear view of the crowd at the bar. Kraemer chose to sit next to her – a little too close for her comfort.

Kraemer opened the conversation. 'So why should a

non-city slicker like you choose this place, Uschi? Do you know the reputation the RCA's got?'

'Yes . . .' Clowes felt indignant at Kraemer's labelling. 'I've been here before.'

'But you didn't pay for anything, though . . . Didn't you realize this was all cash down here? Nobody wants to be traced on a credit check.'

'OK, that was a bit dumb . . . You start then, Kraemer. What's your interest in Coton, the *ex-tile*?' Clowes smiled, she hoped slightly intriguingly.

Kraemer raised his hand at a waiter at that moment. 'Drink, Uschi?'

Clowes ordered a water and Kraemer followed suit.

'Yes, Coton . . .' Kraemer seemed to think for a second. 'I picked up your name from a Sec-services file . . . You know him, don't you?' Kraemer used the present tense intentionally.

'I asked *you* to start, Kraemer . . . I'm saying nothing until you lay your cards on the table . . . And what does the "*E*" stand for, anyway?'

Kraemer grinned and pushed at a drinks mat with a forefinger. 'It's Eugene, but I prefer Kraemer, thanks.' He picked up the mat and flicked it against the knuckles of his other hand. 'OK, Uschi, you seem cool . . . I'll level with you . . . I used to work with Coton, in the Big Mixer, the Sec-services tower. I still do . . . work in the tower, that is . . . Now you can understand why I'm not too thrilled to be here.' Kraemer lowered his voice even more. 'I'm Sec-services . . . a monitoring staffer.'

Clowes almost believed him, but she thought she'd try a further little indicator test. 'Does the name *Piaget* mean anything to you?'

'Hah . . .' Kraemer made the exclamation with some feeling. Clowes felt herself relate to its sound with an odd sympathy. 'Piaget ... He used to be my boss ... and Coton's. He's now the ex-Floor Commandant of Comms Monitoring, engaged in other duties, as I understand ... Now I suddenly get the feeling you might just know what those are ... Am I right?'

'You could be, Kraemer ... Describe Piaget for me, will you?'

'You are *one* cagey woman, Uschi ... Your stuff's going to have to be good after this.'

'You may be surprised.' Clowes was wondering just how much she could tell Kraemer. 'Be really honest about Piaget, I can guarantee none of this will go any further.' Perhaps if Kraemer's view of Piaget tallied with her own, she could really be open with this Sec-services guy.

Kraemer started into his description. Just his detailed observations concerning Piaget's physical appearance convinced Clowes that he was on intimate terms with the man. As he continued, he slipped into a complete history of the events leading up to Coton's Lander crash, then he went into greater detail about his further investigations. Clowes listened, fascinated, as she heard all the references to Coton, Piaget and Renata from this different perspective. There was only a small interruption when their drinks arrived. Clowes encouraged Kraemer to complete his story; the young staffer's guilelessness was clear. She had to really hold herself back from breaking into his tale to put him straight.

Kraemer drained his glass and leant back, stretching his arms along the top of the upholstery. 'Enough cards on the table for you?'

'Plenty, Kraemer.' Clowes smiled in gratitude at how he'd opened up. 'Two decks' worth at least.'

'Do you think I'm stupid, telling you all that stuff? I

know nothing about you ... Only that you're a sci-med tecchie and that you've had something to do with Coton in the past months ... Can you help me with any of this?'

Kraemer's last question, loaded to overflowing with irony, made Clowes shake her head in genuine bafflement at where she should start.

'Uschi?' Kraemer sounded worried.

'Prepare yourself for a shock, Krae –'

A dull bang from the foot of the entrance stairway cut Clowes' sentence and more bangs followed in quick succession. All hell broke loose in the club.

'You bitch, Uschi ... Freakin' bitch!' Kraemer screamed at her.

Clowes gasped as she saw trailing whips of white foam lash across the crowd at the bar. Glue guns ... crowd-control devices. The drinkers scattered, tumbling over one another as they were caught in the strands of epoxy. Kraemer was on his feet, glancing around, uncertain what to do next. There was now shouting, accompanied by bright lights bleaching out the bar as a Sec-services riot squad moved in.

'Get back here, Kraemer! Get down!' Clowes had noticed fleeing figures purposefully skirting past the alcoves; they were heading for the exit underneath the club, the one the Thin Doctor had talked about. Clowes rushed at Kraemer and grabbed him, dragging him along as another person disappeared behind the alcoves.

'Shut it, Kraemer ... Come on!' Clowes pulled harder as Kraemer held back. 'If you want to get out, you'd better move it ...' He seemed to get the message at last and now pushed Clowes on, into the near-complete blackness where the row of alcoves ended. A weak

264

glow was coming from a hole in the floor behind the partitioning, where a man was standing, holding an open hatch-cover. He said nothing, but gestured emphatically for them to hurry. Kraemer followed Clowes as she carefully began to negotiate the vertical ladder down into the bottom half of the disused pressure reservoir.

Clowes was aware of three or four more people entering through the hatch before she heard it clank shut. She looked down and could make out a steel-decked platform, a few metres below; it seemed to hang suspended in the gloom of the hemisphere. She glanced up to see where Kraemer was on the ladder: his progress seemed slow. As she pushed her arms straight, craning to look upwards, a warm spot of fluid splashed on the side of her nose; the fluid ran down to the corner of her mouth and she tasted blood. She spat, disgusted, then began to worry, wondering how he could be injured, as more spots fell on her.

Clowes waited on the platform while Kraemer eased himself slowly down towards her. She told the impatient escapees cursing above him that he was injured and two of them swung round the ladder and passed Kraemer on the other side, leaving another two, possibly three, above him. The two impatient UCs – they had to be, Clowes thought – scowled at her as they landed on the platform, but then they hurried on to a narrow walkway which led out into the centre of the hemisphere. Clowes watched them slow as they reached a point in the middle where the single handrail had completely rusted away. The two men dropped to straddle the open steel planking and continued shuffling towards another platform that she could just begin to make out in the poor lighting.

Kraemer had caught his calf on the jagged sawn metalwork below the hatch opening; it was a nasty gash and needed proper attention. Clowes made him sit on the platform while she ripped a sleeve from her jacket to make a bandage. She had only just finished binding the wound when the pinprick lights in the roof of the hemisphere flickered then went out one by one.

'Oh shit, that's torn it.' Clowes spoke under her breath as she fumbled with the final adjustments to the bandage on Kraemer's leg.

'The bandage or just *it*, Uschi?' Kraemer was in some relief, both at his escape from the riot squad and the skilful attention he'd just received from the sci-med tecchie.

'*It*, I reckon ... Can you make it over the walkway? Did you see it? It's about half a metre wide, with no handrail in the middle.'

'Just give me a few minutes to rest ... then I'll have a go.'

'I hope we've got the time, Kraemer; the riot squad'll find the hatch, you can count on it.'

'Nah, they won't find it ... They've been paid off ... Freakin' bastards.' Another voice spoke in the darkness. 'You've got all night. I'll get down to the bottom an' see if I can get some light back on.' Clowes felt a touch on her shoulder and heard someone shuffle away in the direction of the walkway. It was absolutely pitch black.

'Thanks ...' Clowes called after the toucher.

'Sorry about that upstairs, Uschi. Only when you said ...'

'Prepare yourself for a shock ...' Clowes interrupted him. 'I couldn't believe it either. You were freaked, Kraemer, it's almost funny now.'

A loud bang made them both jump. 'Not again?' Kraemer half laughed.

'I think it must be our friends trying to break out down there.' Clowes remembered the Thin Doctor's mention of the port to the freightway. 'I hope they're not going to crack open a pressure seal. Did you know this is an old pressure reservoir, Kraemer?'

'I guessed it had to be something other than a club basement. Can we continue our talk, Uschi? You were going to shock me, remember?'

'Well, I don't know ... It's a hell of a story, even better than yours. How long are we going to be stuck here?'

'Look, I'm not going to move until they get some lights back on. Tell me now, here.'

'Someone might hear us.' Clowes was nervous about speaking in the dark.

'They all went past us, Uschi ... And who the hell's going to hear us with all that going on?' By now the banging below had assumed a regular rhythm.

'OK, Kraemer ... Get ready for a shock then ... Coton's alive ... in a manner of speaking ...'

'F ... F ...' The surprise needed no face for Clowes to enjoy it in the darkness.

'Don't interrupt, Kraemer, just listen.'

Clowes told her story, sparing Kraemer no detail; she knew how he felt about Coton and his opinions about Piaget. The whole thing stank of some conspiracy and, as Coton's father had told Kraemer, it was time for people to pool their intelligence and resources.

'I don't know whether to laugh or cry, Uschi,' Kraemer muttered in genuine amazed bewilderment. 'Coton a freakin' robot. He must be going out of his mind.'

'I've already told you, Kraemer, he's really pretty

together, all things considered, but I don't know how he'll be in this combat chassis.'

'And he's being prepared for some special mission that you're not supposed to know about. It's just too crazy to be real.'

'It *is* crazy, Kraemer, but it's damned real, too . . . And a *special mission*, just let me work this through . . .'

'Go on then, doc . . .'

'Coton's sister, your *Rapunzel* message has to mean something . . . and did I tell you about the Thin Doctor's reaction to Renata? Do you think it's Electrocorp that's screwing up the whole city?'

'The rumours have always been there, Uschi, right from the first virus alert.'

'I'm getting a horrible feeling about the Supervisor . . . I think she's taking over . . . And Coton's the guy who's been given the job of taking her out. Now does that sound crazy, Kraemer?'

'No more crazy than us stuck in a hole in the ground on a Wednesday evening, surrounded by crazy Azzi dope-dealers.' Kraemer laughed. 'Am I dreaming? Did I buy anything upstairs?'

'Who the freak *are* you guys?' Clowes and Kraemer were interrupted by a voice from the darkness. 'And what the freak are you doing *here*?'

'Hello?' Clowes waved her arm back behind her, and there came a scraping noise as someone moved across to them from the far side of the platform. 'Have you been here all the time? Whoever you are.'

'All the time and every word logged, *Uschi, Staffer Kraemer.*'

'OK . . . So who are *you*, then?' Clowes braced herself, anticipating a physical attack.

'You might say I'm an interested party. My name's

Leach, a *crazy Azzi dope-dealer* and the guy who lives with Renata Coton ... When she's not stuck in Robotics Towers or being impersonated by silver droids, that is ... Yep, I heard every freakin' word ... which maybe makes it your lucky day, don't you think?'

Kraemer started laughing.

'Clarky! Get us a light up here! There's some people we need to get down,' Leach shouted down to the banging crew in the bottom of the hemisphere. 'Whatever you do, keep it stumm on who you are ... I'll get you somewhere safe, then we can talk.'

The motley group of Azzi 'teamsters', as Leach referred to them, had broken the seals on the access to another shaft leading out of the pressure vessel. Unlike the steep stairway entrance to the club in the top half of the sphere, this shaft was broad and inclined gently upwards. It had originally been used for bringing maintenance machinery into the freightway. One of their number, a shortish, wicked-looking individual called Wood, led the way. He had an apparently encyclopedic knowledge of the freightway system under Industry 2; he claimed to have been involved in creating the Real-Club Azzocial. He also boasted that it had been he who had secured the services of the Kings, the undeniably talented band who supplied the live music most nights. Clowes began to lose interest in his stories, once he began to explain how he'd inspired Billy August, the band's xylophone player, to write their cult hit, *Metropolitan Rhapsody*.

'Can it, Wood!' Leach called from the rear of the procession as they made their way up the tunnel. 'He used to be a maintenance monkey on the freightway ... Now he does a bit of software piracy and sorts ent-systems for rage parties.'

'He seems to know his way around, though,' Clowes replied.

'Yeah, he's good, but you have to tell him where to get off every now and then. He'll certainly keep your buddy Kraemer company – a captive audience, he loves that . . .'

Kraemer was at the head of the group being helped along by two of the Azzis, his leg having become almost useless after the descent from the platform.

They emerged from the access tunnel into a large, empty shed – empty, apart from a row of four dusty mobiles ranged in the middle of the building. Their humped shapes looked strangely animal in the cold light from the lamps high in the roof frames. Clowes looked to Leach to initiate their next move.

'Follow Wood . . . This is our little emergency fleet. I guess we'll have to use 'em tonight.'

Leach's apartment was small and spartan. The furniture was an odd collection of pieces, obviously picked up from the junk heaps of sector clearance projects, since no two items matched. In a corner, though, Clowes noticed the curving lines of a new model workstation under a grubby dust-sheet. As she continued her visual inspection, Wood and Clarky pushed past her and lowered Kraemer on to a low, foam-padded couch. Kraemer called after them as they silently made their exit, but his thanks seemed to go unheard. He looked at Leach as if in apology.

'Don't worry about 'em, Kraemer, they're both out of it . . . Were they smoking in the moby?'

'Er, yes, they were.'

'There y'go, then . . . We've got some dynamite stuff just now. Might be good for the leg . . . You want some? What d'you say, doc?' Leach turned to Clowes.

'Always listen to the patient, he's usually right. Do you want anything, Kraemer? It might ease the pain.'

Kraemer shifted on the couch and shook his head, saying he wanted to keep it clear. Leach took the initiative that Kraemer had hinted at.

'OK then ... Let's get this together ... We all know what we want: you want your cyborg back and I want Renna ...'

Leach had an amazing collection of intelligence from Electrocorp. He had lists of Chromium Programme staff and progress reports going back to the start of the project; Renata Coton had certainly been a useful plant. He concurred with Clowes' suspicions about the Supervisor: Renata had reported that the machine seemed to be only barely under the control of the Programme's management. He explained the story of Rapunzel to Kraemer and Clowes and told them how there could be no doubt that the evil sorceress in the fairy-tale had to be a metaphor for the Supervisor. Leach was very well up on fantasy tales – they seemed to sit well with his idealism.

It was interesting to Clowes that Leach seemed to be clearly as afraid of anarchy as was the state itself; he professed great love for an organized society. His azzi motives lay in seeking a means to reset the imbalance that lay between the exploiters and the exploited. The Electrocorp company and its Supervisor droid were to him and his sympathizers the very embodiment of all that was wrong with the system. It was Leach's opinion that Electrocorp was pursuing a blind policy of relentless progress with no apparent regard for the real consequences of their actions. The Supervisor, or a similar development, was for Leach an inevitable disastrous result of their activities. His only hope now was

271

that the situation could be resolved and that lessons would be drawn from this crazy experiment.

Clowes was not surprised when Leach proceeded to condemn the whole Cyborg Project as well, and she found herself drawing closer to the Azzi as he put the project into its global context. She pursued her argument about how she had joined the project, initially disregarding her suspicions concerning the Thin Doctor. It was Coton's life that had been the most important factor to her at the time, but then she conceded that the pure science of the Cyborg Project had also been a powerful hook.

Eventually Kraemer had to interrupt their discussion in order to bring them back on track: how they were going to deal with the immediate problem before them. 'Look, forget the freaking philosophy, will you. We've got to get Coton and Renata out of there.' He was feeling pain from his leg and was tiring of this debate. 'I'm going to contact Coton's old man again and get him to put some political weight into this thing. What the freak are you guys going to do?'

Clowes gave up her struggle to justify her involvement and acknowledged Kraemer's point. 'I need to get back to the Foundation's Facility as soon as I can and see if I can catch Coton ... We still don't know if we're right about all this. You realize we're still only guessing about this *mission* for him.'

'I think it's a pretty well-judged guess, Uschi,' Leach added.

'I've got to get Coton away from the Thin Doctor. Can you help us with that, Leach?'

'I can supply you with my teamsters, if you have a plan, and we can fix a safe house for him. But what about the support he needs? And you forget the deal we've gotta have ... I have to have Renna back.'

'Can't you do that yourselves, Leach? You've got your people ...'

'Don't worry, I'll be doing what I can, but the whole of Industry One's been sealed off ... Your cyborg's going to be in the tower; you've got to brief him about Renna.'

'I will ... But if I can stop him going, then I'll do just that ...'

'And leave Renna to the Supervisor ... You don't care, do you?' Leach interrupted, getting angry. 'We've got to have our deal, Uschi. Your cyborg, Renna's freakin' brother, remember ... It's got to be him who's going to do the white knight bit ... Even if you catch up with Coton – though I doubt it, the way you say this Thin Doctor is ... then you're going to have to tell him about his sister. He'll make up his own mind then ... It's not your freakin' choice.'

'Leach is right, Uschi ... It's got to be down to what Coton wants to do,' Kraemer butted in.

Clowes knew Leach was right and she apologized as she agreed with him.

'Right then ... I'll fix up a safe house and get my guys together, and I'll wait for your instructions. Either from you, or from you, Kraemer ... I'm going to get you out of here now ... And you, Kraemer, just watch what you say to Coton's old man ... No names no places ...'

Leach got Kraemer and Clowes on to an A-train back towards Central; it was a limited service, packed with job-sharers travelling to their first slot of the day. Clowes and Kraemer had to stand. A thought occurred to her as she was asking rather rhetorically after Kraemer's leg – he was grimacing with every smooth sway of the car. 'So they never found Walker after the accident?'

'Nope, no trace.'

'Do you think that might be a little suspicious? Knowing what we know now.'

'Hmm.' Kraemer paused, still suffering with the pain. 'Maybe, Uschi . . .'

Clowes could see he wasn't concentrating. She let it ride.

CHAPTER FOURTEEN

The Lander shuddered as the pilot engaged full thrust to lift the craft from the makeshift apron in the City Park. Coton watched Central 1's shimmering horizon swing away below the window line as the Lander banked east towards the darkened industrial sector of the city. He certainly felt no queasiness in his new body: there was no reminder of the sense of physical frailty that used to haunt him when he set out on missions in his previous, *more human* form. But quite how he felt beyond that he wasn't sure. He had only just begun to explore the sensations of his first composite chassis, Dabbs' pride and joy, and now here he was in the combat version, a combination of flux joints and titan-steel sculpted plates. There was little sense of a wholeness in this form; his only nerve sensors were located in his hands, great knuckly articulations, and he had stress and friction transducers in his joints and on his feet. He felt impervious and invincible, but little else.

Piaget sat across from him in the passenger bay, looking nervously towards the flight deck. Coton could see the sweat beads multiplying on his forehead – he hated flying, Coton remembered. Piaget brushed his brow with the back of his hand and looked back at Coton. He uttered a croak, then cleared his throat. 'Back in the service, eh, Coton?'

Coton couldn't believe the banality of the comment. Piaget was struggling to relate to him after the subterfuge of the Cyborg Project. Coton hadn't known what had hit him when Piaget had appeared that morning with his briefing materials. His recollections of the Floor Commandant had just about all slotted into place – and then he had turned up and launched into this fantastic mission plan against the megalomaniac Supervisor droid.

'How're you feeling?'

'Cool, Piaget, extremely cool.'

'That's good then . . .'

Coton had only had a short time to test his new chassis. The Thin Doctor and Dabbs had reorganized the gymnasium and filled it with various heavy objects in addition to the existing physical exercise equipment. He'd been encouraged to experiment with lifting great lumps of steel and concrete while the two tecchies fussed around with his power settings. His strength was amazing, though: in addition to being able to handle dead weights of over half a ton, his hammer-like fists could punch holes in sheets of mild steel. He remembered how Piaget had hovered behind the glass screen of the gym, his expression somewhere between terror and awe at what he was witnessing.

'Piaget . . .' Coton called out to his ex-commandant, who had gone back to concentrating on the flight crew. No way was he going to start referring to him as 'sir'.

'Y . . . Yes, Coton?'

'Relax . . . It's me doing this thing. You're going to drop me off, and then you're out of it.' Coton felt the lag in his voice as he spoke. This combat chassis' synthesizer was nowhere near as good as the one on the original chassis: there was no compressor, no mechanical parts, and it was so disembodied – Coton hated the sound he made.

Flying in illegal space between air and ground traffic control, the Lander now wove through the dim route canyons below the city skyline. At this height the collision scanners had to work overtime, struggling against the electronic data-fog that spilled from every building. From where Coton was sitting with Piaget the spectacular display across the top of the nav-panel was hypnotic, contrasting sharply with the blue-grey bulk of the industrial structures gliding silently by.

The pilot called back to them on the intercom. 'Prepare to disembark. Setting you down at a raw materials port. We've no monitoring of any detection system ... Good luck ...'

The Lander slowed and yawed into a sideways retro-cushioned landing. As the craft settled on the port's loading deck, Coton rose and moved towards the rear exit lock. Piaget followed behind him and watched as the cyborg scanned the bay for an assault pack.

'No weapons, Coton – there's too much energy loaded in the tower ... If you hit part of the accelerator, then it'd be *Good night, M4* ... We couldn't afford the time to brief you on the machinery. The Thin Doctor has guaranteed that the combat chassis is strong enough for what you have to do.'

It was only Coton's contempt for his synthesized voice that stopped him screaming at Piaget. He fixed the man with a stare from his caricature eyes, then snapped his face mask shut; with his other free hand he reached across the man's shoulder and punched the exterior door release. Piaget didn't flinch as the switch panel cracked under the blow.

'I'll see you later, Piaget ... We have things to discuss.'

Coton watched the Lander disappear into the blue mist of the night, then turned around and strode across the loading platform into the blackness beyond. He couldn't help but marvel as his vision shifted its spectral sensitivity, just as the doctor had said it would. He could see a small doorway outlined in the port's massive sealed arch.

'Cl ... Clowes ... Where've you been?' Dabbs gulped in horror as he saw the tattered state of Clowes' evening wear beneath the heavy winter coat – a man's coat, he also noted.

'It's a long story, Dabbs ... Where's Coton? Is he still here?'

'N ... No, they took him last night ... a special mission.'

'Who took him, Dabbs? The doctor? Piaget?'

'Both. They both went off with some Sec-services people.'

'Did they say anything to you? Did they tell you what the mission was?' At the same moment Clowes wondered why they should.

'No, but Piaget said that I should feel proud to have worked with Coton ... I didn't like it. I don't know what they've got planned for him.'

'I do, Dabbs ... What was Coton like? Did he do or say anything?'

'What do you know, Clowes? And how did you get like that? Were you attacked?'

'Coton first ... tell me about him.'

Dabbs gulped nervously. 'H ... he was powered down. The doctor told me to do it. He was really insistent that it was important, but he was all right ... Coton, I mean ... he told me to go ahead. He said he had something important to do and thanked me for all the work . . . He was asking about you as well, Clowes.'

'What about me?'

'Just where you were . . . he said he was missing you.'

Clowes felt a pang of emotion as Dabbs spoke but she buried it immediately. 'And nothing else then, Dabbs? He just asked about me . . .'

'Yes, that was it.'

'OK then, Dabbs, we've got things to do, you and me . . . There's no one else here, is there?' She suddenly realized that Dabbs hadn't told her whether or not the facility was empty.

'Everyone's disappeared, there's only me here . . . us, now.'

'Good, Dabbs. Follow me, I'll tell you what's happening while I make some TRs . . . What's the comms state right now?'

'It's patchy, Clowes . . . the nets are very up and down.'

Clowes raced down the corridor to the facility's main workstation. Dabbs trotted after her, demanding that she slow down and give him some explanation.

Dabbs got his explanation as Clowes set up the workstation's comms link priorities to Leach and Kraemer. When she had completed her story the technician remained quiet for some moments, clearly giving it all some thought.

Clowes waited for his response as the workstation still clicked through its reconfiguration.

'Oogh . . . You knew about the Supervisor all the time, then?' Dabbs seemed hurt at her not having shared this particular intelligence.

'Yes – sorry, but it was never quite the right time to tell you,' she replied, glued to the screen.

'But that could really have helped me with the net.'

'Shut up about the freaking sub-net, will you ... Don't you care about Coton?'

Dabbs gulpily muttered some further unintelligible comment which Clowes ignored.

'What was Coton's status with the endorphins, Dabbs? Is the combat chassis the same as the original?'

'The ... the ... combat chassis carries bigger reservoir cartridges; he should run for a week on a full load.'

'Well, that's something ... Do you think Coton can survive against combat droids? How good is this new chassis?'

'It's very strong and we tuned it for max performance before they took him away.'

'But will it survive an encounter with a sentry droid? I've seen those things – they're awesome.'

'Coton'll be faster than a standard droid, even if his armour isn't up to a full military spec ... It is titan-steel though, Clowes ... He'll be OK. He'll know that his best tactic will be to avoid the sentries anyway.'

'And what do you think about the Supervisor? How's he going to deal with her?'

'G ... Good question ... From what you've said, it could be difficult. I ... I've no idea how she may be able to defend herself. She's probably loaded with electrical current, that's for sure. It all depends on how much. The combat chassis will insulate against some current loadings.'

The console interrupted their exchange with a comms download whistle: it was Leach. He'd had a contact from Renata. *R. in tower – S. aware – Briefed R. on C. –*

The text stream broke up. Dabbs gulped an amazed exclamation. He had only half believed Clowes' story – he was getting very cynical after recent events.

'Oogh! It's your L . . . Leach.'

The stream picked up again. – *R. now has safe destination info – will attempt to RV with C. – R. is neon freaked!!! – Message ends –*

'There you are, Dabbs . . . Action . . .'

'W . . . W . . . We'd better tell Coton then . . .'

'What do you mean . . . *tell Coton?*'

'Use the chassis' voice link . . .'

'Dabbs, you freaking dweeb! You never said we could contact Coton!'

Dabbs looked hurt at Clowes' insult. 'Y . . . You never gave me the chance to tell you . . . The combat chassis has a direct comms link. It's standard Electrocorp.'

'Where's the terminal then, Dabbs? Let's get on with it . . .'

The direct link equipment had been hooked up to the operating theatre's workstation. As they entered, Clowes saw Coton's old chassis lying headless on the trolley and she felt a horrible chill at the sight. There were bloodstains on the floor. Clowes noticed that the feed vessels from the factorizer had been simply severed; the transfer of Coton's brain had been rushed, with no thought of a future relocation back into the old chassis.

'Have you seen this, Dabbs?' Clowes pointed to the stained raw ends of the tubing. 'The doctor must have just ripped Coton's brain out of the chassis . . . We'll never get it back without a major refit . . . The bastard, he doesn't even intend to re-transplant.'

'I . . . I was surprised at the way he did the op, Clowes . . . he was almost frantic.'

'No time now, though. Is this the comms gear?'

There was heavy military spec casing docked on to the workstation. Dabbs booted up the machine and

Clowes selected the TR frequency. Dabbs stood by her for a while as she waited for a response, then he shuffled off towards the lab suite. Clowes had had no success in reaching Coton when Dabbs reappeared, plonking a set of small polished metal cylinders on top of the console – endorphin cartridges.

'This is the big set, Clowes ... The doctor's got Coton running on the forty-eight-hour regime.' Dabbs' tone was solemn. 'You'd better tell him ...'

'What? He's not on the long-life feed? What the freak's the doctor playing at?' Clowes sensed some awful agenda behind the Thin Doctor's actions. 'This is hopeless ... I can't get a link to Coton ... We've got to try something else.'

'Kraemer, Clowes ... You should speak to him anyway. Get him to use the Big Mixer's equipment ... Give him the TR frequency.'

Coton had spent the night breaking his way through a series of sealed security doors which were barring his way into the Robotics Tower. He was surprised at the way he was feeling. It had only been during the short flight on the Lander that he'd fully realized the power he now possessed. It wasn't just the physical strength which seemed to surge beneath his skull. That was amazing in itself: his consciousness was like a tiny, compressed density of intelligence, the tip of some mountain of power. But it was the purer power which he could wield by just his presence: Piaget was totally freaked by him, and even that crazy tecchie, the Thin Doctor, had seemed nervous when they repowered his system before the flight.

His activities of the past evening had boosted him, too. It was the first time he'd been free, with no controls.

Once he'd got into the main production plant he'd raced up and down the columns of droids, swiping his fists along their stupid heads, whole rows of the things decapitated as he spun and kicked, dancing among them. It was a quite ridiculous activity, but the pleasure . . . superb. There were no signs of life in the production halls: no lights, no power, just his own enhanced vitality. He felt that if he could only find the main power line he could plug into it and light the whole damned place.

Coton now found himself at what had to be the final barrier to the tower, a wide oval door. There was a palm-pad on the wall next to it which glowed intensely in his sensitized night vision. Power . . . He was about to enter the Supervisor's domain. He remembered leaving the Lander hours before and buzzed a strange cackle through his speech synthesizer, letting fly with a high kick at the control box, which flashed sparks under the blow. The door-skin vibrated and shuddered upwards a few centimetres, then stopped. Coton stood back and pondered his handiwork: not good, he was going to have a job raising the door further, it would be locked against the lifting gearbox. He moved to the centre of the panelling and clamped his hands under the bottom edge. Light poured through the crack, playing havoc with his night vision; it switched itself in and out, rendering him effectively blind.

But the door lifted – it moved easily. Coton thrilled at the strength he felt surging through his chassis. His vision stabilized as light flooded across the floor at his feet – then he saw he had company: two sets of steel lifting forks protruded on his side of the door, a pair on either side of him. They had to belong to loader droids. Coton leapt back and watched the heavy yellow machines reveal themselves as they continued to raise the now buckling metalwork. He considered their formidable strength – several tons' lifting capacity.

Coton waited for the droids to take some further action; he could see them locking on to him, selecting him as the next task-item. They lumbered forward together, their hydraulics hissing in rhythm. Coton remembered Piaget's briefing – loader droids: powerful, slow, poor combat-suitability; weak points: exposed hydraulic lines. He stepped to one side to give himself an angle to confront the machines individually. They pivoted around with a speed that surprised Coton, but he chose his moment right to crouch and jab a foot, hooking the front droid's looping hydraulic tubes that ran to its stubby legs. Coton felt the pipe stretch and he pushed nearer to the machine to gain more force. The droid made a sweep with one of its forks, narrowly missing his head, then the pipe broke and he had to quickly regain his balance to prevent himself falling under the now failing machine. Hydraulic fluid sprayed from the break, making a growing pool on the floor; the droid's legs sank down and it lost all motion, only its funny little head still twitching as its sensors maintained their fix on the cyborg.

The second loader was now pushing in vain against its wounded fellow, making no progress towards Coton as its feet slid backwards and forwards in the spilt oil. Coton moved in a wide circle round the struggling droid, testing to see how far it could turn – he had to avoid contact with those heavy forks. The machine's rotating upper body locked as Coton continued his circle. When it paused to swing round in the opposite direction, he dived in and rained two rapid punches from behind, shattering the loader's composite CPU housing. The droid locked solid. Coton applied the same technique to the first, still sentient, droid and left the pair fizzing and popping as he ducked under the twisted door to search for an access to the tower.

He was now in a security zone of some kind: in front of him he saw a row of barriers, individual gates through a check-point; there were no more droids to be seen. Beyond the security gates Coton recognized a familiar diagonal shape, a strut of the lattice skeleton that supported the Robotics Tower. It had to be the root of the structure: the colossal beam shot across the front of a blank grey wall. In the angle where it met the floor a pair of handrails led down. Coton could just make out the top of an elevator bay flush with the head of the ramp. He would test Piaget's theory that the operational security gates would let him through – he was a droid, after all. He strode forward and watched the indicator lamps light up at his approach.

Kraemer had had no success in contacting Coton's father; he was permanently unavailable, in an emergency sitting of the Council of Fathers, his e-mail had said. Kraemer left a string of messages urging him to call back as soon as possible – it was all he could do. The whole Comms Monitoring department was stacked out with TRs, all of them from criminal sources in one way or another; there was no way they could keep up. His leg was really bothering him and he decided to give up on the routine. Tawney, his neighbouring staffer, was going crazy at the workload. Kraemer leant back and watched the messages stack across his screen.

Clowes' TR was unambiguous: *Kraemer – double urgent – contact C. – he has only short life endorphin pack – 24 hrs remain – he is to RV with R in tower – R has location of safe house – use following direct comms link – ends.*

Kraemer dumped the comms link reference on to his own system and rapped the message into his transmission file. His console registered a 'send' message but he saw no acknowledgement of receipt from the cyborg. He played with the frequency code and upped the priority grade, but the TR wouldn't log positively. He cursed the collapsing network system and considered how he could get the message through; he needed to do a direct transmission but from a more powerful, un-jammed system. He would have to try again down in Flight Control: they had a more flexible comms system, which wouldn't be stacked with all the general stuff jamming Comms Monitoring. He pulled himself up out of his seat and mouthed the words *Sick-Bay* to his neighbour, Tawney, who had a headset clamped firmly over his ears. Tawney glanced down at Kraemer's hope-less leg and gave him a thumbs-up sign. Kraemer heaved himself out of the monitoring trench and headed for the elevator bay.

Flight was stupidly busy. Kraemer scanned the banks of staffers at the consoles and doubted his earlier thinking that he'd be able to get a message out from here. He knew no one, not a single face; a favour would be out of the question, there wasn't even a spare console that he could innocently occupy. There was only one other option. If there was a Lander in the docking slots on the floor below, he might be able to use its on-board kit for the TR. Kraemer looked across to the Ops panel at the end of the level: there were two craft with no activity reference. It had to be worth a shot.

When he came out of the elevator on to the docking floor, Kraemer was dismayed to find the first of his selected Landers surrounded by a maintenance crew. There was no way he could get near the craft. That only left Slot 6, a long trail round the circumference of the tower – and his leg was telling him that it didn't want to make the trip. He steeled himself to perform the task and set off, nodding in acknowledgement to the semi-curious maintenance staffers who were observing his cripple's progress.

His lamentably slow tour round the core of the tower was finally rewarded when a lone, unattended Lander came into view. The craft was wrapped by a service gantry with only umbilicals betraying any kind of attention to the machine. Kraemer looked up to the control mezzanine that ringed the tower core; Slot 6's section was as empty as all the other bays he'd monitored on his circuit. He noticed with relief that the mezz had an open elevator, allowing effortless access to the docking control system. He knew that he'd have to open the external launch port for his transmission to stand a chance of reaching Coton.

Kraemer trembled as he limped under the belly of the Lander. The hatch was open and now all he had to do was drag himself up into the ship. The chill air sweeping in from the gaping launch port wafted yet colder vapour across him as it lifted the mist shrouding the liquid oxygen lines. It was warmer inside the Lander and Kraemer eased his way to the comms pit, where he rested for a second. Even though he knew he had to hurry and someone was bound to have logged the open launch port, he gave himself some moments to let the pain from his leg subside. Just as he booted the console, Kraemer thought he felt the Lander sway slightly; the cooling fans had set up some vibration and the whole comms pit hummed. The main screen lit and he rattled the *send* co-ordinates into the control pad. Kraemer smiled against the pain he was feeling as the TR logged positive. Clowes' message flowed from his fingers, followed by an immediate receipt. It was through – Kraemer attached his own ID, it was good to be sending to Coton again, even in these crazy circumstances. Kraemer felt the Lander lurch again: he'd been discovered. So what, he thought, they'd never court martial him when all this came out. He raised himself from his seat to confront whoever it was.

The maintenance droid straddled the narrow comms pit and drove its fist clean through Kraemer's chest and into the transmission desk. Kraemer never knew a thing.

Coton stood watching the elevator indicator panel for a while. There was constant activity throughout the tower: short hops between the floors as the droids carried out the Supervisor's unknown commands. Coton knew from his briefing that he had to make it to at least the one-fortieth floor; from there he would need to transfer to the secure levels of the Chromium Programme. That was where he would be likely to meet concerted resistance: the Supervisor was sure to have deployed a defence force of Electrocorp's latest combat droid types. Coton thought back to the encounter with the two loader droids. It had been a strange experience – life and death for him – but somehow he had felt no sense of mortality during the combat. It had been clean and mechanical: unemotional, machine against machine. He caught a quick flashback of his earlier days in the Security Service, the Azzi clearance sweeps he'd been a part of. Scenes of blasted accommodation units flooded into his mind: red carpets of blood, smashed furniture and bodies indistinguishable from one another. If his chassis had allowed it, he'd have shuddered. He moved forward to summon an elevator.

As he waited to see what the elevator would bring, some droid perhaps, he sensed a communication arriving in his head. It entered straight into his mind like a thought – telepathy. It was the comms link. The Thin Doctor had used it briefly right after he'd been transferred into this chassis. At the time he hadn't been sure if the doctor had been speaking to him or if he'd just experienced some sort of *déjà-vu* aberration. This was real, though; he recognized the *Kraemer* ID tag and then worked back over the words. The message was still just a string of words when the elevator arrived; it was empty. Coton stepped inside and tapped in the number one-forty; the doors hissed closed and the elevator accelerated into its climb.

Kraemer was telling him about his half-sister; it made no sense. She was in the tower and had to meet him – crazy. She was going to get him to a safe house . . . why, he thought. Then he unravelled the mention of the endorphin pack; the short-life carts had been installed, there was also another name in the message: *Clowes* – he'd forgotten about Clowes . . . Her name filled him with some fearful association, then a mass of recollection rushed in: the Thin Doctor, Piaget, the significance of the endorphins and his entrapment in the hands of these manipulators . . . He had lost all these dark thoughts in his power-up before this mission. A full sense of mortality returned when he felt the elevator slow; he looked at the floor indicator: it read ninety.

The military robot held the elevator on lock then disappeared to one side of the door aperture. Coton remained still, contemplating the best plan of action. He had still made no decision when the droid reappeared, carrying a stack of what looked to Coton like insulation plates. They were soft, rubbery tiles, more like a floor covering, he realized. The droid came into the elevator and disabled the lock with a press on the control panel, its head tilted back on its short corrugated neck as it seemed to examine the floor indicator. Coton remained motionless. The droid's head then turned to the cyborg and looked him up and down, and the elevator moved automatically upwards again. Coton rode with the droid all the way to the one hundred and fortieth floor.

The military droid stepped smartly out of the elevator as soon as the doors parted and continued purposefully, carrying its load along the black, shining causeway that led across the grand open hall of the one-fortieth. Regular squeaks from its steps spiked into the hanging silence. Coton let the droid get some distance ahead of him then followed. At the end of the causeway Coton could see only a sheer blank wall, jet-black and completely featureless. As he sharpened his focus, however, he began to make out an archway and a security gate, all fashioned from the same black material. Bringing his eyes back to the droid, he was distracted by another movement at the security checkpoint. There was a second figure in the hall; it moved fluidly and was human. Coton halted; the military droid was now approaching the security gates. Coton wanted to see if the robot had noticed the human. The barrier lights lit green and the droid marched through. Coton was amazed; the human figure was now plainly visible, sitting at the security console, but the droid ignored her. It was a female ... It was Renata, unmistakably – she was eating something, sitting quite coolly behind the sleek reception counter.

'Jon?' Renata spoke with some nervousness as Coton approached.

'Renna!' Coton cursed his awful voice once more.

'You look . . . er, different . . .'

'Is that supposed to be a joke?'

'What've they done to you?'

'It's a long story, Renna . . . But what the hell are you doing here?'

'It's my job – I work here.'

'How did you avoid the freaking droid just then? I was waiting for it to log you.'

'I didn't avoid it – it recognized me . . . Come on, Jon, we've got to get out of here . . . There'll be more 'bots any minute.'

Coton slowed Renata as he demanded more information, so she began to tell him about her job as an Electrocorp security staffer. She hurried her story along, constantly reminding Coton that he had only limited time before his endorphin supply would begin to fail. Leach had briefed her over her voice link when she'd finally managed to get a transmission out from an air-con vent in the service shaft. The story about her half-brother had been a little hard to take on board – but here he was, very much larger than life. She told Coton about the malevolent droid on the exec floor and about her narrow escape.

'But how did you get here? And why didn't the military droid go for you just now?' Coton pressed her.

'I knew I had to rendezvous with you somewhere, and there was only here that was a guaranteed location . . . I guessed you'd have to come up the elevator to get to the one-fortieth. The service shaft doesn't have any access from below, I learnt that myself.'

'Yeah, but you still haven't explained about the droid.'

'Once I'd got down here, I hid behind the counter – you can see there's no other cover ... and then I was discovered by one of the sentries ... I thought that was it, but the thing just ignored me ... I was amazed.' Renata paused.

'Go on, then ... What next?'

'I sussed it out ... All of the droids here have their own mapping system ... It's programmed in so they can get around without beacons and stuff ... I realized that I was in their maps ... I'm a regular feature here; no security droid would pay any attention to me as an intruder because, as far as they're concerned, I'm not ... I've been here for hours, and loads of droids have been past me.'

Coton tried to laugh over his synthesizer, but managed to emit only an odd buzzing.

'What the hell are they all doing then, Renna? What was that stuff the last droid was carrying?'

'They've been shifting stacks of those floor tiles, Jon. They can only be for the Supervisor; I think they're extending her nil-static zone ... That's only a guess, though.'

'Sounds good enough to me ... How do we get up there?'

'Jon ... You need to get out of here ... Forget the freaking Supervisor!'

'No, Renna ... She's got to be stopped ... Come on, show me the way.'

Renata held back and flinched as Coton made to grab her arm.

'There's more to it than just saving ourselves, Renna ... The whole city's under threat ... Believe me ...

You're going to have to help ... I'm not leaving until we've taken out the Supervisor!'

Coton stepped away from her and set off towards the elevator bay for the Chromium Programme. He was standing at the doors when Renata joined him.

'You know I'll be logged, once I'm away from here, don't you, Jon?'

'Yeah, stick with me ... I've already beaten up two droids, you know.' Coton tried to laugh again, but the attempt failed miserably.

Renata looked hard at this weird cyborg thing and worried that it was developing a serious fault. She entered a security code into the elevator panel; the doors slid open and she followed the cyborg into the cube whose themed black interior had now taken on the feel of an exotic tomb, or so it felt to Renata.

'Floor One, Jon.'

Coton swept the entry pad, but the elevator had already started into motion; he said nothing to Renata.

When they cleared the elevator bay, Floor One's security gates stood unguarded and completely open. Renata tucked herself behind the cyborg as he stepped forward into the nearest scanner channel. They passed through with no acknowledgement from the machinery; the only noise came from the bay behind them; its doors had closed and the elevator had gone into descent. There was a choice of three corridors in front of them, each curving away concentrically.

'Which one, Renna?'

'The left one, Jon; they all run in a spiral. It'll take us right to the Supervisor's control centre, if that's where you want to go ...'

'And the others?'

'Support labs and crew rooms.'

'OK, left it is . . .'

'I *do not* like this, Jon, it's too quiet . . . I know that there must be at least twenty droids up here – I saw them all go past me downstairs.'

'Maybe they're all at it, building the zone extension . . . Or on other floors – they don't all have to be *here*, Renna.'

It was small reassurance for her: she remembered the sentry droid that had gone for her on the exec floor.

'Take it easy, Jon, and let's check out some of the rooms on the way. I think I need some kind of weapon.'

Coton agreed to her request and led the way into the corridor. It was narrower than the other two and its curving nature afforded only a limited view ahead. The first two doors that Coton tried were secured; when they reached the third, it too was locked. Coton weighed the door's construction; it was the same black composite as the rest of the corridor. He cautioned Renata to stand back then thrust his fist at the space just above the recessed handle. The material crazed over and, with a couple more blows, Coton had it open. He paused for a moment to see whether this activity would summon an investigator, then he motioned for Renata to enter.

'It's the Pyro-Control system, Jon,' Renata said as she walked across the chamber to a bank of large pressure cylinders and valves.

'The what?' Coton could see it was some sort of pressure regulation equipment for gas or a fluid.

'Fire control, dummy . . . This thing governs the sprinklers and the halon gas circuit . . . Look what I've found . . .' Renata slid a compact cylinder out from a rack of similar ones. 'A hand extinguisher, foam and gas . . . They must fill them here.'

'Great, Renna – you can put me out if I blow a fuse.'

'Don't joke, Jon, this might just disable a droid ... spray it over its sensors ... You never saw the monster that went for me up there.' Renata raised her eyes to the ceiling as she adjusted her shoulder bag, now weighted with the extinguisher.

'OK, so you're armed; do you think that's the best we'll find?'

'Guess so, Jon.'

They left the chamber and continued along the corridor. Renata cautioned Coton that they were approaching the security gate to the Supervisor's inner sanctum. 'There'll have to be droids there, Jon ... You go on in front and I'll hang back a little ... Call me if it's clear.'

Coton froze as he rounded the final curve of the corridor. There were five droids busy with stacks of the insulated floor tiles. He could see beyond the gate that the further corridor was completely carpeted with the black rubber material. The droids logged the cyborg's presence and halted in their labours, each one turning its head towards the silver figure. Two of them were huge, red, sentry robots and the other three were smaller, military models, like the one that had ridden in the elevator with him. None of them moved its position.

Coton took a step forward but there was no response from the droids. He shot a glance behind him. Had they seen Renata? But the corridor was clear; she was still well back. Coton walked across to the nearest stack of tiles and picked one off the top; the droids merely tracked his action with their heads. He walked over to the nearest military droid and offered the tile but the machine made no response. He looked straight at the sensor eyes of the droid, vainly looking for some kind of reaction, but the machine betrayed nothing. What was the thing doing? Did it think that he was the

295

Supervisor? There were no other silver-coloured droids in the Electrocorp range ... No, it couldn't be so dumb – the droid had to be under some kind of control. Coton took the floor tile and placed it on the machine's head ... still nothing. He pushed at its shoulder and the machine just moved with the pressure in a sort of shrug. It was live but for some reason was not bothered by him. Coton moved across to the security gate and entered the scanner channel. He walked right through it and back again with absolutely no response from the robots. There was only one other test he could make, so he moved back to the centre of the space and called to Renata.

She came into view, stepping gingerly. Coton looked back to the droids and watched them lock on to this second visitor. They still made no other movement.

'Renna, come right up behind me, we're going to walk straight through the gate. Don't worry about the droids – they're all paralysed.'

Renata obeyed silently and Coton lost no time marching directly onwards as he had said.

'Are we OK behind?' Coton called back to Renata as they proceeded on down the rubber-tiled corridor.

'Nothing at all, Jon, they're all still stopped.'

Coton slowed as the corridor began to widen and slope upwards, the conventional warm lighting fading, giving way to a cold blue.

'This is it, Jon,' Renna hissed from behind the cyborg, 'the Supervisor's control station.'

The floor levelled out above and, as he crested the rise, Coton caught his first glimpse of the stunning Supervisor droid. She was standing in the centre of a wide horseshoe of control consoles, stark and beautiful in the icy light; she seemed to have her back to him.

Coton moved his arm back to Renata, silently urging her to remain where she was. He walked slowly forward, making no sound on the tiles laid by the droids, but he knew that the Supervisor was aware of his presence. He had walked right up to the lip of the slightly raised nil-static zone when the droid turned, sending ultra-blue flashes of current discharging across the floor. Coton stepped back, suddenly realizing that he had no clear strategy to meet the power of this creature. He sensed his brain pushing all sorts of fear signals against the endorphin blockers; his head felt fit to burst and he knew he wanted to panic, but his mind wouldn't let him.

Coton, I've been waiting for this – The words just came into his head: the Supervisor was using the telepathic link ... Coton battled to clear his mind, but the words seemed to echo, looping into a continuous noise. *More, Coton?* It was a weapon: she was going to drive him mad ... His vision blurred but he could still see the silver form distort and come rocketing towards him in a swirling bolt of energy. He found himself instinctively ducking then rolling down the gentle slope towards the ramp from the corridor. He was on his hands and knees by the time he gathered his senses; the Supervisor was standing some way above him on the edge of her zone, looking down at him with her blank face. *And some more* – Coton tried to block the words out again, but he was transfixed as the droid's face began to ripple and distort. Every face he knew seemed to merge and twist across the front of her head. *More, More, More!* The words came like a data-scream command on a nightmare comms link. He knew he had to get away from this monster; he pushed himself further down the slope.

Renata had watched in horror at the Supervisor's

advance; she couldn't understand what Coton was doing, just rolling and buzzing awfully through his speech synthesizer. She knew she had to do something though, and she ran forward, brandishing the fire extinguisher, letting go a long blast on the trigger. The droid suddenly seemed to become aware of her, and Renata felt herself become rooted with hypnotic fear as the robot took on her own face, gnarled into an agonized expression. The Supervisor shrugged off the extinguisher attack and extended a morphing arm, knocking the cylinder from her grasp. Renata was blinded by the blue flash and fumes as the punctured device rattled away down the ramp behind her. Her only instinct now was to flee, and she turned, tumbling in panic, her bag and its contents scattering in front of her down the ramp.

Coton had recovered while Renata was diverting the Supervisor, and he now saw his only chance to attack; he had to do it: physically throw himself at the droid. The monstrous female was coming at him again now, moving swiftly down the slope. He braced himself on the rubber tiling and sprang like an animal.

Renata heard the thunderous crack from the hall above and waited long, anguished moments, praying for her cyborg brother to appear. A flash of silver appeared at the head of the ramp. 'Jon!' She called out, but the flash re-formed to become the Supervisor, heading straight for her. She felt Leach's lighter under her hand, the one thing she had left. She lit it and opened the gas jet wide, sending a long yellow flame out of her hand. She raised herself up and watched the Supervisor pause for a second, then continue towards her. Renata waved the flame and saw the droid hesitate again. Then the idea struck her . . .

She thrust the lighter up above her head, brushing the mass of conduits with the flame. A jet of white gas shot out from the wall-skirting and then she felt a splash on her hand. The sprinklers opened with a roar, sweeping a moving curtain of water from behind her down the corridor. She was drenched in moments. Awestruck, she watched as the liquid hit the Supervisor, just a few metres in front of her. The droid froze rigid then shattered into a million tiny shards of silver that hit Renata like powdered snow. She stood, breathless, watching the glittering speckles wash from her and stream away in the flood now at her feet.

Renata stood for what felt like an age, mesmerized by the swirling gas and water. The sprinklers had triggered an alarm which shrieked, blanking her hearing. It was a dull vibration through the floor which brought her back to her senses. She turned to see behind her the rapidly advancing hulk of a sentry droid bearing down the misted tunnel. She spun back and set off, splashing through the silver-flecked water towards the ramp up to the control centre.

The cyborg was raising itself as she raced over the rise, its left arm hanging, useless, from a melted shoulder.

Renata called out to her bizarre half-brother: 'Jon! We've got to get out!'

Coton had straightened when she reached him and was pulling at the limp dangling mess of metal.

Renata could see an elevator bay in the dimness across the nil-static zone, and she tugged at Coton to get him to turn. 'The sentries are right behind us ... Come on, will you!'

She broke away from him and charged across the blue floor; looking over her shoulder, she could see the cyborg begin to lumber after her. He must still be sentient, she thought with relief. Coton caught up with her at the elevator and thumped inside. Renata scanned the controls and saw they could only go up. She slammed the top button and the elevator hummed into motion.

'Roof level three.' The elevator voice seemed comically calm to Renata as the car came to a halt and opened its doors. A cold blast of wintry night air whipped away her body heat through her sodden clothing. She pushed at the cyborg and the two of them walked out into an open-sided shelter on top of the Robotics Tower. Renata looked across the flat expanse of the roof which was floodlit and empty. The backs of the transmitter dishes ringing the circumference gave it the air of an arena – a fitting location for a final showdown with the droids, she thought. The elevator had returned to the Chromium Programme level – the sentries would be up with them at any moment.

'Jon! Say something, you fabricated freak-ass! What are we going to do?'

Renata kicked the cyborg's leg in frustration. Coton hummed an uncertain response.

'I'm going to check out the roof – there's got to be some other way down! Are you coming?' she bawled at the cyborg as she set off into the bright light. She was freezing and was seriously beginning to doubt how long she could take this exposure to the bitter cold. When she looked back to check on Coton, she saw with amazement that they had been standing under a landing platform, an apron with a Lander craft sitting, waiting, on top. She saw a metallic flash in the shadow beneath the structure – the cyborg was coming across to her. She ran back to meet him, pointing up at the Lander.

'Sorry, Renna, I've been really blasted . . .'

Renata could have cried with relief as he spoke. She interrupted his apology. 'Can you fly a Lander, Jon?' She thought that every Sec-services officer had to have some flying experience. 'Look up there . . . behind you . . .'

Coton turned and saw the craft on the raised deck. 'Not very well . . .'

'But you could get us off this tower, though? Come on . . . I'm going to die if I don't get out of this wind.' Renata ran back to the flight of open steps that led up the shadowed side of the platform. Coton seemed brighter now and he came close behind her. He pulled himself up into the Lander's belly hatch with his good arm. Renata watched his smashed limb catch under his body and she gasped when, with another pull, the arm ripped from its shoulder, clanking on to the decking below.

'Come on, Jon . . .' she urged him as she stood back in the empty freight hold, powerless to help the heavy machine. As Coton got to his feet, they both became aware of the humming that preceded the motor ignition phase. The Lander had a pilot already on board.

CHAPTER FIFTEEN

Clowes fell backwards with a crash as the facility's main workstation popped loudly, throwing sparks that fountained up the wall. Somewhere else in the complex she heard at least one other loud bang.

Dabbs came rushing out of the lab suite, summoned by the noises. 'C . . . Clowes, are you all right?'

'I think so . . . I . . .' Clowes' voice faded out as the lighting dimmed slowly to black. 'What the hell's going on?' Then the facility gently illuminated again.

'P . . . Power-surge, Clowes.'

'I thought we had an isolator, Dabbs? That shouldn't be possible . . . should it?'

'No, not really.'

Clowes dusted herself down and looked at the black smoke-stain up the wall. She turned back to Dabbs to check how he was progressing with their preparations for Coton's return.

'That's a hell of a mess . . . How's the endorphin factorizer? Did it catch the surge?'

'It's as good as useless, but nothing to do with the power. All the distillation-phase data's scrambled . . . There's nothing I can do.'

'Well, that's it then . . . We have to have the doctor.'

'But where do you think he is?'

'With Piaget and his Sec-services cronies, most probably.'

'What makes you think he's going to come back here?'

'If we have Coton, he'll be back ... The cyborg is his baby, Dabbs, and he'll be wanting the glory when the story gets out.'

'You really do have faith, Clowes. Coton *and* the Thin Doctor.'

'I've got no choice ... We have to prepare for an immediate transplant if we can't get an endorphin match.'

'But the chassis is nowhere near ready, Clowes ... It'll take me a week to prepare it.' Dabbs paused, thinking. '... And you'll still need endorphins ...' Dabbs gazed at Clowes and began to shake his head.

'Not for his own biological body, Dabbs ... There's a crew bringing it down from upstairs right now.'

'B ... But ...' Dabbs gulped.

'But nothing, Dabbs ... Coton's body is perfect ... he was never injured in the Lander crash.'

Dabbs gulped to answer her but found himself speechless.

'You remember the original transplant ... The doctor left me with the cerebration while he concentrated on the torso ... he didn't want me to see. He stopped Piaget looking as well ... Remember?'

'I thought that was strange ... He's uninjured ... Oogh ... Apart from a freaking g ... great hole in his head ... We wrecked a perfectly viable subject ...'

'Under the direction of the Thin Doctor, Dabbs,' Clowes interrupted him.

'But what made you suspect?'

'I began to suspect every damned detail after I'd spoken to Kraemer ... Once I had my suspicions, I only had to ask the right questions upstairs in the foundation.'

'And you're sure Coton'll come back? And what about the safe house you were talking about?'

'Well, I can't be a hundred per cent sure, but we have to be ready, or Coton will have no chance at all ... I want the safe house so we can keep Coton out of the doctor's hands until we get his father in on the act ... The pressure, Dabbs ... With Coton's father's influence, the doctor will have to do what we want.'

'It's all a big ... g ... g ... gamble, Clowes.' Dabbs struggled with the two g's. 'Have you heard from Kraemer, then?'

'No, not yet. I can't raise him at his station.'

'So no Coton, no father and no Thin Doctor.' Dabbs' tone was equivocal.

'Well no, not yet ...'

The Lander's motors fired into life and the pilot switched in the lift thrust. Renata hung on to a grab-rail as the belly hatch, damaged by the cyborg's entry, flew open. When the craft keeled away from the top of the apron, she could see the long shadows of the pursuing droids reaching out from the elevator bay.

'Where are we going?' Renata shouted to Coton above the whine of the motors.

'Ask the pilot, Renna?'

'Do it then!'

Coton started to move along the freight bay towards the flight deck bulkhead; he could feel himself becoming dizzy through the motion of the craft. He stopped to steady himself but Renata called out to him to hurry.

'I'm losing my balance!'

Renata remembered Leach's warning about the endorphins and wondered if this could be an indication that they were giving out. He could have been damaged anyway; the left side of his head was discoloured following his contact with the Supervisor. She crawled along after the cyborg, not trusting herself to stand as the Lander dipped to the left then the right. When she got to Coton, he was just short of the hatch to the flight deck.

'OK, Jon . . . Open it . . .' She pulled herself up against the bulkhead as she spoke.

Coton pushed the release catch and the door slid sideways. Renata shrank back as the figure in the captain's seat was revealed. Coton sensed her horror and eased forward in the cramped space to see what had caused her reaction. It was a silver female droid, but, in the dark of the cockpit, a gleaming black, elegantly spattered with the reflections from the instrument panel. The droid seemed to be ignoring their presence and simply continued with her manual control of the Lander. Coton's night vision came in with a delay and he began to make out the lines of joints in the droid's chassis. It wasn't a Supervisor-type droid at all – it was a beautifully crafted electro-mechanical replica.

'Renna, come back.' Renata had retreated to the rear of the freight bay. 'It's not the Supervisor, it's a clone . . . a mechanical clone.'

Renata came slowly back up the bay. The Lander had gained some altitude after its dip down amongst the city blocks and was now flying straight and level. Coton could read north from the flight instruments, but he was beginning to feel bad again. The droid was flying the Lander wonderfully smoothly – that wasn't what was making him ill – and he began to sense panic building as he remembered the endorphins. But the droid distracted him: there was something about it. He decided to speak to it directly; it had auditory sensors: he could see the fine, pepper-

pot punctures in the side of its head. When he asked
the machine where they were heading, she responded
with a short series of buzzes. He tried again and received the same response.

'She can't understand my freaking synthesizer, Renna
. . . You try . . .'

Renata repeated Coton's question, and the droid answered in a polite female tone: 'Lorus Depression. Thank
you.'

'Where?' Renata was stunned by the reply and repeated herself more out of surprise than for any further
clarification.

'Lorus Depression . . . Co-ordinates on the nav-panel.
Thank you.'

'Let me see, Renna!' Coton leant forward past his
half-sister. The nav-panel gave him a familiar reference:
the heading he and Walker had had for their Azzi TR
search.

'Jon, I know what this droid is. It's the Server from
the Supervisor visitor suite. I'd only heard about her till
now . . .'

'That's correct. Thank you,' the Server interrupted.

'She might just do anything we ask. Like new co-
ordinates, y'know . . .'

'Go on then, Renna . . . Tell her.'

'But I've lost the freaking reference . . . It was in my
bag.'

'Look, Renna, don't do this to me, I'm beginning to
suffer here . . . I think it's the endorphins.'

'The Farm Park, er . . . Server . . . Can you take us to
the Farm Park? Abort Lorus destination.'

'Please be more specific. Thank you.'

'Er, Agri-Business district . . . North eight.'

'Over North eight now. Thank you.'

306

'Teh ... Teh ... Tell it to do a visual approach!' Coton buzzed at Renata. She heard the cyborg struggle launching the sentence – certainly he wasn't a hundred per cent.

'Drop us in for a visual approach on the Farm Park. I'll guide you.' As she issued the command, Renata prayed that she'd be able to spot the boulevard, her only real reference for finding Griff's shed. The droid acknowledged and put the Lander into a steep sideslip.

'Hang on, Brother Cyborg ... She's doing it!' Coton made no sign that he'd heard her; he seemed to have locked himself to the overhead grab-rail.

The Lander made two passes low over the illuminated boulevard and, as the obliging droid turned for the third, Renata saw a flash of light at the corner of one of the flat oblongs of the Farm Park's sheds. It had to be Griff – he must have heard the machine passing overhead.

Coton's body lay motionless on the trolley from the coma control centre. Dabbs had removed the top half of the protection capsule and was muttering to himself at its perfect condition. The ape brain still sat in its cranial floor, mounted into the linked support console. Clowes ran through the diagnostics and wondered at the genius of the Thin Doctor to have stabilized the subject so successfully.

'He's in perfect shape, Dabbs ... It's quite remarkable.'

'I ... I still can't get over what he's done.' Dabbs spoke quietly, closing the inspection cover of the preservation housing on Coton's head. 'He's not going to come back and answer for this.'

Clowes felt her positive mood vanish as Dabbs voiced the fear she'd not dared to admit to herself. 'I know, Dabbs . . . Will you help me?'

They were interrupted by a hammering on the theatre doors. All hell seemed to have broken loose in the corridor outside. Clowes could see a scramble of shapes in the translucent partition: she could hear Piaget's voice booming over others that were unfamiliar to her. She rushed across into the glass bubble airlock. It was Piaget's face that met her as she slid back the outer door. Behind him, the blasted cyborg lay on an industrial truck. Renata Coton stood, chained to its control arm, with Leach and some other roughly clothed Azzi next to her.

'Tell them, Clowes!' Piaget barked the words in her face. 'The cyborg is state property!'

Clowes noticed two armed security staffers and another man moving down the corridor towards them.

'You can send *them* back first, Piaget!' She turned to the advancing security people.

'Clowes, Coton's out of it, you'd better do something!' Leach butted in.

Clowes looked down again at Coton the cyborg and pushed the call button for Dabbs to join her from the theatre. 'I'll get him inside . . . Can you get that chain off, Renata?' Leach handed Renata a small clicker box. 'It's Coton's sister, Piaget.' She could see his incredulity as she spoke familiarly to the azzi-girl.

'My daughter . . . and my son.' The voice of Jon Coton Senior came booming up the corridor. Clowes and Piaget turned to see the middle-aged politician hurrying ahead of the security staffers.

Dabbs had now appeared out of the airlock and was

poring over the cyborg chassis, mumbling gulpily at the damage.

'Get Coton hooked up to the support console, Dabbs ... Get him inside!'

'Ms Clowes?' Coton's father had now reached the group and spoke urgently. 'Is he all right?'

'I won't know that until he's hooked up, Mr Coton.' Clowes' mind raced. No Thin Doctor and a (no doubt) rapidly failing Jon David Coton. 'Let Mr Dabbs through, everyone ... Don't any of you go into the theatre!' Dabbs was struggling to guide the powered truck — it was all getting chaotic.

'Will you let me know as soon as you can? Is the Thin Doctor in there?' Coton's father nodded towards the operating theatre door as he spoke.

Clowes was scarcely listening to Coton's father as she rapidly thought out her strategy for the burning reality of an unassisted brain transplant. 'Er, no, Mr Coton ... Excuse me.' She pushed past him — mention of the Thin Doctor reminded her about the transplant data carts in the scientist's office.

The Thin Doctor's small office lay diagonally across the corridor. Clowes slid the door open and gasped as she saw the Thin Doctor sitting silently at his work-station, a pained expression on his face. There was a large smoke stain up the wall at the back of the work-station, just like the one by the facility's main console.

'Doctor?'

She touched his shoulder and felt her hand meet no resistance as it pressed through into a powdery mass. She stood rooted as the whole figure of the planet's most eminent scientist crumbled before her eyes into glittering silver dust.

Out in the corridor, Renata Coton saw a thin cloud of

silver dust billow out through the open door; she shrieked.

*

The Comms Monitoring floor hummed with routine activity. From up on the management mezzanine, Piaget surveyed his domain with satisfaction. He'd just cancelled his Staff Officer selection review and confessed to himself that he was happy with the decision. His workstation beeped an incoming e-mail message and he strolled back to the machine. He read the text box and closed down the console. He'd been waiting for this message: Lander 3 had arrived back from its pick-up in the Lorus Depression ... It would be interesting to take a look at the alien deep-space transmission equipment. It was loaded with coded sci-medical data, the recovery tecchies had said.

**Exploring New Realms
in Science Fiction/Fantasy Adventure**

Calling all fantasy fans!

Join the

FANTASY FAN CLUB

for exciting news and fabulous competitions.

For further information write to:

FANTASY FAN CLUB

Penguin Books Ltd.,
Bath Road, Harmondsworth,
Middlesex UB7 0DA

Open only to residents of the UK
and Republic of Ireland